EXITUS

Works by T.S. Petersen

Evanee Sheperd Series:

Moribund

T.S. PETERSEN

EXITUS

AN EVANEE SHEPERD NOVEL

Exitus: An Evanee Sheperd Novel

Copyright © Tammy S. Petersen 2019

The moral right of the author has been asserted.

This is a work of fiction. Names, characters, places and incidents are either the product of the author's imagination or are used factiously, and any resemblance to the actual persons, living or dead, business establishments, events or locales are entirely coincidental.

Cover art © by Amanda Pillar of Smoking Hot Covers

To Dannielle, Danielle and Helen thank you for your incredible editing and critiquing. I'm a better writer because of you three.

To the Love of My Life thank you for supporting me and encouraging me. Love you, Sexy.

Prologue

Hand in hand, Erick and I stepped through my portal, leaving behind the carnage that was once Aeternum's Science Laboratories at Acrasin General Hospital. The scents unique to Murder Point Bay drifted enticingly through one of the open French doors lining the top floor. The shadowed wrap-around veranda beyond the doors beckoned, whispering of rest and relaxation as the sounds and scents of sunrise cast their spell over me. With a tired sigh, I ignored the call and focused on the door that led to Erick's room.

A sudden shift in the pressure turned Erick's, Jordan's, and my head towards the veranda. Jordan stopped short and inhaled the new scent drifting into the hallway on the cool air. The air surrounding him responded, growing denser as the shadows in the hallway crept along the floor and roof. His hands clenched into fists, the dried blood that caked them cracking. He was frightening in this moment, and I was glad the focus of his attention wasn't on me. Erick dropped my hand, placing his body between me and whatever, or whoever was responsible for the shift.

Focusing on the power emanating from outside, I sensed my mother's presence seconds before she emerged from the shadows, her hands raised to show she meant no harm.

"Relax Jordan, I'm not here to reap."

Jordan visibly relaxed as Mum stepped further into the hallway.

"Apologies Reagan, we didn't realise it was you."

Dropping her hands, Mum spoke with a quiet urgency. "No need to apologise, it's me who has dropped by unannounced. There's something I feel needs our attention—sooner rather than later. Jordan, where's that prophecy you were referring to at the hospital?"

"I asked him to put it in my study for safe keeping," Erick responded.

"Good. The fewer people who know about this, the better. Erick, if you would lead the way, I don't have much time." Nodding at my mother's request, Erick moved towards his bedroom doors.

I stalled momentarily, not sure I wanted to know what the prophecy said.

I don't know how much more drama I can take.

Jordan's raised eyebrows had me sighing with weariness, and my shoulders slumped in defeat. The action forced the dried blood covering my body to crack, pinching at the tiny hairs on my body. I grimaced at the unpleasant sensation.

Entering Erick's room behind my mother, my gaze zeroed in on the turquoise love seat near the fireplace, reminding me of the vision Fate bestowed upon me before my death. My eyes darted away, and I made my way towards Erick's desk in the corner.

"Hello sweetheart, sorry for the haste."

Mum's rose-lipped smile was laden with hope, and I cringed inwardly.

"Hi Mum," I mumbled. Things were far from being resolved between the two of us, but that didn't mean I didn't love her. She was my mother.

Looking for Erick, who'd disappeared into his walk-in closet as soon as we'd entered his room to retrieve the vampire's prophecy from his safe, I prayed he'd hurry. I wasn't even close to being ready to talk to my mother about her years of betrayal and lies. If she forced me to address it now, I knew we'd both walk away feeling worse than we did now.

Mum looked me up and down as though she finally noticed my bloodied appearance.

"I hear you kicked arse at the hospital. Jordan said you were magnificent."

Wow, she didn't even bat an eyelid at the blood. At least now I know who Jordan was texting before we left Acrasin General.

"Apparently. Let's not forget I also started an interspecies dilemma, and all in my first month of being a vamper. Personally, I call that talent. Erick will probably refer to it as a pain in his royal arse."

'Play nice, Evanee.'

Erick's hiss slithered through my mind as he emerged carrying a small leather-bound scroll.

"Vamper. That's cute. Vampire and reaper combined, am I right?" Mum asked.

Nodding silently, I stood back from the desk making room for Erick.

Together the four of us crowded around the desk as Erick gingerly unwound the brittle paper. We took a few minutes to absorb the words scrawled across the middle of the page.

"Well, that settles that." Mum recovered first. "The good news is we found the correlating prophecies. The bad news is that the one I have in my possession is one of our forbidden prophecies, which was why my memory was vague. What the Mors family prophecy refers to is something my parents have worked hard to ensure didn't come to pass."

Mum looked to Erick and Jordan.

"Mors... wait that's what... umm," I stalled, realising I hadn't informed my mother about everything that had happened before my death and during my conversion. "Someone called me that name just before I died. Your maiden name was Mors?" The pieces were sliding together, everyone seemed to have guessed who I was except me.

"Yes, it was."

Mum stared at me for a heartbeat before she moved on.

"One reason my family cut me off was because they worried my marrying a human meant I was the woman in the prophecy."

"What does the Mors prophecy say, Mum?"

Pulling a torn, rolled piece of tanned paper from her pocket, Mum placed it on the table in front of Erick and stepped to one side. I leaned forward and gazed at the looped writing on the piece of what I prayed was paper. It was far too thick and rubbery to be paper, and a shudder of foreboding clawed at my skin.

Order out of chaos, chaos out of order. Death she comes, uniting the divided. Sword and shield at her side; she is their salvation, or their doom. For she will rule, her King beside her. All Hail Regina Populi Mortis.

"Interesting. The prophecies are the same, with one exception the last sentence." Erick tapped on the ancient scroll just in front of him. "Ours indicates she will sit upon the throne, beside her king. It also leaves out the 'All Hail the Queen of the People of Death.' I take it your family doesn't have a ruling monarch like ours does?"

"No, we don't. If there is a ruler of any kind, it would be my grand-père—Death," Mum clarified. "As you three are aware, my grand-père has not been seen since the day of my naming ceremony as an infant. My father, sensing the chaos approaching, tasked himself with overseeing the family and reapers; however, his abilities have waned substantially since I last saw him, as has the rest of Death's remaining direct living descendants. Except... umm... myself and... umm you, Evanee."

Curious. I wonder if any of Great Grandfather's reapers have noticed any changes?

Mum cleared her throat, distracting me from my thoughts.

"Now, it's been some time since anyone's seen Death. My father has grown accustomed to his rule, and fears being overthrown from his position. From what I've been able to gather since my return, there has been no attempt to locate my grand-père. I'm not exactly in any rush to remind my father about the prophecy or my suspicion that it refers to Evanee."

I could just imagine how that would go over with my mother's family. *'Hey Papa, I'm back. Oh, and by the way, your long-lost granddaughter is your new queen.'*

"I can see how they might not accept that with open arms."

I rolled my eyes at Erick's dry tone, as he echoed the words he'd surely heard me think.

"I don't see your family or that vampire council you're all so afraid of taking the news any better." Sarcasm dripped thicker than honey as I spoke.

"Evanee." Mum's note of warning did nothing to deter the fear churning my gut.

"What? You're all standing around insinuating that some cockamamie prophecy that that bitch, Fate, concocted, is supposed to be about me. How would you like me to react to this?" Looking between my mother and Erick, I resented the hell out of the fact I was once again being thrown in the deep end with no floaties.

"I mean, if this prophecy is really about me, then that would make you and I." My hands jerked angrily towards Erick. "Nothing more than Fate's pawns in some morbid game of supernatural chess."

Erick stood immobile, as he took in my words.

That would mean what we feel for each other is all a farce, something programmed into our brains by Fate.

"What did you say? Evanee, tell me. What did you mean by Fate concocting the prophecy?"

Mum's worry fell on deaf ears. I was done being a pawn in everyone else's game.

"You heard me, Mum. I know Fate drummed up this useless prophecy. She admitted as much the night she appeared to Erick and me while we were in the cocoon." Shocked into silence by my confession, it took a second before the wheels in my mother's mind began to churn.

Stepping around the desk, I bade my farewell. "Now, if you'll all excuse me I think I've had enough bullshit and drama over the past few weeks to last the rest of my undead life."

I made my escape, leaving Erick's room as Mum rounded on Erick firing questions at his startled face. I couldn't care less what they had to say. A hot shower and peace were what I sought.

Chapter 1

Curlews crooned softly in the cool night air, their eerie cries drifting around me. For some their cries were haunting. To me they were lovers beckoning to their mate, gently reminding them they would always find each other no matter how great the distance between them.

Chaotic thoughts swirled through my mind, but I pushed them aside instead focusing on placing one foot in front of the other as I forced myself to walk at human speed. My powers showed no signs of abating since my death three months ago. While this wasn't a bad thing, the downside meant it was harder for me to function as a human.

I gazed up at the twinkling stars and cheerful moon smiling down at me, mocking me and my sombre mood. Being dead had not been as fun and carefree as the books and movies made it out to be. I still stared down that black tunnel some days, hoping the light would eventually emerge. The hunger, which Erick and Jordan had assured me would go away, only seemed to get worse. Not that I was in any hurry to reveal this to Erick or my mother for fear of their reaction. The last thing I needed was my freedom curtailed any more than it already was.

Breathing deeply, the familiar scents of tea tree and eucalyptus saturated bushland drifted along the breeze to surround me. My one attempt at showing Erick I could be strong, that I deserved the title I would inherit, had ended with a beheaded vampire. Not to mention Erick fearing some all-powerful vampire council would come swooping down from the sky to bring justice upon me. You could cut the air in the mansion with a butter knife, it was that tense.

A gentle pulse of my birth mark at my lower back elicited a shiver of anticipation from me. Whispering, my words drifted along the breeze. "It didn't take you long to find me."

With a weary sigh, Erick stepped from behind a magnificent Paperbark tree. "I didn't want to disturb you, but I thought you should know I just got off the phone with Bob. I'm sorry, *mic luptător*, they lost the last infected human last night."

I cringed at his endearment, *mic luptător*, little fighter. I didn't feel like a fighter tonight, I hadn't for a while now.

"Thank you." I said between gritted teeth, trying my best to hold on to my temper. I had no desire to lose control over my power and accidentally kill anything around me.

"I know what you're thinking, I can see it in your shoulders. They carry the weight of the world, when they don't need to."

When I remained silent, he continued.

"You couldn't have known this would happen. The humans appeared to be stable, and there was nothing any of us could say to tip the doctors off about what happened without causing more drama and getting the government involved."

"You think I don't know that, Erick? Why the hell do you think I kept my mouth shut all these months? It sure as hell wasn't for my benefit." *I should have just let Jordan kill everyone that night in the laboratory and saved them and their families the months of agony.*

"You weren't to know that the decomposition of Jared's creatures would be lethal. How were any of us to know that?"

I knew he was trying to make me feel better, but the more he spoke the more I wanted to punch something or someone.

"No Erick, you're wrong. I should have known." A resounding thud of my fist hitting my chest did little to comfort me. "I mean, come on, the initial virus and her eggs lived in an acid, not to mention the creatures were made up of an acidic compound. I should have known they'd need to be removed surgically; but no, I was too bloody distracted with all the bullshit and melodrama of becoming the first ever vampire-reaper." My body shook with fury, and I refused to turn and face him just yet.

"So, do me a damn favour..." Breath hitching, I paused. "Please, just stop talking, okay. I was a self-centred bitch, and as a result innocent people lost their lives." The slow unfurling of something ancient and powerful rose from deep within me, responding to the overwhelming anger and pain squeezing my dead heart. My clenched fingers loosened their tight grip, flexing so onyx and electric blue sparks drifted down to land atop of the brittle foliage beneath my booted feet. The leaves that had once held life in them, turned to ash as the embers touched down.

"Evanee, you need to calm down. I know what you're feeling, because I feel it too, but now is not the time to fight about it. Aeternum compensated the families of the victims. I've had my people monitor transactions to the victims' families to combat possible lawsuits. I wanted to keep you up to date, so that it wouldn't be something else you could put between us."

"You want to choose your next words carefully, Erick." Hurt pierced my heart, but I pushed it aside, choosing to embrace the anger simmering beneath the surface instead.

"I understand you're angry with being sequestered to the mansion. But you can't deny that when it comes to your mother and I, your temper ignites quicker than drought-stricken bush during an electric storm these days."

He wasn't wrong. Staring into the distance, my mind drifted back to the night I'd finally set eyes on Fate's prophecy. The realisation what I felt for Erick, and what he felt for me in return, might be nothing more than a result of Fate's interference had really hit home. To think under normal circumstances I wouldn't have been someone Erick would've chosen of his own free will, hurt. I'd withdrawn into myself, choosing to spend my days reading, walking in the state forest, or training with Jordan and Aunt Paige whenever she was at the mansion.

Breathing in deeply, I struggled to pull my power back within, when what I wanted was to lash out at anything and everything. Reigning that ancient power in, the hunger lurking in the dark corners of my mind, assaulted me once more. Despair followed close behind it. *Why am I so hungry? Surely it should simmer down by now?*

"Evanee, you need to give yourself credit. You've made so much progress in such a short amount of time. The hunger will gradually become easier to control."

"Reading my mind again?" My lips quirked to one side.

Cheeky bugger.

"I only caught that last thought, but I try not to. Although, I'll take advantage of whatever opportunity presents itself, if it means I'll be one step closer to healing this rift between us."

His confession hurt. A part of me wanted to build on the friendship we'd initially built, but a larger part of me was too afraid of being hurt or worse—hurting him.

"Give me some credit, Erick. At least I'm trying. Being cooped up at the mansion all day, every day, isn't helping. Neither is the fact that I'm cut off from everything I once knew. I haven't seen or spoken to Ellie or Brad for over two months," I said, the venom clear in my tone.

"Enough Evanee. You need to accept there'll be things you'll never be able to do again without betraying the supernatural community. Seeing Ellie and Brad would still be out of the question if they were in Murder Point Bay, because you're still having problems controlling your hunger and speed."

Holding up a hand to silence me, Erick stepped closer as he spoke.

"Don't bother denying it. It's only been a little over three months since your conversion, and we still don't know what powers you've inherited."

"And what about you? I can't have been the only one who inherited new powers. As I recall, you were trapped in the cocoon right along with me."

Huffing in frustration, his pale hand combed at dark spiky locks, only for them to spring back into place.

"You're being purposefully obtuse, Evanee. I have over 500 years of experience with controlling the powers I already have. I don't think my new powers will be any harder to control."

Gesturing at me, Erick's exasperation came across loud and clear.

"You barely knew your abilities before the conversion."

So, he has received new powers. He could have at least given me a heads up.

'That would've been hard considering you've been avoiding him since the prophecy. Give the poor man a break.'

My inner bimbo snapped in frustration at my bull headedness, all the while applying a fresh layer of red lipstick.

Erick was speaking again, dragging my attention back to him.

"Without testing, we have no idea what your weaknesses are. You've built an immunity to the sunlight at an accelerated rate. We're yet to determine if a stake to your heart will kill you. We have no idea what vulnerabilities reapers have, as you keep avoiding your mother like the plague. Aside from Death, his creations, and your extended family, is there something or someone else who might pose a risk to your life? Then there're your damn temper tantrums, and the fallout from them."

Silence settled around us as he registered what he'd just blurted out.

The power I'd been struggling to contain barrelled upwards, a cold rage settling over my mind. My anger lashed at the surrounding air and I snarled, "You want a temper tantrum, Erick, I'll give you a tantrum like you've never seen before."

Erick's calmness further fuelled my temper as my voice rose. "Who exactly gets to determine whether I have a handle on my newfound abilities, Erick? Who determines when I will regain my independence? You?"

The surrounding air thickened, compressing my empty lungs a little more, and I was grateful I no longer needed to breathe as Erick stared unblinking at me.

Finally, his power receded, and he addressed me with a composure I'd have imagined him using to address members of the council or during his many staff meetings, but not during an argument.

"Stop this now, Evanee. I will not be held accountable for my response if you continue to behave like a child."

Passion and conviction drove me onward as I yelled at the steadfast male before me. "If I'm behaving like a child, it's in response to your shitty parenting skills. I want to see Uncle Bob, Aunty Marg, Steve, Brad, and Ellie. I miss my work and the help I gave to those needing justice. Instead, I'm stuck here listening to Tristan and Jordan bitch at each other day in and day out."

A sudden intense urge to scratch at an itch at the top of my spine, between my shoulder blades, distracted me. As it continued, my eyes shifted around the area, subtly looking for the nearest stick. Argh, m*an that's itchy.* Erick's retort drew my attention back to the now seething vampire before me.

"Your ungratefulness astounds me, you know that? I've been putting out the damn fires you started with your little stunt outside the lab. I have my father pressuring to meet you, and the council isn't far behind him. Between the transformation and my absence during it, your poorly timed killing at the lab, and that damn prophecy, I've had my hands full. So, you'll have to put up and shut up until things quiet down. I don't have the time to deal with your insecurities and melodramas right now."

Power glowed from the depths of his eyes, as he lost what little patience he'd been holding on to. If he'd been human, he'd have been breathing heavy from sheer anger and frustration.

Needing a distraction from the itch that had re-emerged at my shoulder blades, I stepped forward so Erick and I came face to face. We stared unblinking at each other, neither willing to budge first.

When the itching grew too much, I blinked, whispering, "I'm drowning here and all you can see is that I'm a pain in the arse."

Erick stood unmoving and non-pulsed, the glint in his hooded gaze betraying his resolve. Tugging me closer, he bent his head to whisper in my ear.

"You will not leave this property, Evanee. I have my reasons for limiting your access to the outside world, and they're my own. You leave without my consent and I will lock you in the basement right beside your best mate, Jared. I'm your sire, Evanee, and I won't tolerate your insubordination. Don't screw with me on this."

Releasing my hands hard so I stumbled backwards, he turned and disappeared into the darkness from which he'd emerged.

Clenching my jaw against the sob of anguish lodged deep within my throat, I dashed at a single tear making its escape down my cheek, the itch in my spine forgotten. "I'm done. I'll give you bloody insecurities and temper tantrums."

Summoning my reaper's portal, I stared into a darkened bedroom beyond. Sounds of beeping machines drifted through from beyond, at odds with the crickets and rustling leaves of the eucalyptus trees swaying in the light breeze around me.

I'm done being everyone's little puppet, and we all knew this was a long time coming.

Without hesitation I stepped through the portal and into another kind of hell.

Chapter 2

Shadows clung to my curves, hiding me as I studied the still figure in the centre of the king-sized bed. The heart monitor beeped over and over, annoying me. I'd been standing here for the last fifteen minutes, the stench of decaying flesh stinging my nostrils. Yet I remained unmoving, used to the numerous odours bodies made in their various states of decay.

At last, I glided forward, silently approaching the man who'd haunted my nightmares for the past three years. The man who'd been the firing gun at the race to my descent to hell—Brian Turner.

A slight disturbance in the air behind me was my only warning I was no longer alone. Turning my head slightly, three figures appeared in the spot I'd stood not moments before. Glowing garnet and emerald orbs gave away one intruder, as did the giant outline and glowing amber and carmine eyes of the second figure. The third, could only be my mother, considering how quickly they'd found me.

I glanced back at a slumbering Brian, ignoring my audience. Anger and sorrow ripped at my still heart. He'd taken so much from me that night. My trust and self-confidence had disappeared the instant his hand clamped around my mouth. I was the lucky one who'd escaped relatively unscathed. I'd not experienced the rape, torture, and degradation the other women had, and I was both glad for it—and guilty because of it.

Three years later, he'd once again put me in a position to fight for my life. Oh, sure, he wasn't wholly responsible for the attack, but he'd played a part in it. He'd succeeded in a way he hadn't the last time. I'd lost my life. Well, my human life at least.

An eerie, soft pearl glow emanated from my body, bouncing off the sterile white sheets encasing his decaying body. Around the room, writhing shadows rose up the walls in response to my heightened emotions. The cries of the damned wailed softly, reaching for freedom, yet never able to achieve it. The snow-white strands of my hair lifted on an unfelt breeze. Looking towards the mirrored cupboards that sat along one of the bedroom walls, the now familiar image of a ghostly woman in a decaying and tattered dress stared back at me.

Turning from my haunting image, I considered Brian, debating my next step. *Do I reap him and be rid of him forever, or should I leave him in this perpetual state of hell?* His eyelids quivered and flicked open to reveal grey eyes that fixed on me with confusion.

His dry lips opened, and he wheezed, "Are you here to take me?"

I wonder who he thinks I am? Devil or angel?

"I'm wondering that myself, Brian Turner. I'm unsure as to whether I should grant you peace from this curse I've inflicted on you or do I leave you to suffer like so many of your victims, myself included?"

Seconds ticked by before he realised who stood at his bedside.

"You're no angel… You're the bitch who ruined my life," Brian spluttered.

Wow, he really thought he was going to heaven.

"Oh, come now Brian, don't be such a sissy. It's not that bad." Bending down, I pinched at the sheet, drawing it up to see what lay beneath. It wasn't pretty. "Okay, well maybe it is that bad, but on the plus side at least your outsides now match that disgusting soul of yours."

"You fu—"

He trailed off, overcome with racking coughs that shook his depleted body. I stared at him impassively.

It looked like Desmond, was right. The decay had spread from his penis to above his kneecap and halfway up his chest. Sitting on the edge of the bed, I no longer feared him. He wasn't going anywhere in this state.

"Here's the thing, Brian. I could reap you right here and now. I could send you drifting off to Death, allowing you to pass on to whatever awaits you beyond the veil. I believe my mother would jump at the opportunity to reap your rotted arse. She's here by the way, behind me in the corner of the room." Twisting around, my fingers wiggled at my mother. Brian's hate-filled gaze drifted to where I was waving. I had no idea if he could see her, or whether he only saw the other two shadows. "It'd be so easy, you know. All I'd have to do is reach into that spot where that putrescent soul of yours sits and pluck it out."

Watching him carefully, his expression never changed, and it dawned on me then he would never be sorry for his crimes. He'd never understand the hell he caused and given half the chance he would kill me slowly and painfully.

"Well, what the hell are you waiting for then? Get it over with." Wincing, he slurred through the pain.

"Nothing, really."

Rising slowly, my knee and hand grounded my body as I leaned across the mattress to place a translucent hand just above where the sheets and his night shirt stuck to his pathetic body. I hesitated momentarily, thinking out loud.

"If I reap you, you'll be released from the hell you're in. There will no longer be any reason for your parents to look upon their spoiled and sadistic son. I've seen your parents, and I have no doubt they are equally to blame for the self-entitled brat they raised."

Looking deep into his grey eyes, I gave him one last chance to show any signs of remorse. When none appeared, it made my decision easier.

"Then again, where would the fun be in releasing you from the hell you're locked in? Did you think I wouldn't find out about your cousin's plans for me? Oh." I chuckled slightly. "Desmond will meet you on the other side when your body finally gives in."

Shock filled his pain-hazed eyes. Looking carefully at Brian's handsome features, I could see how so many women had fallen for his tricks, myself included. That straight nose and strong jawline accompanied with those steely grey eyes.

I didn't smile as I whispered my confession. "No one told you, did they? Desmond died in a rather unfortunate lab incident. I ripped his throat out and left his body to decompose in acid; but not before I allowed him to become infected by the very creature I extracted from my back."

He spluttered in shock at my confession, but I held up a finger to silence him.

"Shush, I'm not done. As for you, I think I'll approach things differently. Look long and hard into these… What did you call them again? Ah yes, that's right. 'Fuck me' eyes. Know I won't do a damn thing to ease this never-ending pain. You don't deserve peace Brian, not after the pain you caused so many of my sisters." Smiling savagely down at him, I pushed lightly off the bed to stand beside it.

"You bitch. I will kill you. I will see the light bleed from those eyes!" Spittle dribbled down his chin as he yelled.

"Brian, Brian, you're too late. You can't kill what's already dead. Didn't you notice the light display and ghostly appearance? No? Well, here's a little something just for you." Fangs extending, I smiled the biggest smile I had in my arsenal, my swirling eyes never changing.

"You whore. I hate you, hate you, do you hear me? I won't die until you're dead and rotting in the ground where you belong."

Turning from him, I waved at the sliding door to the balcony, stepping through it as it opened. The three beings who had borne witness to my revenge followed.

Embracing Brisbane's muggy night air, I was grateful to be away from Brian and the putrid odour of his decaying flesh. Behind me the doors drew closed, silencing Brian's hateful words. My relief was short-lived when Erick stepped up behind me and put his hands around my upper arms.

He hissed into my hair, and I stared stubbornly ahead as he spoke.

"I expressly told you not to leave the property. You've put not only yourself in danger tonight, but other humans near you. I told you what would happen if you disregarded my warning."

I had nothing left for Erick tonight. I was hollow inside, my emotions depleted.

"I harmed no one tonight, and I heard your warning, Erick. Frankly, I just didn't give a shit. But I'll tell you what. I'll just go right ahead and put myself in the basement right beside Jared, shall I? Save you the trouble and all that. Is it the room to the right or the left? You know what, never mind. I'll just choose one." Ripping my arms from his grasp, I jumped atop of the railing, staring down at the traffic ten stories below me.

"Evanee, what are you doing?" Jordan approached the railing warily.

"I'd heal if I jumped from this height, right?" My question was a whisper along the connection Jordan and I shared.

"It'd hurt like all hell, and you'd be bed ridden for a while, but yeah you'd heal."

I could always count on Jordan to answer me honestly. I respected him for it.

"Thanks." Not looking back, I stepped off the railing, plummeting to the ground below. The exhilaration of the fall was exactly what I'd hoped for. The adrenaline exploded to life, replacing the bleakness and hopelessness I felt.

My spine tingled and tightness travelled across my upper back. A distinct ripping sound echoed in my ears as the skin ripped open. Shocked by the sensation, I summoned a portal, dropping through it as something erupted from fresh slits on either side on my spine. Landing heavily in one of the dark rooms of Erick's basement, my legs gave out. I landed hard on my knees.

Loud cracks released as they connected with the cement floor, the pain of my shattered kneecaps mingling with the panic of what I was feeling at my back. Breathing deep past the pain, I summoned every last drop of courage I had to look over my shoulder, dreading what I might find at my back.

Flared out in an impressive display of brilliance were a pair of transparent moth-like wings resembling the dress I wore in reaper mode shredded at the tips. They flared once before they curled in on themselves, retreating from where they'd erupted. Ripping at remnants of my shredded shirt, the rags dropped forgotten to the ground as I gingerly patted at my back, expecting to feel lumps, only to feel smooth skin.

I sagged in relief, and the world tilted, the corners of my vision darkening. I had seconds to realise what was happening before falling face first into the coarse cement, as I blacked out.

My eyes snapped open to the clicking of the lock giving way. I had no energy to move from the cramped position I'd fallen in when I'd blacked out, nor did I have any desire to do so. I had no idea how long I'd been like this but judging from the bruised feeling of my face and my numb arms and legs, it must have been at least a few hours.

The door opened slowly as Erick's power pushed its way into the tiny room. At last he silently stepped inside. Jared's hoarse screams of terror reached my ears, only to be silenced when Erick shut the door behind him. I didn't care about any of it. For once I'd had a dreamless sleep and not woken to my own petrified screeches. Down here in the sound-proofed rooms, silence ruled, and I was grateful. There were no scents, no angry yells or side looks.

"I know you're awake, Evanee. Why are you lying on the floor like that?"

His low growl tickled along my sensitised back, but I didn't move.

"I was practicing some yoga." The hunger was returning, but I pushed it aside. Erick's strong arms rolled me over gently before he scooped me up and deposited me on what could be the world's most comfortable bed.

"Really? Funny, it looks like you landed on your knees and passed out." Sighing in frustration, he disappeared briefly, only to return with a blanket. "Why won't you just listen to me? I have my reasons for wanting to keep you in the mansion. It's not just your safety I'm concerned for, but those you come into contact with. I'm not doing it to hurt you, *mic luptător*."

He laid the blanket over my shaking body and slowly stretched my cramped limbs out.

I remained silent until he finished, then tugged at the blanket until it sat just below my nose. *This bed really isn't half bad. Although, that could be because I passed out on the floor for who knows how long.*

"Look, I overreacted," Erick admitted, "and I know threatening to put you down here wasn't the right thing. I've had to be firm when dealing with fledglings in the past, and perhaps that's not the best way to deal with you. You just make me so furious some days, when all I want to do is protect you, but you won't let me, and I don't understand why."

The bed dipped gently beside my legs as he sat.

"Why do you keep pushing me away? Why did you jump from the balcony, *mic luptător*? Am I that unbearable that you'd inflict harm on yourself to be away from me?"

His questions hurt, and I wanted desperately to tell him it had nothing to do with him. I wanted so badly to tell him taking that step, feeling the wind rip at my hair as I plummeted ten stories, was the most exhilarating thing I'd felt since the conversion. I wanted to tell him seeing Brian had been the only way to re-establish control over my life again. But I feared how he would look at me if I told him I'd needed to feel something other than hunger, or anger, or hopelessness and sorrow. There'd been so little happiness since I'd died, and it'd taken its toll.

Erick sat patiently waiting for me to respond, but there was nothing I could say he could understand.

"Like you, I had my reasons, Erick. I would like to be left alone for a little while."

"That's it? The tough and unbeatable Evanee Sheperd is giving up?"

Anger shook his voice, and I imagined him clenching his fist.

"No one is unbeatable, Erick, not even me. I don't know why you're so angry anyway. If I'm down here, I'm out of everyone's hair and not creating messes for you to clean up. I'd have thought you'd be happy about that. Now please, just leave me alone." It hurt to have him near me. I'd bounce back when I was ready, but for now I needed to be alone.

As if sensing my fragility, Erick sighed.

"Okay, I'll go. Come out whenever you're ready, the door won't be locked."

My eyes shut as Erick stood. I thought I heard him whisper 'I'm sorry' just as he left the room, but I didn't call him back. It allowed me to escape the reality that was my life.

⁐

"So, this is where you've hidden yourself, is it?"

A deep, calm voice jolted me from my sleep.

Rolling over in haste, I shrieked as I tipped over the edge of the single bed I'd been peacefully slumbering in.

"Crap, that hurt." Pushing up, I shoved at the tangled blankets around me rubbing my upper arm that had taken the brunt of my fall.

"Do you need a hand?" came an amused drawl.

Head darting up in surprise, I realised I hadn't imagined that dark voice. Looking around the tiny shadowed room I searched for the owner of it and came up empty-handed. Except for me, the room was vacant.

"Is someone there?" I wrapped the blankets tighter around my bare shoulders.

"Don't be afraid, little one. I would, could, never hurt you. You are too special to me." A dark outline detached itself from the dark corner of the room, morphing out of the shadows themselves.

"Death?"

Wow, now that's a man who knows how to make an entrance.

Chuckling at my astonishment, he responded.

"The one and only, though I'd prefer you called me Grandpa or Grandfather. I'd say Great Grandfather, but it's rather a mouthful, don't you think?"

His shadowy figure loomed above me; a perpetually changing hand extended out to me. I stared as it morphed from a young man's hand to an elderly lady's, and bulked slightly as a clawed and furry paw, much like a lion's, replaced the aged ravaged hand. Hesitantly I reached up from beneath the blanket, placing my own skeletal looking hand in his.

"I guess I should say thank you for the scythe then. It came in handy." A small smile was all I could manage as I was still a little stunned the one and only Death was standing in this tiny room with me. His soft chuckle reminded me of leaves rustling in a gentle wind, and it was strangely soothing, yet at odds with the cloaked figure before me.

"Oh, I saw your battle. You made me immensely proud. I have to say though, watching you battle Erick was a little harder to watch. I could have swatted that little brat for hurting you like he did that night in the forest."

His irritation made me grin. "I think I landed my fair share of punches. He had me at a disadvantage, considering the life was being sucked from me. Still, I thought I did rather well." Standing at last, I moved to sit on the bed, weak from lack of blood.

"Here, drink this. It should help you regain some of your stamina."

A unit of blood materialised in front of me, and I latched onto it, not bothering to hide my starvation from him. The bag drained, and another appeared. I took it, draining it too.

"Thank you. So, what brings you to my neck of the woods?" Sitting back, I tried to make myself as comfortable as I could against the hard brick wall.

"I thought it might be time to introduce myself. I've spent so long watching over you and your mother, I'd forgotten you weren't even aware who I was," he said matter-of-factly. An arm chair materialised behind him, and he made himself comfortable.

"You've been watching over us? How did my mother never sense you, or me for that matter? I thought our DNA would call to one another, kind of like how I know whenever my mother is near?" I sipped at the new unit of blood that appeared and waited for his response.

"Sweet child, I am Death. I could stand in front of you, and you'd never even know I was there. Reality is something I bend to my whim. It's one perk of the job. That and a few others."

I studied where his face should have been, feeling slightly disorientated as it shifted like his hand had.

"Fair enough. I was right, then. You were the man who spoke to me the night Brian attacked. Why didn't you help me if you knew what was happening?" Hurt tightened my throat at the thought he'd not cared enough to help me when I needed it most.

"Sweetheart, if I'd been able to help you I would've, but, I'm not at liberty to change a person's fate, no matter how much I want too."

Mouth opening and closing, I may as well have been a fish on dry land. All I'd need to do was flop around a bit and the image would be complete. "Are you kidding me? That night was one of the worst nights of my life, and you're telling me you couldn't at least have flung the idiot across the parking lot to give me a head start? All because of my so-called fate. What the hell kind of excuse is that?" An angry red tinge crept into the corners of my visions, and my fists clenched.

His dark chuckle caught me off guard, and I bristled.

"That temper of yours, Evanee, it's always been such a delight to watch, but to have it turned on me is refreshing. I can't remember the last time someone reprimanded me."

Are all gods bat shit crazy, or is it just the ones who visit me? "That's all well and good, but you still didn't answer me, *Grandfather.*" I hoped the reminder of our familial connection might push him to answer me.

"Well played, granddaughter. It's not an excuse, it is just how things are. Now it's your turn to answer me. Why are you hiding down here?"

He gestured to the windowless room around him as he spoke, and I suddenly realised we were having this conversation in the dark.

The joys of great night vision.

"I'm not hiding." My high-pitched retort belied my words. Grandfather sat silently, watching me, waiting for the truth.

"Okay, fine. Yes, I'm hiding. It seems to be the only place I can get any peace. Not to mention, I've had the best sleep down here since my untimely demise."

"I see, and why have you not been sleeping well?" He questioned.

There was a curiosity to his voice, and I wondered whether I'd inherited my own curious nature from him.

I sat for a moment, debating whether to tell him the truth, or lie as I'd been doing whenever anyone asked how I was going. *What harm could it do? He might be able to help. After all, he is as old as time itself.*

"The truth?" He nodded his incorporeal head, and I continued. "Because I'm starving. Blood isn't cutting it anymore, and then there're the incessant nightmares and this horrible feeling that the other shoe is about to drop. Oh, and then there's the prophecy that has me questioning everything

I thought I knew. It's too much." Placing the now empty blood bag beside me, it disappeared instantly.

"Is blood the only staple in your diet?"

His question stumped me. Out of everything I'd just said, he'd focused on my hunger, and it baffled me.

"Uh, yes. I can't exactly eat human food anymore, which I am seriously missing by the way. I'd kill for a piece of dark chocolate cake."

"Dear child, human food and blood are not the only food source. Everything needs sustenance to survive."

His amusement at my conundrum was not helping to suppress that temper he loved so much. My power rose to greet my anger as if they were old friends.

"I'm really not in the mood to beat around the bush, Grandfather, so if you know what's missing from my diet, it'd be brilliant if you could just spit it out."

"All right, I'll give you a clue. Humans eat meat, vegetables and fruit; vampires drink blood; ghouls consume flesh and blood; werewolves consume raw meat; so, what do my descendants and creations survive on?"

Hang on, there are werewolves and ghouls out there? Fan-bloody-tastic.

"You'll have to give me a second, I'm still stuck on the existence of werewolves and ghouls. Mum has always eaten human food. I don't think I've seen her eat anything other than human food. As for your other descendants and creations, I've never met them, so I really wouldn't know what they eat."

Sighing, Grandfather got to his feet, leaving me to scramble to mine.

"Wait, don't leave, please. If you know what I need, please tell me, then maybe I can right at least one thing in my life." I thought of Erick and the hurt in his voice the last time he'd been in this room.

"I would love to stay longer, but I have a soul to reap in the room next to this. Think on what I told you, and you'll figure it out. Consider this a test of sorts."

"A test. Why the hell are you testing me? It's not like I don't have enough on my plate as it is. Did you not hear what I said before about impending doom and that forsaken prophecy?" I screeched in desperation.

He chuckled. "Evanee, you're probably one of the smartest of my descendants, other than your mother. I have every faith you will figure it out in time. As for righting things in your life; my child, there is more to life than trying to right things that cannot be changed. You are who you are. Perhaps if you stopped fighting it, and accepted yourself, you might not have so much trouble making the decisions that need to be made."

Words of wisdom if ever I heard them.

"Fine, I'll work on it. Did you know I was the one who'd fulfil the prophecy?" I desperately wanted him to stay, I had so many questions.

"Yes, and no. I thought it might be your mother, but when she fell pregnant with you, I knew it would be you who'd unite the species of death. I once ruled over them all, and now it looks like you'll take my place."

Bending ever so slightly to accommodate my 5'7" height, Death reached out with his eerie hand; a gentle damp mist drifted gently over me as he tilted my head up ever so slightly, placing the lightest of kisses to my forehead.

He stepped back into the reaching shadows, his figure engulfed in darkness, but he imparted one last piece of wisdom before he left.

"Remember, be who you are and not who everyone expects you to be."

Then he disappeared, and I was once again alone in my tiny windowless room.

"Hang on, did he just say he was here to reap Jared?"

I frowned. My great grandfather was an odd man, or was he a god?

He showed little emotion, yet his words were heavy with meaning. Shaking my head at just how odd my life had become, I summoned a portal with a sigh.

"I guess it's time to get my arse into gear."

When a buzzing took up residence at the back of my skull, I turned to stare at the wall separating Jared's room from mine. With a pop, the buzzing stopped. With a shudder I stepped through the portal and into the guest bathroom I'd been using since my arrival.

Chapter 3

Wandering through the mansion, my mind drifted as I slowed my pace once again, concentrating on mimicking a human's walking speed. The quicker I learned to act human, the quicker I'd be able to return to work. My only dilemma was my current dietary requirements and what was lacking within it. My initial thought was I needed souls, but I found the thought of consuming someone's soul repugnant. I pushed the thought from my mind, not ready to deal the idea I needed to eat the very things I had worked so hard to release to their final resting place.

Approaching the converted gym, the thud of a body hitting the mat followed by a deep-bellied laugh drew my attention. The stretching sensation of my birthmark at my lower back preceded Jordan's deep-bellied laugh. My birthmark had become a homing beacon of sorts for not only Erick, but Jordan as well. The vibrations of my phone in my palm drew my attention, and I looked down at the smiling face and name lighting my screen.

"Doctor Death speaking." Grinning like an idiot, I stalled outside the grand wooden doors to the gym waiting for my boss and adopted uncle to respond.

"Good evening, I was wondering if you might have a spare moment to chat with your senile boss?"

Laughing at his chirpy tone, my heart ached a little. We'd only spoken on the phone since my conversion, feeling it too risky for me see him and his wife Margaret. I'd missed them both, especially since I'd finally revealed my dark secret. They still loved me, despite me being a monster.

"Mm, senile boss, you say? I recall having one of those. I believe I kept having to show him how things were done during our shared autopsies." A happy warmth infused my body as we joked, it made me feel normal again.

"Yeah, yeah, laugh while you still can. If memory serves me correct, you cheated. Having superpowers equates to cheating you know." The steady click of his fingers hitting the keyboard filtered through the line.

"Me, cheat? Never. But in all seriousness, Uncle Bob, what's up. Is everything okay?" I worried when he'd called. Although we were close, our phone calls tended to either be about work or something more serious. Considering they'd revoked my clearance after my supposed death, I was assuming he had called for personal reasons.

"Everything is fine, relax. I'm calling to let you know I received your identification cards, and that you are all clear to come back to work."

Say what now?

"How did you manage that?" I was in awe. I had only submitted the paperwork declaring I was 'alive' a week ago.

"I called in a few favours with some friends in high up places. I really can't say any more than that, or I'd have to kill you."

I giggled, a weight lifting from my shoulders. This was good. My life was getting back on track. The only issue would be to convince Erick I was ready to re-enter civilization.

"When can I start?"

"I have you rostered for Monday. I thought I'd give you the weekend to get your ducks in a row before you dive into the hustle and bustle of work life again."

"Really? That's fantastic, will you be there, or will I be taking the shift on my own?" Fingers crossed behind my back, I prayed he'd be taking the shift with me.

"Oh, I'll be here. I wouldn't miss it for the world. I've also rostered Mel on. I believe Steve reorganised his schedule to be on the night shift when you come in too."

And the team was back in action. Fist punching the air, I did a little happy dance, stopping short when I caught sight of Jordan leaning against the door frame, smiling at me.

"That's fantastic news. Hey, I umm… have to go. Is it the same start time as usual?" Watching Jordan's eyebrow rise, I didn't have to guess what he was thinking.

"Yup, 4pm start."

"Fantastic, I'll see you then. Say hello to everyone for me. Speak to you later." Saying his farewells, the line went dead.

"He'll never go for it, you know that, right?" Pushing off the door frame, Jordan unwound his arms, dropping them loosely to his side.

"It's not really up to him, Jordan. I'm done being dictated to, and I'm done being 'poor Evanee'. I want a normal life, even it means only going back to work and living in my little cottage. I'll settle for that." I would get my arse out of this depressed mood I'd been in lately. Grandfather's appearance had been the wakeup call I needed. I was Evanee

Sheperd, and I never gave up no matter how down and out I was. I'd forgotten this over the last few months, but I'd be damned if I'd forget it again.

"I hate to break it to you, but it is up to him. You need to under—"

I stepped around Jordan, and into the gym, interrupting his speech. With a sigh, he followed me in and stood beside me as I observed Tristan sparing with another vampire in the centre of the room.

"Where is the lord and master anyway?"

"In his office, I believe. Someone told him you left the basement." Jordan shrugged at me apologetically, and I focused on Tristan's fluid movements.

"Did elf boy tell him?" I knew he'd hear me, and right on cue he stalled, leaving him open to his opponent's strike. Tristan sailed through the air, landing with a thump on the other side of the mat. Grinning, I sauntered over to greet them.

"I heard that you know?" Tristan complained.

"You did? I'll be sure to whisper next time." I replied in mock seriousness.

"You're in workout gear. That mean you're here to challenge me, or are you still too chicken shit?"

I glanced at my exercise leggings and crop top and met his glare with a grin.

"You bet your arse I'm here to challenge you; except, no sharp pointy things. I really can't afford to keep replacing my clothes just yet." Jumping lightly, I sailed through the air, landing softly in the middle of the enormous blue mat.

"No rules, all out?" His grin was slightly menacing.

In other words, he'd snap my neck if he got me in the position. I had a little more confidence now than when I'd first stepped onto this mat for training. He and Erick had no clue Jordan and I trained when they weren't home. Knives, swords, scythe, all my weapons of choice. Hand to hand combat was a must according to Jordan, whereas guns were crass and a last resort. He wanted to be certain I could hold my own if challenged to combat.

"You're looking forward to snapping my neck, aren't you?"

Jordan snorted in exasperation as he straddled a chair he'd somehow acquired. Tristan waited patiently for me to give my final okay.

"I think I can handle that."

Meeting me at the centre, we shook hands before assuming our fighting stances. Silence settled over the gym as we eyed each other. My hands curled into fists, while Tristan tensed ever so slightly.

"FIGHT!" Bellowed Jordan.

We circled each other, assessing each other for signs of weakness. My concentration was complete, just as it was when I stepped up to my autopsy table. Circling once more, Tristan struck, a blur of movement. My head ducked to the left, narrowly avoiding his white-knuckled fist to my face. Straightening up, I regained my footing before he struck again. I met him mid-way, shackling his clawed hands in my grip.

"Hey! I thought we agreed no sharp or pointy things." Panting with the effort to stop his strike, I watched as a vicious smile lit his transformed face.

Wow, he's going full vamp.

He was still handsome, despite his skin being just a little tighter around his cheekbones and forehead. Lavender glowed brightly from within his eyes. Flecks of garnet swirling chaotically to the surface before disappearing once more.

"What's the matter *princess*, you scared?" His hiss taunted my own powers.

Hissing back, I grinned savagely. This is what I needed; someone who wouldn't take it easy on me. Someone who wasn't going to sugar coat things.

"Bring it on, elf boy. If you're lucky, I might even remove that stick shoved up your arse."

Releasing him, we backed off before circling each other once more. My long lean fingers flexed, talons erupting to replace my fingernails. Mist exploded from beneath my feet in a white tsunami. My new wings itched to be released again, but I refused them the freedom they sought. Fighting wasn't the only thing I'd been practicing. It was all about control.

Together we were a blur, slamming into each other as we met in the middle of the mat once again. Sharp claws ripped at the soft flesh of my belly, blood seeping through before the wound could heal. I responded in kind with a savage swipe to his face. We were a match, landing blow after blow on each other, healing as quickly as the cuts and breaks were inflicted.

I can't keep this up much longer. I'm expending far too much energy. Knowing there was no other way out, I did the only thing I knew he couldn't.

He stepped forward, his claws circling my throat as my own talons reached for his heart. He was none the wiser, his look of victory premature.

"I win, *princess*," he spat, his grin savage.

"I hate to break it to you mate, but she has you."

Erick spoke up from the sidelines, where Jordan whooped, and wolf whistled at me. I'd been so focused, I hadn't registered his entrance.

Jordan's cheerful boast sang throughout the gym. "Atta girl. You see that Erick. My protégé is a chip off the old block."

"What the hell are you all talking about? I have her around the neck, which I will snap in a second, by the way."

Tristan looked back at me as he finished speaking.

"Not before I remove your heart, *elf boy*."

Looking down, his face was comical as he finally registered just how screwed he was. There, sticking out of his chest, was my solid arm, while tightly wrapped in my corporal hand was his heart.

"All it would take is a thought and you'd have a solid hand inside your chest. Now, I don't know about you, but I don't think I'd be recovering from a missing heart any time soon." Smiling sweetly at him, I watched as he carefully lowered his hand from around my neck, trying not to jar my hand or arm.

Stepping into his face, I hissed softly, "Do you concede?"

"I do."

He still hadn't moved. Withdrawing my arm, it once again solidified. Tristan rubbed at the spot my arm had been protruding from, before he shook his head, a small smile creasing his lush lips.

"You've come a long way, Evanee."

It was as close to a compliment as I'd get.

I'll take it.

"Thank you, Tristan."

"He's right, you have come a long way since we last sparred."

Erick watched me curiously.

"I've been training with Jordan and on occasions, Aunt Paige, every spare minute for the past three months. Keeping up a human appearance isn't the only way I've been preparing myself to re-enter civilization." I stood loosely, but alert. The last time we'd spoken about me leaving the mansion, it hadn't ended well.

"I see."

Not this crap again. Can't he give me a damn break?

"Do you really see Erick? Because I'm sensing you're about to put your foot down once again, when you really have no right to."

Erick's eyebrow rose, and I tried hard not to stare at his arms crossed over his chest, bulging ever so slightly. It was very distracting, as was his dark chocolate locks and stunning emerald eyes framed by winged eyebrows. If he turned around, I'd be done for. The man had an arse and back that would leave me in a drooling mess. He was talking again, and I mentally dragged my mind, which was clearly on heat, back to the present.

"Evanee, I do have a right. It is a law within our species for the sire to have the final say on whether a fledgling is ready to once again walk amongst the humans. We risk alerting the human authorities to the supernatural community if we don't adhere to these laws, and as your sire, I don't believe you're ready."

I looked towards Jordan, who nodded sympathetically at me. This was what he'd been trying to warn me about earlier.

"Are you kidding me? There is no way in hell I'm abiding by that law. I'll never get out of this place if it's left up to you to decide when I'm ready. You treat me as though I'm some new toy, and you don't want to share me."

"And what if I don't want to share you?" Erick hissed in frustration.

That was a little left of field. We hadn't approached the topic of what our relationship was exactly.

"You can't keep me hidden forever, Erick. I'm a living, not-quite-breathing woman who led an independent life up until the shit hit the proverbial fan. I've allowed you to take the lead until things simmered down. I'm grateful for the help and kindness you've shown me, but it's time for me to put my big girl panties back on and get on with my life."

Pausing briefly to regain my composure, I continued. "Bob reinstated my security clearance and I start my first shift on Monday evening. I'd like it if you could support me, even if it is only as a friend, but if you won't." I shrugged nonchalantly, while my gut squeezed anxiously. "Well, there's not a whole hell of a lot I can do about that. I will return to work, and I also plan on returning to my house. I love the mansion and all, but I don't have the fondest memories of this place and I miss my house and creature comforts."

I watched Erick closely as he considered my words. His growled response shocked me.

"No."

"Excuse me?" A red haze drifted over my eyes, and I clenched my fists against the rising need to punch him.

"I said no, Evanee. You're still not ready. Your little temper tantrum at Brian's apartment proves my point."

He was gesturing towards me, still speaking; but I couldn't hear past the blood pounding in my ears. After everything I'd just said, he still hadn't listened.

"Each fledgling needs to pass a series of, let's call it tests, before their sire is satisfied they have enough control. The fledgling needs to protect themselves, which I see you've vastly improved on. They must have control over any inherited powers; and, they must have control over their hunger. The last two concern me the most with you. Your powers respond to your moods, which have been temperamental at best. Then there is your appetite, which has not diminished or settled as it should have," he explained calmly. "Everyone in this room has had to undergo this process upon conversion, and so will you."

"I don't need your permission, Erick; I'm going back to work on Monday come hell or high water." *Why can't he just get on board for once? Why can't he just trust me to know myself?*

What do you care what he thinks of you? I thought you delegated him to friend status after he banned you from leaving the mansion.

My inner bimbo chose that moment to make her grand entrance.

I don't care what he thinks, but it would have been nice if he could get behind me in front of the others. Even if it was only as a friend.

Honey, the only time that man will get behind you, is in the sack.

Sipping at her Cosmopolitan, she was all elegance.

You keep trying to defy him, like I would.

And cue the inner teenager.

It's the only way to get through to him.

Is it? Maybe stop trying to act like a child and start acting like his equal.

She had a point. I'd never earned his respect, because he'd only ever seen me as the damsel in distress. Things were different now. I had my powers, things were somewhat repaired with my mother, and I had my friends and my career.

"Let's fight for it." I spoke suddenly. A look of surprise flickered across his eyes.

"If I win, I'm ready to step out into the big bad world. If you win, I'll wait until you give the say so." It was risky, especially considering he was an excellent fighter in both hand to hand combat and the majority of the weapons lining the four walls of the gym. But he wasn't fighting for something precious like I was. He had nothing to lose in this battle, I had everything.

"I suppose we could test your ability to protect yourself now. That still leaves your powers and control over your appetite. How do you plan to convince me you're ready in those areas?"

Oh, I'll convince you, with my foot up your arse.

"You've seen me fight Tristan, and you've seen just how much I've learned in such a short time. Who's to say it's just my fighting I've improved on? Could it be that I've mastered control over my powers too?" I taunted him, knowing he would be curious to see if I'd improved as much as I was hinting at.

Sure, I'd lost my temper in the woods, and yes, I should have held my temper in check. That didn't mean I hadn't been practicing mindful meditation or learning control over the powers I knew I had.

"So, are you going to come onto the mat, or do I need to drag you up here and kick your arse." Posturing was a fantastic little trick Jordan had taught me. Feign confidence to throw your enemy off, no matter how much you're shaking in your boots—and I was shaking.

"All right, I'll agree to your terms. No weapons or powers. You cannot back out of this if I best you, Evanee. I mean it. Trust goes both ways, and while I know I've broken yours in the past, you haven't been far off breaking mine lately."

His words stung. My stunt at Brian's apartment had hurt him more than he'd let on. Nodding stiffly, I looked on as he approached me, light on his feet. Pulling his shirt overhead, he dropped it to the ground.

'He'll use dirty tactics to win this, Evanee. He'll target your weakness—your temper.'

Jordan's warning tumbled through my mind.

'Oh, trust me, I know. He's already got a head start and the fight's not even begun,' I responded dryly. The sight of Erick shirtless was a definite distraction, and the cheeky bugger knew that.

Why can't I turn this attraction off? It'd make my life so much easier.

Jordan's demand lashed through my mind, demanding I pay attention.

'So, what are you going to do, woman?'

'*Fight hard, fight dirty.*' I recited Jordan's words of wisdom. He'd prepared me to fight to the death, whereas Erick and I had only ever fought to train. I'd lost count of the amount of times Jordan had sliced my abdomen open, almost gutting me, or snapped my neck with far too much ease. He was ferocious during our training. I was always an opponent to be defeated and bested.

'*No matter what though, I gotta say I'm proud of you. Now kick his arse, will you? He needs schooling.*'

Looking at Jordan, he winked and I gave a hard nod.

"Hey! I heard that. There will be no coaching from the sidelines you two. Utter silence."

Erick looked between the two of us.

"Why? You scared he'll expose a weak spot?" Smiling cheekily to hide my nerves, we stepped up to each other. His smooth palm brushed my mine and butterflies danced merrily within me as I stared up at him, heat simmering between the two of us.

Damn he's hot. I really don't know how much longer I can hold out if he keeps looking at me like he wants to devour me.

"You wish. Ready?"

His whisper felt intimate, but I knew better. Nodding, I released his hand and stepped back, watching his retreating back. Distance was good. My brain took over from my hormones when there was distance between us.

All that glorious muscle rippled and flexed, distracting me as intended. Erick spun suddenly, pouncing upon me.

Tricky bastard.

Erick's solid fist rammed my chest sending me sailing through the air to land on my back.

"Wake the hell up, Evanee! Use your damn brains upstairs, not downstairs. FUCK ME DEAD!" Shame washed over me at Jordan's bellow.

Rolling to my knees, I dodged yet another one of Erick's fists.

Come on Evanee. You're better than this. Remember what you're fighting for!

"Already going for the pep talk, Evanee? Tsk, tsk, I thought you could fight, or was it an excuse to get up close and personal with me?"

Swinging inward, Erick dodged my right hook before he landed a kick to my stomach. This time I stood my ground, absorbing the kick as I latched onto his ankle. Looking up from the leg in my grasp, I hissed long and low. I wasn't here to play; I was here to fight for my independence.

Throwing his leg to the side, I leapt for his throat. Large roped forearms smashed downward, dislodging my hands, but I was ready, my head coming down hard to land against his nose. A crimson spray glittered through the air, landing quietly on the mat. Ignoring his broken nose, Erick clawed deeply at my abdomen and connected; his nails no longer short and trimmed. Blood soaked into the top of my pants as my wounds healed.

"Son of a bitch." Panting, I stumbled backwards.

"All is fair in love and war, *mic luptător*." Snapping his nose back into place, it healed instantly. "That was a good first round, but I have to hurry this along. I have another conference call in fifteen minutes."

His matter-of-fact tone hit home, stinging more than it should have. From the sideline I caught Jordan palming his forehead, while Tristan was busy looking everywhere but at me.

"This is supposed to be a test to see if I'm ready to re-enter human company, and you make it sound like I'm just a distraction between your precious meetings. You don't give a shit about what I want, do you?"

Erick looked to the side in confusion before looking back at me.

I didn't give him time to respond. Blurring my features, I went low tackling him hard into the ground. Rearing back, my right fist came down only to be caught. He held it hard, increasing the pressure until bones snapped and popped. Yelping, I smashed my left fist into his sternum, and he released my aching hand at last. His next punch landed against my jaw, the crack dredging up memories of the night we'd fought in the woods all those months ago. Rolling off him, I snapped my jaw back into place mid roll. Crouched low to the mat, I reached deep within grasping that ancient part of me before I dragged it to the surface. I couldn't best him with only my vampire strength, I needed more.

"I will leave this mansion, Erick. You forget, while you may be a prince and my sire, I am the great granddaughter of Death himself. I will not be treated like some inconvenience or a distraction."

A dense and glistening fog burst from beneath me as shadows clawed at the navy walls. The wails of the tormented forever locked in purgatory cut through the silence of the room, pleading to be set free. They would never be free. Trapped for all eternity, they were mine to call to arms.

With a single step, the room blurred, and my taloned hand latched onto his throat. My other hand lay at my side, onyx and electric blue flames creeping towards my elbow. Raising his hands to mine, a garnet and gold flame I'd seen the night he'd rescued me from my room of doors within my mind, sizzled at my skin, forcing me to drop him.

"You need to calm down, Evanee. Your powers are getting out of control."

He stood tall and proud, all the while trying to coax me as he might a frightened child.

"No, Tenebris, it isn't. You think the only thing I've been doing is training physically? Those long walks in the bushes weren't about me only practicing passing as human."

Skeletal hands reached from within the fog, shackling Erick's denim-clad legs as I spoke. His flames spluttered before surging to life once again, this time moving from his feet upwards.

"You cannot hurt that which does not exist." My body rose gently above the fog, and I walked gracefully across it, as though it were my stage and I, its model. Circling him, I brought my right hand up, watching the colour leak from it as it became transparent. I lowered and deliberately pushed it through the muscles at his back, reaching for his heart. My left hand reached around, talons drawing tiny droplets from his throat as they held him in place.

I was losing myself to that ancient power flooding me, but I was too caught up in the moment to care enough to reign it back in.

"Yield Erick, or I will give you a taste of what it felt like to have an acid barb pointed at your heart; scraping at it upon each rising." I waited as he decided his best course of action. He could play my bluff, and I'll admit I probably wouldn't rip his heart out, but the less he knew the better.

"I yield."

His low growl vibrated the length of me, rubbing against me with enticement.

'If I wasn't so mad at you right now, I'd be tempted to see just how far we could take things, and whether that fire of yours lights up your whole body.' That ancient part trapped within reached for Erick and the power he now held within him.

Closing the small gap between us, my breasts pressed against his back. My seductive whisper drifting through his mind had the desired effect as the scent of his arousal reached my nostrils. Inhaling deeply, I smiled a lioness with her prey in sight.

'I can never get it right with you, mic luptător. I'm always misstepping when it comes to you. I try to protect you; you throw it in my face. I try to help you; you throw it in my face. I can't win with you. I don't understand why you won't give us a chance.'

I removed my arm from within him, placing my palm at his back.

Lowering my chin to his shoulder, I whispered sadly. "Stop trying to fix things for me, Erick. All I've ever wanted was a friend, someone I could trust. I'm not worthy of anything more than that. No matter what that prophecy says, I am not someone you want to attach yourself to romantically for all eternity."

My heart clenched saying those words aloud.

I dropped back to the ground, recalling the fog now coating the entire gym floor. As it raced back towards me, I turned and summoned a portal to my cottage. Jordan's question was the last thing I heard, before I shut it.

"Has she always had a tattoo on her back?"

Looks like my wings are visible after all. I made a mental note to inspect my back in the mirror.

Chapter 4

I stared despondently around my little cottage as the stillness and loneliness cocooned me. A short time ago the place had felt like home; I'd been happy and content. Now, it felt empty, much like me.

Padding barefoot into the lounge room, my fingers trailed the table behind my couch, coming away dusty, and I looked down at it miserably. Entering the kitchen, I retrieved disinfectant, wood polish, and cloths before I turned, setting my sights on the dining room.

For the next couple of hours, I wiped, dusted, polished and cleaned the wooden floors at human speed, using the chore as a distraction from my self-destructive thoughts. The scent of beeswax and lemon scented disinfectant drifted up as wood shone under my cloth and mop, restoring the house back to its former self, but I was a long way from healing my heartache.

I stood in the kitchen observing my handy work, all the while rubbing the area over my heart. "Bath, that's what I need." I decided.

Water splashed into my clawed tub, and I emptied a portion of my favourite vanilla scented bubble bath in the churning water. Meeting Grandfather had been so surreal; knowing he was out there, and wasn't disgusted at what I'd become, as I'm sure his other descendants would be, was a small relief.

Shutting the taps off, I deposited my clothes into my wash basket, relishing something utterly normal.

The empty towel wrack caught my eye, and I sighed in exasperation. "Of course, I'd forget a fresh towel."

Padding into the hallway, I snagged a fresh towel from the linen closet before retracing my steps into my room. The sight of my reflection in the full-length mirror stopped me short. Stepping closer to it, I held the towel away from my body, studying the small yet noticeable changes that had occurred since my transformation.

My hips, which had always been on the curvier side, still hadn't regained the weight I'd lost during my infection with Jared's creation. I'd gained a little weight after my conversion, and since getting rid of the creature, but my body struggled to recover without the proper sustenance it required. Long platinum blonde hair hung loosely around my pale upper arms, glittering ever so slightly in the light from above me.

I turned side on and gasped when I caught sight of the tattoo Jordan had been referring too. There stamped into the middle of my back on either side of my spine sat a pair of silvery wings. The ends trailed down the length of my spine, stopping just shy of the dimples above my bum. I watched as the tattoo flexed, then smoothed again. Jerking, I stumbled backwards, horrified that there was yet again something trapped beneath my skin, waiting to erupt.

I hightailed it into the bathroom, chased by the fear I was transforming into something that might be considered a monster by most, including myself.

Shivering, I stepped into warm vanilla scented water and reclined against the porcelain, pushing my fear to the back of my mind, only to have unbidden thoughts of Erick slam into me.

I hadn't lied when I'd said I was the last person he wanted to tie himself to. Death and mayhem tended to follow in my footsteps. Dad had died on his way back from the falls near Erick's mansion, then there'd been Brian. Reducing a man's penis to a piece of rotting flesh wasn't something a normal person did. A normal person wouldn't release a blast of magic when being attacked, catapulting poor Detective Brand, Erick, and Tristan through the pathology lab. It was lucky they'd escaped the explosion without serious injuries. I was grateful Mel, my forensic nurse, had escaped injury too.

Despite being a forensic pathologist, I still held the same beliefs as any doctor. I truly had believed in the Hippocratic Oath, and still did—to a point. I understood being what I was, there would come times where I would have to defend myself and that would require killing someone in extreme circumstances. As Jordan had said, "it's you or them Evie, and you have many people depending on you here, so don't let it be you."

I didn't want to sink into the dark world I had when my father died, nor did I want to feel the anxiety and depression I'd suffered after Brian's attack. It'd taken me years of hauling my arse into the psychologist before I began the long journey to a place where I felt safe enough to smile again.

How can I expect someone to stand by me when this will inevitably reoccur throughout the rest of my life? I had no right to drag someone I loved through the agony and despair when I inevitably relapsed.

Erick had been the one to make an effort to talk to me during my teen years when we'd waited on Uncle Bob to return from a meeting. The man had saved my life more times than I could count, and I had no idea how to repay him. If I wasn't so broken, tainted, and unworthy of his love, I'd have readily accepted what he offered. Then there was Fate's continued interference, and the thought she'd forced Erick to settle for someone like me.

Erick was a shiny beacon. I'd seen his soul burn as bright as his eyes, and I refused to be the one to put a shadow in those gems. *I can't let the black dog that was depression near him, I will be the only one it drags to hell.*

Tears of heartache and resentment seared a trail down my cheeks, the tiny pink droplets plopping into the surrounding water. My eyes shut and I drifted into my room of mirrors, where I sat at the centre of the room and gave my heart permission to mourn what could have been, just this once.

The beautiful, shimmering door of emerald, garnet, and gold drew my attention. The door Erick and I shared. A testament of what might have been if Fate hadn't doomed me long before I was born.

The ripple within my mind was my only warning before Erick, seemingly summoned by my thoughts, stepped through our connecting door and into my round room of doors.

'What can I do for you, Erick?' I whispered between my raised knees, my hair hiding my now silent tears.

'Why are you crying, mic luptător?'

'What makes you think I'm crying?'

'Besides the wobble in your voice? I can feel your tears and heartache.'

Damn it all to hell, I needed to brush up on blocking my emotions.

When he remained silent, I whispered, *'Who else knows?'*

'Jordan felt your grief. He thought it best not to disturb you, but I've never been very good at avoiding things. Do you want to talk about what's worrying you, and what made you jump from that balcony?'

He was like a dog with a damn bone. He would keep gnawing at it until I finally relented.

My head didn't move as I murmured, *'I wanted to feel.'*

'Feel what, Evanee?' He moved closer.

'Anything. Leaving Brian to suffer like that, it didn't feel like I thought it would. I don't think killing him would've been any better either, to be honest.'

The outline of his jeans came into my peripheral vision as he dropped to his haunches beside me.

'Revenge never feels good Evanee, no matter how much pain we've been through.'

Lifting my head at his sigh, he tucked the loose tendrils of my hair behind my ears, concern creasing his handsome face.

'You sound as if you're speaking from experience.'

His eyes held mine with a loving caress and a small smile curved his lips, breaking my heart just a little more.

'You could say I have an inkling of what you're talking about. I've lived a long time, mic luptător. I've lost those I've loved to madness and chaos, and I've sought revenge on their behalf, but it never changed the fact they were dead.'

Nodding in understanding, I allowed silence to descend for a moment.

'Would you mind if I asked you a question?'

I couldn't hold back my smile. *'You may as well. I mean it's not like you haven't already been asking them.'*

'Fair enough. When you said I shouldn't attach myself to you romantically, why'd you say that? Why warn me away from having feelings for you?'

And there it was, the heart of my despair. The reason I was sulking like a teenager who's crush thought she was plain and boring.

Sighing heavily, I dropped my legs down, crossing them as I hunched over. *'Erick, I meant what I said. I'm not the right person for you. I know there's a prophecy, and Fate declared it and all that crap; but prophecy aside, I wouldn't be a woman you'd want to be with for all eternity.'* For a brief second I thought he wouldn't answer.

Sighing in frustration, he finally responded. *'That's bullshit. Who're you to decide what I want and don't want?'*

'Erick any feelings you think you have are probably just a side effect of the prophecy and the conversion,' I beseeched, hoping he'd see reason.

'Evanee, you wouldn't have a clue what I'm thinking, let alone feeling. The only one who gets to decide what I do and don't want is me. I understand you've had a rough run. I get that becoming part vampire, part reaper wasn't what you planned, but it's not necessarily all doom and gloom.'

Large hands hung loosely over his knees, and I stared at their smoothness, at odds with the warrior I'd seen in Aeternum's lab and during our battle.

'You forget I was once part human, part reaper. Me being part vampire doesn't really worry me all that much. Okay, the drinking blood thing is slightly gross, but not intolerable.' I tried for humour, hoping it'd distract him from his current line of questioning.

'Is it me?'

His whisper of uncertainty hurt, and I turned my head so he wouldn't see the tear that slipped from beneath my lashes.

'Yes and no, Erick. There are so many hurdles set in stone long before we were even born that I worry would be impossible to overcome. We are so different in how we approach things.'

'These are things all couples have to deal with, Evanee. Guaranteed, I have a couple hundred more years of conditioning than other perspective partners might, but it wouldn't be impossible to meet in the middle.'

Reaching across, he stroked my hair, trying to comfort me the only way he knew how.

'What was the no part?'

Moving away from his comforting touch, I surged up in agitation and paced, my pale pink maxi dress swirling around my ankles. I was grateful my current state of dress wasn't a true reflection of my corporal state.

'Erick, I'm trying to save you here. You have an out. Take the damn thing and run.' I gestured to his door. *'Run as far from me as you can. Find some other vampire who will adore the ground you walk on, who will look pretty with a crown on her head and do what's required. You don't want the chaos and drama that comes with being close to me. You don't want the hell and anguish that will come.'* Frustration coursed through me, replacing the sorrow I'd felt moments before.

'What the hell are you talking about? That's life. It's full of challenges. It's how we deal with them that matters.'

He spoke heatedly as he sat back looking up at me.

'And what if my way of dealing with life's downs is being dragged down to the very depths of hell by the big black dog of depression? What if every time I smell the deodorant Brian wore that night sets off my anxiety? What if every time I fall asleep, I wake screaming, scythe in hand? You don't deserve to be dragged down with me when I inevitably descend back into hell. You deserve better than that!' My hands gestured every which way as I laid myself emotionally bare before him, the truth finally out. *'I can't be the person who kills the light in your eyes. I'd rather just kill myself now, somehow, and be done with it.'*

Erick's shoulders went rigid. His shock at my confession would have been comical if I hadn't been hurting so badly. Opening his mouth, he shut it with a snap. Together we stared at each other, the air thick with tension, and the silence deafening in its intensity, neither of us knowing what to say next. Suddenly he looked towards his door, a frown creasing his features.

'Damnit all to hell. Evanee, I have to go, but I want to finish this talk. Tristan has just informed me that my father is waiting to talk to me.' Erick stood, his fists tightly clenched at his sides.

Relief travelled through me and I replied softly, *'Go. I'm guessing your father calling can never be a good thing.'*

Nodding his confirmation, he stared at me for a second longer and I could see how torn he was.

'Shit, I have to go. I really want to finish this conversation though, in our physical forms.'

Striding to where I stood, he placed a tender kiss to my forehead, holding it for a few seconds longer than necessary. Turning, he left without so much as a backwards look.

Erick's presence and lack of it left me confused and aching. I sunk back to reality and opened my eyes to the soft flickering of candlelight across the pale sage walls of my bathroom. Stepping from the now cooled water, I dried myself before making my way to bed. Tugging at the top drawer of my dresser, I cursed as I realised my pyjamas were still at Erick's. Not feeling sexy enough to sleep in one of my many lingerie sets, I opted to sleep naked instead. I crawled under the covers, too worn and tired emotionally to care about anything except the sweet oblivion sleep would bring me.

If Grandfather or my mother come for a visit tonight, they'll be in for a shock, but at least it'll teach them to call first.

Chapter 5

The double doors at the front entrance to Acrasin General's morgue loomed before me, my stomach a ball of knots as I stood finger poised to ring the bell for Bob to let me in.

Shit! Am I sure I'm ready to be back? What if I've forgotten all my medical training?

Darling, you just spent the entire weekend catching up on the latest medical journals, and forensic updates while you waited for Erick to turn up. You'll be fine.

My inner bimbo lay reclined on a love seat, sipping on a glass of chilled white wine.

You're right, I've got this. I've been doing this how many years now? And don't remind me of how Erick was a no show.

A tall pot-bellied figure stepped beside me. He stood silently, looking between my poised finger and the steel grey doors.

"Are we inspecting the quality of the doors?" Steve asked gruffly, his hands behind his back.

"Yup, that's exactly what I'm doing. I noticed a rather suspicious looking substance near the doorbell," I responded dryly.

"Do you want to tell me what's got you looking so scared?"

He didn't turn to face me, as though he understood I was teetering on the verge of turning around and returning home.

"Nothing and everything. I've changed so much. What if I've forgotten how to be who I used to be?"

"Now you listen to me, Evanee Sheperd. You are one of the best forensic pathologists I have ever known, and I've seen a few in my day. Now get in there and do what you've always done."

This time he turned and faced me.

"Get in there and help the dead speak."

"Help the dead people speak, hey? You realise I am technically dead right?" I lowered my voice and glanced behind me.

"Yeah, yeah, I know, but you're still Evanee to me. Slave driver of diets, quirky, full of mischief, and someone who likes to give me heart attacks when she goes off exploring dead people's souls."

His kind words drew tears into my eyes, and I clenched my jaw hard to stop them from escaping. Instead I hugged him, taking comfort in his warmth.

"Thank you. I needed to hear that. I missed you, Steve."

"I missed you too, sweetheart, but you'll always have me. I'll haunt you if I have to."

Giggling at his joke, I released him from my hug.

"Now, let's go in shall we." Reaching across, he scanned his ID card, the doors opening with a soft hiss to reveal Bob and Mel standing at the reception desk inside.

"There she is. Hello Evanee, we thought you might have changed your mind about coming back."

Behind them, a series of monitors stood mounted to the side wall. Feeling silly, I wondered how long they'd seen me standing at the doors.

"Nah, just a moment of self-doubt; but Steve here thought it best I get in here and show you all who's boss. You know how it is."

A chorus of laughter filled the sterile corridor, and Bob stepped up, his arms open wide. Dropping my handbag to the floor, I stepped into his arms.

"It really is good to see you up and about, princess. I worried we'd lost you there for a second." His hug was tight, and warm, exactly how I remembered him.

"You did lose me, but I can't seem to stay dead. Then again, Fate probably knew you needed me back at work to haul your arse out of tricky situations, being senile and all that nonsense." Pulling back, Bob held me at arm's length, searching my face.

"Who you calling senile? I'll have you know I've been holding the fort on my own since we reopened, and not one body has gone undiagnosed. Senile… please."

His mock sternness was a breath of fresh air, compared to the solemnness and fighting at Erick's mansion. This was what I'd been missing.

Ellie and Brad had been non-existent since the night we'd revealed the prophecies. We'd spoken only by text, hoping to keep my location quiet for as long as possible. They were no closer to finding out who the head of Aeternum was. Every lead ended with a dead end, despite the convenience of technology.

"Okay, okay, let me put my bag away. Do I have my old locker or a new one?"

Bob shook his head, turning to lead the way to the staff change rooms. Waving a hello to Mel, who was preoccupied on the phone, I followed after him with Steve at my side.

"You have your old locker, Evie. I couldn't bear to let anyone else near it. Mel just about decapitated an intern when they put their things in it after the refurbishment." Lowering his voice, he whispered conspiratorially. "But don't tell her I told you that. She said she'd neuter me if I told you. I get no respect around this place."

Giggling, I looped my arm around his slight shoulders. "Of course, we respect you, and even love you. We just can't afford for you to get a big head. We have to keep you on our level somehow."

Bob's rumble of a laugh reverberated through me, bringing the feeling of home and belonging back to me and righting a world that had turned topsy-turvy.

"Ah, so that's what it is. Conspiracy at its best, I see."

Pushing the door open to the staff change rooms, Bob stood aside for me to enter.

"Here you are. I hope you don't mind, but I took the liberty of ordering you a new coat and scrubs. You had a spare pair in your locker, but your mother removed them, as well as your scrub caps. I'm not sure what she did with them. Worst day of my life that was. Even though I knew you weren't dead, I still cried like a baby. Goodness knows what your mother must have thought of me." Removing his glasses, Bob wiped at them out of habit and agitation.

"Oh, I wouldn't worry about what my mother thought. She had just as many tears the night she told me my whole life was a lie." Okay, so I was still a little sensitive about being lied to my whole life. I'd forgiven my mother— kind of.

"Evanee, I know this isn't what you want to hear, but please listen. Your mother did what any caring and loving mother would do for their child. She tried to protect you the only way she knew how."

Raising his hand to silence the rebuttal on the edge of my tongue, I shut my mouth choosing to listen to the man who had been a second father to me.

"She told me the entire story when she came to collect your things. I knew you were part human, part supernatural creature after you became infected, I'll admit it came as a shock to find out your mother wasn't human, but she's not the first person I've met who wasn't."

"Erick?" I queried.

"Yes, Erick. I always thought you were psychic, but I'd never have dreamed you were the offspring of a reaper," Bob confessed.

"I think it came as a relief to all of us knowing that you weren't entirely human. If you had of been, we'd have lost you a lot sooner than we did. There was no way you'd have survived that creature without your supernatural heritage," Steve added.

My throat tightened at his hoarse whisper.

"Agreed." Bob cleared his throat. "Now getting back to what I was saying about your mother protecting you. I would've done the same thing, and I know your dad would've felt the same way. That's what love is, princess; protecting those closest to us any way we know how."

Bringing me in for a hug, Bob's arms tightened around me.

"Now get dressed and let's get to work?"

Stepping back and around me, Bob headed towards the door, Steve following behind him.

"I'm glad you're back, sweetheart." Steve shut the door behind him.

Left to my thoughts, I reached for my lab coat, and contemplated what Bob had said. Could it be possible I'd overreacted to my mother's betrayal? Yes, she'd broken my trust, but it'd been to protect me. Bob was right, love was about protecting those you cared about the most, and I would have done the same to protect my child. On impulse, I reached for my phone, taping a quick message to my mother.

I understand why you did it. I love you.

Sitting across from Bob, he explained some new forms on bio-safety protocols and new policies revised in my absence. Not a lot had changed. We were in the midst of discussing the newest article in The Journal of Forensic Sciences when a knock came at the door announcing Mel's arrival.

"Sorry Bob, Evanee, a call just came in. We have incoming."

"Thank you, Mel. We'll be there in a second. I guess you'll get to perform an autopsy after all. You ready for this?"

Am I ready? The last time I performed an examination I had a mutated jellyfish cross witchetty grub attack me.

Standing, I stumbled slightly as an image of the creature erupting from the corpse on the autopsy table seared my synapses. Muscles seized involuntarily at my spine, the remembered pain from the acid as real as it had been all those months ago. My back cracked as I straightened and shook off the fear crowding my senses and smoothed my coat down before fiddling with my ID card around my neck.

"Ready as I'll ever be. I'll change into my gear, and then perhaps familiarise myself with the layout of the morgue." Excusing myself, I beat a hasty retreat. Changing into my scrubs and a pair of spare gumboots, I sat staring at the door to the morgue with trepidation. Logically I knew I wouldn't have another mutated creature jumping out at me, but that didn't stop the horrific images dancing around in my mind.

I clomped towards the door, my hand hesitating for a split second over the metal handle. I sighed heavily as I depressed it and stepped into the transformed room. As I looked around the room, a sense of familiarity flooded my veins as I noted the morgue's layout hadn't changed drastically from the previous footprint.

The two-way freezer remained where it had been before the explosion, with the exception of its new shiny metal door. They'd replaced the glass window between the morgue and the viewing room. New chairs lined the wall where the three men had blasted through. The style and colour of the chairs differed vastly from the old ones. The wash bay, steel benches, autopsy table, and attached sinks glistened under the florescent lights with their newness. New implements and instrument trolleys waited patiently in the new supplies area. The shelves and counter surrounding the trolley brimmed with new stock neatly filed away in their designated spots.

Walking towards the table at the centre of the room, I trailed my cold fingertips along it, remembering a saying from my studies.

"*Mortui vivos docent,*" I whispered.

"What was that, Doctor Sheperd?"

In my distraction I'd not heard Mel and Bob enter.

"Nothing. Just a saying that came to mind. '*Mortui vivos docent*'." Looking up, I smiled.

"Ah yes, the dead teach the living. Something we as pathologists should never forget, and neither should the rest of the medical community for that matter."

The loud chime of the bell at the loading bay echoed through the room bringing us to attention and away from our morose thoughts.

With a quick shake of his head, Bob addressed us gruffly.

"Well, let's see what this body has to teach us, shall we?"

Gingerly, I slid into a disposable cover suit, slipping on sleeve protectors, a plastic apron, and face mask. A pair of face visors joined the already prepped instrument tray. I wheeled it across the room towards the metal table. I started to stretch, then remembered I was a supernatural being who didn't need to limber up.

Through the window to the loading bay, I watched Dan and yet another new employee wheel a blue bag into the two-way freezer. The man had a high turnover of assistants. Waving shyly at Dan as he appeared in the morgue, he rewarded me with a bright and cheerful smile.

"Well, well, look what the cat dragged in. How are you doing, Dr Sheperd?"

As far as Dan and everyone else was aware, I was injured in the explosion and placed in an induced coma. To avoid another attack on my life, my family and friends had faked my death until they'd caught the person responsible. At least that's the story the human community was being fed.

"I'm doing fantastic Dan, thanks for asking. It's lovely to see you again. How's business going?"

"I could say the same. Business isn't too bad, nothing exciting ever happens at the funeral home. We have a fresh one for you. Don't suppose you'd indulge an old man with a little game of guess the sex and death?"

Laughing, I shook my head in fake exasperation. Nothing had changed, and it was an immense relief.

With an exaggerated huff, I conceded. "Oh, go on. Let's have a bit of fun then." Movement in my peripheral vision drew my attention to a grumpy looking Detective Bernard and a striking female detective finding their respective places in the viewing room.

"Evening, Detective Bernard." I called out. Nodding his hello, it was reassuring to see he was still a man of few words. Clapping my hands together for show, I approached the blue bag. I hadn't done this in a while, and a small part of me worried I wouldn't be able to oblige my work colleagues.

Looking at the body, I didn't bother closing my eyes, as the translucent image of the woman within floated above the bag.

"Right. We have a Caucasian female: approximately thirty years of age, blonde hair, blue eyes. She's roughly 5'7'''. Cause of death is—shit me—cause of death is a mixture of things. There's a slash to the throat, multiple slices to her abdomen and little to no remaining blood in her. Each of these would have caused her death given long enough." Looking around the room in horror, my gut churned at the mutilation someone forced this woman to endure.

"One day, Doctor Sheperd, you'll have to tell me just how you do that."

Turning to the young and rather awestruck female employee beside him, Dan said, "You have just met the infamous Doctor Death, young lady. One of the best pathologists in the business in my opinion. Aside from our Bob here of course."

Winking at Bob, Dan turned back to the rest of us, before motioning for the young girl to assist him. They made quick work of positioning the body beside the autopsy table.

Stepping up beside the young woman, we each grabbed a corner of the blue bag.

"On three. One, two. Three." Bob stood beside Dan, counting down.

Together, we each heaved, the plastic hissing as it scrapped the metal bench. With a heavy thwack we placed our newest charge on the autopsy bench.

"Right, well my job is done. Have a lovely evening everyone."

"You too, Dan."

Bob nodded and watched on as Dan and his assistant wheeled the trolley out of the morgue, and slowly past the windows connecting the sterile room to the loading bay beyond. With a final wave, they disappeared from site. Mel manned the roller door, shutting it once the white van had cleared the door.

"Let's get started then," I said breaking the thought-laden silence. Looking around the room, I reached for my clear glasses settling them in place.

The dead will talk loud and clear tonight.

Chapter 6

The three of us stood paralysed by the carnage that lay before us. What should have been ash blonde waves of hair, now lay matted with blood. Hollow sockets stared unseeing where her bright blue corneas had once sat. Her hourglass figure and taut stomach were now nothing more than raw open wounds, with strips of skin and muscle tissue laying uselessly against her rib cage and lower abdomen.

"Anyone else grateful they haven't had dinner yet?" Bob's voice wavered, his gulp audible even without my heightened hearing.

"What were the coroner's instructions?" Looking between Detective Bernard and my boss, I hoped we'd received permission for a full examination, although given the time frame I highly doubted it.

"At the moment, it's only an external examination. Officers are notifying Miss Martin's family. We'll notify you if they give permission for a full autopsy; although judging by the state of the body, I'll hazard a guess that we'll be getting it." Bernard's arms crossed over his chest, bulging slightly beneath the navy-blue shirt he'd chosen for the evening. His auburn curls blazed under the fluorescent lights.

"I'm going to agree with you on that, Bernard. Were there any dingoes or feral dogs spotted nearby?" Bob bent over the body as he looked closely at the slash marks across the young woman's abdomen.

If you stared hard enough, you could make out part of the intestine peeking through. For once, I was grateful my diet consisted only of blood and nothing solid.

"No dingo or feral dog did this, Bob. These are definitely scratch marks, but the measurements appear off. Something else attacked her."

My acute eyesight may have felt like a curse after my transformation. Now I appreciated it for the gift it was. "Let's strip her down and get started with the photos, shall we? Whereabouts was she found, Bernard?" Mel and I cut through the remains of the black maxi dress our newest charge wore.

"We found Miss Tracy Martin at Mermaid Close on the south side. Her handbag was untouched beside her."

The scissors in my hand stilled briefly. A fleeting memory of a little restaurant tucked away in Mermaid Beach on the Gold Coast flickered behind my eyes before disappearing. It'd been Brian's favourite restaurant while he'd been trying to court me.

Coincidence. That's all it is. It's fresh in your mind because you saw him the other night.

"Evanee, you okay?"

Mel's smoky voice cut across my inner pep-talk.

"What? Sorry Mel, what was that you said?"

"Are you okay? You went very still just then. Do you need to sit?"

Mel had deposited the black cotton material in an evidence bag without me even noticing.

I really need to stop spacing out so much.

"I'm okay. The street name just reminded me of something unexpected, that's all. I'll collect her sandals while you take photos, Mel."

I retreated to the end of the autopsy table, Bob following close behind, a look of concern etched his face.

Whispering, Bob looked at me over his glasses.

"What's going on? And don't fob me off."

"Nothing, really. The name of the street where they found her reminded me of Mermaid Close on the Gold Coast, that's all." At his perplexed look, I continued. "It's where Brian took me a couple of times. In fact, it was the last place we visited before I called things off with him. I guess visiting him the other night left me more rattled than I thought." I removed her brown leather sandals and deposited them in a new evidence bag.

The soft click of Mel snapping pictures of the body distracted us for a second before Bob murmured beside me.

"You visited him?"

Sighing, I was tempted to smack myself upside the head for being so careless in bringing up such a sensitive topic.

"Let's just say I paid an impromptu visit that was meant to end with me providing eternal relief but resulted in me leaving him to the fate I inflicted on him three years ago." I set the clear bag aside for analysis and stared hard at Bob, hoping he would understand what happened.

"I see, and how do we feel about this new development?" he asked cautiously.

"I'm not sure yet, but when I figure it out, I'll let you know." I flashed a quick smile. I appreciated his concern.

Bob nodded before moving back to the middle of the table.

"Sorry Detective, please continue. You mentioned Tracy still had her handbag beside her and everything appeared to be intact. So, this likely wasn't some mugging gone wrong."

Five sets of eyes focused on the poor soul before us.

Putting aside my personal feelings, I looked critically at the body before me. "Judging by the damage done, I'm going with a hate crime. Give me a second to double check something."

Bob knew what that meant. I was going in. I needed to be sure her soul had passed on before I began my inspection. I hadn't noticed its presence when I'd first inspected her for Dan, but I hadn't been looking for it either.

I focused, searching for the tiny orb that was her soul. On the verge of withdrawing, a slight flicker of light caught my eye. Frowning, I leaned even closer to the body, knowing full well it wouldn't make any difference to my power, but doing it out of habit. The flicker came again. As I focused harder on it, revulsion hit me harder than a full body slam and I stumbled backwards.

There, cradled in Tracy's naked chest, lay the shattered remnants of what'd once been her soul. Stepping back up to the table, I gripped the metal edge tightly. My power circled that shattered orb, assessing it from every angle. It was as though something had drained the delicate, yet resistant part of her so all that was left were remnants of pain, anger, and despair.

"Bob, could you please clear the room and go stand with Detective Bernard until I say it's safe to return? I will explain everything in a second. Mel, perhaps you might like to show the new detective the staff room. I thought I noticed some lovely looking pastries someone brought in earlier."

Looking up at Bob and then to Mel, she didn't need asking twice. She scampered towards the staff room, her boots squeaking as though they had toy squeakers strapped to them. She motioned for the detective to meet her out in front of the viewing room. Bob scurried behind Mel at an equally fast pace.

Beside Bernard, the new detective questioned him about the break in protocol. She wasn't happy at being asked to leave the viewing room and thought it unprofessional. Bernard explained I'd activated the bio-hazard safety drill. Snorting, I shook my head at his rather pathetic explanation.

"Hey, no judging, Dr Sheperd. I'd like to have seen you come up with something better."

Bernard glared at me once the other detective left.

"Yeah, yeah." Coming towards the window, I stood side on, dividing my attention between the viewing room occupants and the body.

"What's going on, Evanee? What did you see?"

Bob's hands were sans gloves, indicating he'd dumped his previous pair on the way out.

"I'm concerned we might have another bio-hazard and want to check the body without worrying about casualties. Her soul appears to have been partially drained, similar to the souls I found in our previous victims before my attack."

"Shit!" Bernard and Bob proclaimed simultaneously.

"There's no real point in putting on a bio-hazard suit is there?" Bob queried.

"No, there isn't. You should be safe behind there if there is something present. There's no real damage that can be done to me. Not anymore."

Bob looked to Bernard, and it hit me then he assumed Bernard knew what I was since he'd been present the night of the attack. The truth was, I hadn't said anything to Bernard, but I had a strong feeling he knew exactly what had happened to me all those months in isolation. Looking at his fiery aura, I made a mental note to query Bernard about a few things, including the part about him not being entirely human. If his fiery aura hadn't given him away, his body being flung through a couple of solid brick walls and him still standing here would've.

"I'll flip the body now and do a quick examination of the spinal cord. The crime scene officers didn't mention anything about back wounds, did they?" I approached Tracy's body, wary of disturbing whatever might lie within.

"No, there was no back injury. Nothing that raised my suspicions."

Bernard was on edge, and so he should be. I guessed he had no interest in being blasted through the walls behind him again.

Approaching the table, I bent down beside the corpse and was again grateful for my new strength as I pushed her onto her side with ease. Examining the area quickly, I returned her body to its previous position.

"There are no recent or old injuries near her spine, but that doesn't mean she's not infected. I'll need to conduct a full examination of the body psychically, considering we aren't able to conduct a physical autopsy yet. You'll be able to talk to me, and I should be able to respond. I have better control now." *I hope.* Waiting for their nods of confirmation, I turned back to Tracy's body.

As my eyes shut, I drifted into my mind and its round room of doors. I padded across the soft carpet towards the window affording me a view into the room housing my newest charge. I stood for a moment, studying Tracy's lifeless form floating horizontally mid-air. A thudding noise from the direction of Jordan's and Erick's doors distracted me momentarily. My unease must have seeped beneath my barriers.

'Not now guys. I can't afford any distractions.' Adding a layer of steel, my equivalent of a 'do not disturb' sign on the door, I turned, ignoring the slightly muted knocking. Stepping into my mental morgue, I closed it firmly behind me, embracing the silence within.

I approached Tracy's body, crooning softly with each step. *'Let's see what happened to you, Tracy. I promise to give you whatever semblance of peace I can once I'm sure nothing nasty will jump out at me.'*

Right hand rising, I twisted my wrist, suspending the body vertically. The sheet of mist covering her, dissipated, leaving a now naked Tracy to hang by invisible strings with me as her puppeteer. Circling to the back, I studied her cervical and the first couple of thoracic vertebrae between her scapulas, looking for any hint of an incision wound. Finding none, I stripped the body of both the epidermis and dermis; careful not to strip too much too quickly. When nothing peaked through the hypodermis, I stripped it as well, careful to keep the organs in place.

"There's nothing there, well, nothing that's showing up on my radar. She's not infected. I'll look at the soul a little closer, see if perhaps there's any residual left from whatever attacked her." Speaking out loud, Bob's okay echoed loudly within the room.

Stripping the body back until I reached the soul peeking from beneath stark white bone, the tiny cracked orb floated weakly before me. I stood before the violated thing, examining it as closely as I could without alarming what was left of it.

"There are no entry points to the soul, nothing that'd suggest that a creature similar to the one that was in me, has been in Tracy. However, something *other* definitely did this, and judging by the cracks and lack of colours, I'd say they were interrupted, or they left the soul like this on purpose." I spoke aloud.

'Right Tracy, let's see if I can't help you find some peace.' Reaching within the chest cavity, I grasped the soul tenderly, feeling its shudder at the action, leading me to wonder what torture this poor woman had endured before her death.

'Sshh. Don't be afraid, I won't hurt you. I'm going to extract you gently, then release you. It won't hurt, I promise.' When the shuddering stopped, I withdrew my hand and the orb with it, my body tense.

At last the soul was clear of the corporal body. My arms rose up, my hand opening to release what was left of Tracy. Unlike previous souls, she didn't skyrocket, exploding into fireworks as she hit the roof of my mind, instead she floated limply before dispersing in a pathetic shower of obsidian sparkles. I cringed at those sparks.

Turning back to the corpse before me, I replaced the organs and flesh until it was once again whole before me. Coming close to her abdomen I studied the four slash marks, the angle of the puckered skin, and the width between each groove.

"The width between each slash is approximately 4.5mm to 5mm. We have four slash marks in total. Judging by the external puckering of the epidermal and dermal I'd say claws of some kind are responsible for the slashes. It's unlikely that a dingo, wild dog, or even a big cat did this. If I were to hazard a guess, judging by their span, I'd say a human hand did this."

Splaying my hand over the area, my fingers bent slightly at the proximal phalanges and intermediate phalanges to form a loose claw. Dragging them just above the wounds, a shiver of apprehension ran through my body.

Lowering the body slightly, I looked towards the gaping wound at the neck, shuddering at the sight before me. Someone or something had ripped the skin from her throat revealing the bloodied oesophagus beneath. The diameter of the wound reminded me of images Erick had shown me of an unrestrained fledgling vampire in the initial blood lust after their conversion. The damage the fledgling had created had been nauseating. Seeing a sight like this in person, I understood why Erick had been so stubborn about my walking amongst humans before I was ready.

I may owe him an apology.

My temper and need for independence had clouded all rational thought. But it was one thing to see images of an event, and another to be confronted with the reality of it.

Moving on, I focused on the eye sockets, and the whiteness of the socket edges peaking from beneath the drying blood. Observing the puckered tissue around the area, it became evident the young woman's eyes hadn't been removed with a blade or smoothed edged weapon of any kind.

Someone's gouged them out. Why the hell would someone be so cruel?

Returning her body back to a horizontal position, I recalled the mist to cloak her, affording her the privacy she deserved, even if it was only in my mind. Once I was sure I'd ascertained all her body had to tell me, I'd release it from my mind long before the decomposition process took hold.

Leaving the room, I secured the door tightly. Looking to Erick and Jordan's doors, they were quiet, and I was grateful for the silence. Foreboding and dread churned and clawed at my gut after seeing Tracy and learning where they'd found her.

This has to be the other shoe dropping.

'Or it could be that you're simply hypersensitive because it's your first day back at work' my inner teenager

replied around a mouth full of chocolate coated peanuts. *'Give yourself a little credit. This case is all kinds of messed up. I mean what are the chances this would have anything to do with you?'*

Knowing what she said made sense, I sighed and allowed myself to drift back into my body.

Another perk of being dead meant re-joining the corporal world no longer drained me to the point I was left shivering in cold or my hair whitening from the near-death experience. All I'd require was a bag of blood to satisfy the munchies, and I'd be good.

"We need to talk in the office. Perhaps the young detective and Mel could monitor the body until we return." Bob and Bernard were now seated in the chairs overlooking the morgue. I'd been gone a while judging by the coffees, they each held.

"I'll get Mel. You two go on ahead of me." Bob stood, moving towards the door. Bernard nodded, before standing and following him out.

~

Striding into my old office, now Bob's office, I shut the door quietly. Looking at Detective Bernard lounging in the spare seat at the front of the desk with his ankles crossed before him, I sat beside him, determined to get some answers.

"We need to talk before Bob gets back. I need to know what you are?" I demanded.

"I have no idea what you're talking about." Bernard's tensed body said otherwise.

"I know you're lying, Detective, so cut the crap. I saw your aura the night I was attacked. It's as though flames surrounded you. I can see it right now. So, I'll ask again, what are you?" Hands on my hips, I refused to back down.

Sighing, he leant forward, his forearms coming to rest on his thighs. "There aren't many in this world who can see my true nature. I know of only one other, and I'm cursed to follow him for eternity. Together we symbolize balance and harmony."

"Death." My eyebrows shot up.

"Yes." Bernard sighed tiredly. "I've known you were a creature of Death since the first time I met you. You were such an oddity, a perfect balance of life and death in one little vessel. My heart broke the night you were attacked. I knew then the same bitch who cursed me, had gotten her claws into you as well." He huffed in frustration. "Fate really is a heartless bitch, isn't she?" Bernard spat.

I snorted at his declaration. "I'd say she's bordering on bipolar with a touch of schizophrenia if you ask me. She may even be a tad homicidal. She's a contradiction of things all rolled into one misty package. You still didn't answer me though. What are you?" Taking a seat beside him, I waited, hoping he'd answer my question before Bob arrived.

Bernard rose, shedding what I could only described as a shield. I sat back further into the chair as bright fiery wings flared out around him, brilliant white lightning forking across them in tune to a rhythm I couldn't hear. The entire room shone with a fire no mortal could ever survive. Tears coursed down my cheeks as I gazed at the raw beauty before me. Bernard's blazing auburn curls reflected in the shinning glory of his ruby eyes. His face resembled Death's, perpetually shifting from one face to another; then just as suddenly, the light disappeared so that I once again stared at Bernard.

"I am Life, or a version of it, anyway. I'm the reason the myth of the Phoenix exists. My corporal body disintegrates to ashes, whilst my soul emerges in the form of the firebird, taking off to reform in the shape of a man or woman. It's happened so many times I've forgotten my original form. Although, I wonder at Death's reaction at times. It's almost as though he knew me before Fate cursed me."

The door opening signalled an end to our conversation. Scrubbing at my wet face, I had no intention of letting the topic go, but looking at the hurt in Bernard's eyes I decided it best to let it drop—for now.

"Right. Talk to me Ev. What's going on with that body?"

Taking a seat behind his desk, Bob's fingers formed a steeple beneath his chin as he gave me his undivided attention. His frown at the state of my face forced me to clear my throat and answer his question, before he could ask any more.

"Uh, um the body? Oh, that's right, Tracy." Shaking my head infinitesimally, I did my best to clear the image of the Phoenix now burned into my synapses. "I admit I may have overreacted, but the state of her soul hit a little closer to home than I anticipated. The cracks and colour of her soul were similar to those of the souls of the bodies I autopsied during Jared's experiment. When I went to help the soul pass on, the poor thing refused to let go and seemed petrified I would hurt it too."

Massaging my scalp, I continued with my findings. "The slash marks and their diameter, I feel confident in saying, were not done by an animal, neither was the torn throat. If I was going to say anything, I'd say a fledgling vampire did it, but I'd need to show Erick for his opinion. I'm still new to the world of the living dead. The gouged eyes, well that feels personal, a trophy piece perhaps." I looked at Bernard to see if he concurred with the last part of my observation.

"I'd have to agree with you, Evanee, which only makes my other observation that much more disturbing. Did either of you notice her appearance?"

I knew where he was going with this because I'd already been there. The slap of Tracy's driver's license on the desk made me jump. While she may not have been smiling in the photo, her eyes still shone with happiness and laughter. They were a shade darker than my own, but only just.

Bob looked down at the image and details before looking up at me, dread paling his handsome features.

"Yeah, I noticed the similarities, but was hoping I was the only one." No one spoke as we all stared at the young woman whose life had been taken so cruelly.

Chapter 7

Stepping through the portal, my feet shuffled under the weight of my workday. My first day back hadn't gone the way I'd hoped, and my mind kept flashing back to the clear-as- day image of Tracy when I'd been playing the guessing game. She'd been so beautiful.

Distracted by my churning thoughts, I slipped my old orthopaedic shoes off at the front door. I didn't really need them anymore thanks to my new healing abilities, but I would keep them for appearance's sake.

The sudden fluttering of my birthmark stiffened my body. Turning towards my front door, I inhaled the all too familiar citrus and vanilla scent. Flicking on the hallway light, I unlocked the door, stepping onto my dark front veranda.

Handbag still clutched tightly in my hand; I approached the large figure reclining in one of two rocking chairs. Sitting softly beside Erick, I looked out at the quiet street.

"Did anyone ever tell you that lurking in the shadows of a woman's veranda is just plain creepy?"

"I wouldn't have had to wait in the dark if you'd answered my multiple calls?"

Sliding my hand into my handbag I retrieved my phone. I looked at the black screen and realised I'd forgotten to recharge it the night before.

Oops.

"My bad. I forgot to recharge it last night. It must have switched off during my shift." I waggled my phone at him to prove my innocence.

Standing suddenly, anger radiated from his stiff posture.

This is going to be a long night, or is it dawn?

"Don't play ignorant with me, Evanee. I know you felt Jordan and I trying to connect with you. You barred the entrance when all you had to do was reassure us that you were fine, and I want to know why?"

When I didn't respond, he snapped.

"Now, Evanee."

I stood as I responded with a weary sigh, "Not out here, Erick."

I stepped tiredly around Erick, depositing my handbag on the hall table. I trudged into the dining room, phone in hand and turned to see Erick enter the lounge room.

This was the last thing I needed after today, but it didn't appear Erick was going anywhere until I explained what'd happened. "I was at work, Erick. I can't always take yours and Jordan's calls during an autopsy." Making my way into the kitchen, I retrieved two units of blood from the fridge.

"Well, it must have been one hell of an autopsy for us to feel your discomfort and alarm all the way from here. You're lying to me, and it's pissing me off. I'm trying to give you the chance to explain things to me, but I'm fast approaching the point where I'll just read your thoughts to get the information I need. Did you come close to hurting a human?" He hadn't moved from the lounge room and I turned my back to him as I warmed my dinner.

"No, I didn't harm any humans, and I'm not lying, Erick. Now who has trust issues?" I was baiting him, I knew it, but tonight had been tough and I was wired, tired, and starving.

"It's not a matter of trust issues, Evanee. You've been so hell-bent on shutting me out that you can't see why what you did was alarming to not just me. Your issues have you destroying whatever little connection we have before we've even explored it. You're keeping me at arm's length, and I'm sick of it."

"Erick, tonight isn't the night to discuss my issues. I know you're frustrated by my actions. I thought we'd cleared up a few things the other evening. I thought you understood keeping you at arm's length was my way of protecting you. You're so determined to throw my multitude of issues in my face, but you've completely ignored the fact that my actions are more than just self-preservation." Opening the microwave as it dinged, I retrieved my warmed blood and slammed the door shut.

Stunned silence met my confession, and I was glad for it. Walking to the table, I ignored the tall, brooding male standing stock-still in the lounge room. Taking my first sip, my eyes drifted shut as I fought not to gulp the entire lot down.

"No one asked you to protect me, Evanee. I've got soldiers who do that. It isn't your job to ensure my safety."

Gliding towards the table, he sat opposite me.

"There's more than one way to hurt a person, Erick. Your guards protect your body, but not your heart or mind. Brian isn't the only reason I've remained single for so long. Yes, I'll admit to never being interested in anyone as I have been in you, but the attraction and interest mean nothing if, like I said, I drag you to hell with me."

Or if it's a by-product of Fate's meddling.

Sipping at my mug, I hoped it might alleviate the tightness in my throat. It didn't.

"Why would you drag me to hell, *mic luptător*? Who says I can't take hold of your hand and walk that path right alongside you, or hell carry you in the opposite direction? Shouldn't I be the one to make that decision?"

His statement encased my heart, shutting around it and I knew despite our differences, and our numerous arguments, he cared. I looked down into the mug, not wanting to meet his eyes. He wasn't wrong. It was his right to decide whether he tied himself to me, burdens and all. But how much of that decision was influenced by Fate's meddling?

"Can we talk about something else, please? Just for tonight. It's been a day from hell today, and I just don't have the energy to do this tonight."

He obliged, changing the topic to the very thing that had bought him to my front veranda.

"What happened at work that's left you all nervous and on edge?"

Sitting back, his arms crossed over his broad chest, momentarily distracting me.

"Um… we got a DOA in. Female in her late 20s. It was nasty and brutal. There wasn't one of us in that morgue whose stomach wasn't churning with nausea. I was going to come to the mansion tomorrow and discuss it with you before work. I was hoping for your input." Offering an olive branch, I drained the rest of the blood.

"Well, I'm here now, we could discuss it if you like. It might alleviate some of your worries."

Nodding, my mind was going around in circles.

"Thanks. I don't think I could nap without going over and over what I saw and talked about tonight. Can we go to the lounge? My chair is looking good right about now."

At his nod, I approached the world's most comfortable sofa. I'd missed it while I'd been away and had considered dragging it to the mansion. Sinking into its embrace, I sighed in relief. It felt good to be back in its welcoming arms. My eyes snapped open when Erick sat at the end, motioning for me to give him my feet. I hesitated for a second before lying down and depositing my feet onto his lap. He held them in his hands and began pressing my pressure points.

I studied the man sitting beside me with his broad shoulders, strong jawline, and hair that begged to have my fingers running through it. Despite my bitchiness, my brick walls, and temper tantrums, Erick was still here, massaging my feet of all things. The man had the patience of a saint; but from our conversation tonight, it appeared he was fast running out of that patience I envied.

Massaging my temples, I shut my eyes. "I'm thinking the best way to explain what the body looked like is to show you," I explained. Opening my eyes, my weary gaze focused on him, as I asked. "You mind going on an excursion into the chaos that is my mind?"

With a quick nodding, Erick closed his eyes and dropped his head back onto the couch, prompting me to do the same.

Appearing on the carpeted floor in my mind, I looked down at my bare feet and then to the soft pale pink silk slip hugging my body. I smiled at its prettiness, knowing it wasn't something I'd have worn unless I was home alone. The white waves of my hair drifted softly down my back, tickling my shoulder blades as I turned towards Erick's door. With a thought I unlocked it, and in he stepped, clad in dark blue jeans, while his broad shoulders fought against a midnight cotton t-shirt.

Mmm, yummy.

To my right two figures appeared as though summoned by my X-rated thoughts.

'Hey Erick, long time no see.'

The teenager waved cheerfully. Apparently, I wasn't the only one who'd come dressed to impress. Clad in tight black denims and a blood red crop top, the teen was going all out to impress Erick. Beside her, in a short as all hell arctic blue bandage dress, stood the bimbo.

'Evening handsome. You've finally come back to visit us.'

Rolling my eyes at the bimbo's dramatics, I stood silently waiting for them to have their turn in the limelight that was his attention.

'Good evening, ladies. You are all looking beautiful this evening.'

Both versions of myself preened and blushed at Erick's praises.

'Tell me, who do I speak too about putting in a good word with Evanee here about possibly going on a date with me?'

A date? Say what now? This was the first I was hearing about us possibly going on a date.

'Oh, either of us. We can be persistent and persuasive when needed.' The bimbo smiled radiantly at him, while the teenager swayed from side to side.

'Do you have any recommendations of where I should take her?'

I groaned as he finished his sentence. It was the worst possible question he could've asked.

'Bed.' replied the bimbo as the teenager responded, *'Between the shelves at the library.'*

'And that's enough from you two this evening,' I spoke stiffly, mortification pulling my shoulders back tightly. Walking towards me, Erick chuckled at their confession.

They make me sound like some sex deprived woman. Oh wait, I am sex deprived. Never mind.

With a cheerful wave and a blown kiss, the two versions of myself dissipated.

'Have I told you how much I like those two?'

Snorting at him, I turned towards my viewing window and the steel door beside it, but not before I caught him studying me with a discrete, yet appreciative look.

'I can feel you looking at my arse, Erick. And, you only like them because they're always on your side.'

'I can't help if my eyes are drawn to beautiful things. Anyway, I'll take all the help I can get. If two versions of yourself like me and want me to visit you more often, isn't that telling you something?'

Ignoring his logic, I twisted the doorknob in front of me, stepping to one side as I entered.

Unlike the previous time Erick had been in here, he didn't circle the room looking for imminent threats. Instead, he stood and waited for me to shut the door, before we proceeded towards Tracy's covered body at the centre of the room.

'Would you like to see her horizontal or vertical?'

'She's fine the way she is. Do you want to run the specifics past me?'

'I'd prefer not to just yet. I'll remove her covering and allow you to examine her first. I want to hear your initial thoughts.' I swallowed hard when he nodded for me to go ahead. My hand waved delicately over the body, dispersing

the mist covering the poor creature beneath. I stepped back, giving him room to move around her.

Dark, winged eyebrows shot up before resettling into a frown. Erick moved around the body, bending close to examine each wound at her abdomen and at her neck.

'This is an exact replica, right?'

I nodded, and he stood back, shaking his head.

'I feel for this poor woman. What she experienced before her death would've been sheer torture. Looking at the neck, missing tissue, and the size and pattern of the wounds at the edges, it appears to point towards a fledgling attack. But I'm guessing you already suspected this and wanted my confirmation on the matter.'

I nodded at his deduction.

Together we stood side by side, our arms crossed as we observed Tracy silently.

'There's more, Erick. There is something about this body that is hitting a little close to home for me, and it's got nothing to do with it being my first one since I was attacked. Why take the eyes? A fledgling in a state of blood lust has no thoughts but to feed. Taking the eyes was personal. Anyone of these wounds would've killed her. She has no blood left in her, and I suspect the amount they found at the scene wouldn't add up to what she's missing.'

'I agree, which would rule out a fledgling.'

His deep voice rumbled around the room, vibrating across my bare skin. I shivered, knowing what I needed to do next, and dreading it.

'I'm going to revert her to her previous state before she died. You ready?'

Erick stood back, and I wasted no time ripping the proverbial band-aid off. Together we watched as her abdominal wounds stitched together to show a smooth taut stomach, her neck came next as it knitted itself together, skin replacing the missing tissue, revealing a slender and beautiful neckline. Her eyes were last, the bright light blue of them shinning even in the stark light of the room. She really had been a beauty.

A long, low hiss erupted beside me as Erick's arms dropped to his side.

'Erick, I'd like you to meet Tracy Martin from Acrasin City. She is 5'7" with ash blonde hair and light blue eyes according to her driver's license. They found her body at Mermaid Close in Acrasin City yesterday evening. We are yet to perform a full autopsy but judging from the state of her body I have no doubt the Coroner will approve a full examination.' Breathing deep I continued, knowing full well I was about to get an even stronger reaction from the already tense vampire beside me. *'I thought her soul had departed, but I was wrong.'*

I looked up above the body, and a screen appeared showing the state Tracy's soul had been in when I'd first come upon it. The shuddering, fear and pain left behind in that little orb dulled the room so that shadows reached out from the walls in despair. Erick was in front of me before I could blink.

Grinning, I giggled at the absurdity of him trying to protect me from my own mind.

'You realise we're in my mind, right? You can't exactly protect me here, even if I wish you could some days.'

The screen before us disappeared, taking with it the shadows of despair. The room was once again bright with white light.

'So that orb like thing we just saw, was that a soul?'

I'd forgotten he didn't know what souls looked like. *'Yes, that's what a human soul looks like. Supernatural creatures have a different shape and the base colouring is different. What you saw just then is an extremely damaged soul, one in so much pain you can't fathom how it remained intact. It's what mine would've looked like had my power not raced it away when Jared's creature attacked.'* I watched as the realisation of exactly what I'd just implied sunk in.

'Are you telling me that we have another one of those viral creatures out there?' he exclaimed.

'I'm saying that whatever did this to her was more than just a vampire, and Aeternum has been rather quiet of late, wouldn't you say?'

Together we looked at Tracy, sombreness uniting us.

~

The scalding cascade of water hit my chilled body as I tried to scrub the memory of Tracy's empty eye sockets down the drain along with my coconut and elderflower shower gel. Knowing Erick had the same thoughts I'd initially had wasn't comforting. I hadn't told him about the similarities in the names of the street where they'd found her. I would, but I wasn't sure how I should approach the topic, considering what'd happened the last time I'd seen Brian.

Turning the taps off, I stepped lightly from the shower, wrapping a towel around me. Looking around the room, it dawned on me I had nothing to wear to bed. I'd have slept au naturel, but that wasn't going to happen with the hunk now taking up half of my bed. Standing with my hand on the doorknob, I heard Erick's chuckle as I contemplated my next move.

"I can feel you thinking in there. What has you so indecisive, Evanee?"

The playfulness in Erick's tone elicited a smile from me.

"I … um… I have no pyjamas."

"I see. I'm totally fine with you sleeping naked. You won't hear any complaints from me," came his cheeky reply.

"I'm sure I won't." Why was I so shy about being naked in front of him? I'd been nude after I'd awoken from my transformation, and then again during the first month when I'd needed to shut my body down fully after my transformation. Waking to bloodied clothes had become an inconvenience. However, after I'd removed the creature, and the weeks had rolled on, I'd been able to avoid waking up with blood-drenched clothing. And I could resist the sleep of the dead more and more with each sunrise. I had no doubt my reaper genetics had played a role in my sleep resistance.

"Evanee, come out. I've already seen you naked, and I promise not to lose control at seeing all that gorgeous nakedness."

His exasperation forced me to step out.

"I never said you couldn't control yourself, Erick. I just didn't want you getting the wrong impression. I was trying to be respectful." Stepping through the open door, I stopped short at the sight before me.

"Thank you for being so considerate, *mic luptător*. I'm fine with whichever way you decide to sleep." He leaned against my headboard, his bare abdomen on full display.

How the hell am I supposed to resist all that? I bet his mother used to wash her clothes on that stomach.

"Uh… are you sure you want to sleep here? Won't it be a little disconcerting sleeping here with no one to guard you?" I padded towards my chest of drawers that housed my secret lingerie addiction.

"I'm over 500 years old and have slept in dungeons that smelled and looked worse than anything you could imagine. I'm sure I'll handle it. Now stop stalling and get into bed. It's time for you to rest."

I selected an emerald teddy; the colour reminding me of eucalyptus leaves on a bright summers day as it shimmied enticingly down my body. Retrieving my towel, I returned it to the ensuite before making my way back into the room. True to his word, Erick didn't make a big deal of it, although I was sure I'd felt his eyes tracking my every movement.

"There is something else I didn't mention about where they found the body." Climbing into bed, I pulled the navy Egyptian cotton sheet over myself.

"What's that?" Lying on his side, we stared at each other, and I prayed our friendship would continue to progress as it had this evening. We'd had what felt like a minor breakthrough.

"The name of the street they found Tracy in; it was Mermaid Close." At his confused expression, I continued. "Whenever Brian and I would go on a date he would always book a table at this little restaurant he liked in Mermaid Beach on the Gold Coast. It was a pain in the arse getting there and back to my apartment." Smoothing at the sheets below my palm, I hesitated before speaking on. "Would you think I was crazy if I said that it's a little too coincidental for my liking?"

His searching gaze pierced the layer of bravado I'd been keeping in place since I'd seen Tracy laid out before me; and just like that the tiredness, hunger, and fear caught up with me.

I crumbled at the thought I might have to face yet more pain or another one of those creatures created by Aeternum. The tears I thought I'd released that night in the basement of Erick's mansion rushed back to the surface. Tugging at the sheet so it covered my face, a broken sob escaped before I could stop it.

The bed dipped as Erick scooped me into his chest, tugging the sheet from around my face.

"Hey, you don't have to hide when you're upset. I can't help you when you're hiding beneath the sheets."

Reluctantly I allowed him to pull the sheet down. I stared hard at the wall beside the door to my room, willing my tears to stop flowing, but they didn't.

"You're not crazy for seeing the similarities. In fact, it's brilliant that you've considered so many directions when looking at Tracy's death. She's the only dead woman so far, so let's not jump to conclusions just yet, okay? That doesn't mean you still shouldn't be on the lookout or have your guard up. Patience is key to battling an unseen enemy. We have Ellie and her brother making silent inquiries within the government about any new projects being pitched by Aeternum. Brad is attempting to wade through the dead ends and paper trails of the owner of Aeternum. You've been training in case you find yourself in a tight spot, and after the other night's fight, I have no doubt you'd be able to handle anything thrown your way."

The kiss he pressed to the crown of my head, was solid and reassuring.

"I do have one question though?"

He muttered the words into my hair.

"What's that?" Craning my neck, I looked up at him.

"Just what did Jordan teach you when you had all those lessons with him?"

He was trying to lighten the mood, and I adored him for it.

"Fight hard and fight dirty. Win by any means necessary, because if you don't, you're dead." I muttered the chant I'd said repeatedly as my arse hit the mat hard, or he'd snapped my neck, or slashed at my exposed flesh.

"I see. No more training with Jordan. I can't have you beating me whenever we get in the arena for practice."

I giggled at his mock sternness, relaxing a little more as I settled against his chest. "You and I both know that you took it easy on me, but if it means not having my neck snapped repeatedly, I can get on board with that."

My eyes were growing heavy, my tiredness taking hold of me.

"Thank you for listening to my crazy thoughts, and for staying with me. I know what a bitch I've been, and that I'm hard to deal with," I murmured sleepily.

"You're most welcome, *mic luptător*. Thank you for trusting me enough to stay with you tonight. Now go to sleep, please." He once again pressed a silent kiss to the crown of my head, and I let sleep wash over me knowing I was safe, for now.

Chapter 8

Darkness surrounded me, broken only by the eerie lights from the car's dashboard and radio. Frowning in confusion, I tried to recall why I was sitting in the middle of the back seat of a car when I had no recollection of getting in one. It was then I realised my father sat in the driver's seat, singing along to a Phil Collin's song I hadn't heard in years.

I sat back, smiling at Dad's off-key and frankly horrendous vocals, when the sudden painful pulse of my birth mark took my breath away. Breathing deeply, I tried to ignore it as I stared at my father's silhouette, drinking him in. It continued to pulse the pain increasing, refusing to be ignored any longer. As I rubbed at it, I thought I caught sight of a shimmering silhouette in the passenger seat.

Staring at the spot where I'd seen the shimmer, I frowned at its emptiness. I was sure there'd been something or someone sitting there. Focusing hard on the seat, the outline of a man slowly appeared before my eyes. At first, I thought he was a ghost, but then his appearance slowly solidified until a tall, raven-haired man sat impeccably dressed beside my father.

"Daddy, look out!" I screeched too late as the raven-haired man tugged at the wheel. There was no stopping what was coming.

My father hollered as the world became a blur of colours, the car rolling and tumbling down the embankment. Metal crunched and screeched, and dirt exploded into the air as the car hit the embankment. A deadly silence filled the night air, as the dust and debris finally settled.

I stood outside the vehicle, dazed at what'd just happened. I stared down at my hands, realising they were much younger than they should have been. I lifted my head, taking in the sight of the ball of metal that had been our family car, catching sight of my father's unconscious body still shackled to his seat by his seatbelt. *How'd I get out of the car?*

A light mist tickling at my bare feet distracted me as I looked down in bewilderment and back up to see a dark hooded figure standing sombrely at the crushed bonnet. Shock clouded my mind, giving way to panic as I wondered if this was the same man who'd yanked at the wheel. However, the waves of sorrow emanating from him were at odds with what I'd witnessed.

"You should not be here, sweet child. No child should bear witness to a parent's death."

His softly spoken words offered little comfort.

Adrenaline seized my body as I registered his gentle words. Rushing forward, I screamed. "Daddy!" When no response came, I yelled louder. "Daddy wake up. Come on Daddy, open your eyes, it's me, Evanee."

"Don't just stand there, help him!" I beseeched the dark figure. "Help my dad, please!" When the strange man didn't move, I tried to yank the car door open, only to have my hands pass through the metal of the door. I looked at them in uncomprehending confusion. I tried once again to grip the door handle, but my hands disappeared into the metal.

"There is nothing you can do, sweetheart. He is beyond help. His loyalty, devotion, and love for you and your mother is why I'm here personally. He's earned my respect and gratitude for the joy he's brought to your mother's life and the precious life he helped create with her."

"Who are you?" I whispered with trepidation.

"I am Death, sweet child. Now go. Forget this night."

He was beside me now, his hand on my shoulder as silent tears of grief and fear coursed down my cheeks.

With the blink of an eye, the world expanded before it collapsed in on itself.

Jerking awake, reality crashed upon me, and I wailed in despair and sorrow.

A dark figure hovered above me, their eyes glowing as they yelled down at me in concern.

"Wake up! Evanee, come on wake up, baby, it's all right!"

Erick? His yells filtered through my pain, and I realised I was gripping my scythe, its steel edge pressed against his neck.

I closed my mouth, my scream cutting off just as the door slammed open. Our heads moved simultaneously as a furious and battle-ready Jordan burst through, followed closely by the illuminated ghostly appearance of my mother, sword in hand.

Erick's low hiss stopped everyone in their tracks. The bed dipped slightly as Erick reached across to switch on my side lamp. Squinting at the harsh light, I dropped my head back to the soaked pillow, my hand dropping and loosening to let my scythe fall onto the floor. I took a deep, shuddering breath as I worked to clear the fog and fear from my sleepy mind.

"Guys, it's okay. It was just a bad dream," I croaked.

The tension in the room eased, though Erick remained on edge, unwilling to move from above me. I'd rarely seen Erick in vampire mode, and I took a moment to study his subtly drawn features and sharp fangs resting against his bottom lip.

"What the hell do you mean?" came Jordan's surly response.

He stomped around my bedroom checking the bathroom and my walk-in closet for any possible threats.

Together, Jordan and my mother approached my bed, and I tugged the sheet closer around me self-consciously as I mumbled, "As in I had a nightmare, and now I'm awake."

Erick still hadn't moved from above me, but I was happy to lie there soaking in his strength and protection while my mind replayed the nightmare. Mum came to a stop beside me, picking my scythe up off the floor to place it on my bedside table.

"Sweetheart, that was some kind of bad dream. Your mark on Jordan's arm went ballistic, refusing to balance or pick a side to land on."

She smoothed my tussled hair back as she had whenever I'd had a night terror as a child.

"Ballistic! The damned thing near on burned a hole through my bicep. What the hell were you dreaming about that freaked you out that badly you needed to call for my help?"

Jordan sat on the bench chair at the foot of my bed, his power finally subsiding.

"I was dreaming of the night my father, John, died. Although, I suspect it wasn't a nightmare but rather a memory." I looked to my mother, who frowned at my confession. I patted at Erick's arm to get him to move.

"Evanee, why would you think it was a memory?"

Erick settled himself against the bed head, drawing me into his body, his face once again human.

"I thought my powers emerged after my father's death, but after visiting with Brian, I'm willing to bet some of my nightmares have been memories trying to resurface. Most recently, it's been my memory of the night Dad died."

"*Mic luptător*, what happened after your visit to Brian?"

Erick tensed beneath me.

"I had a visitor who, let's just say, persuaded me to get off my arse and stop wallowing." At everyone's dumbfounded expressions, I sighed, not really wanting to give away our conversation. "Death paid me a visit not too long after the incident at Brian's place. Oh, Grandfather said to say hello, Mum." Looking at my mother, I would have laughed at her surprised expression if I hadn't still been reeling from my nightmare.

"Grand-père visited you? Why wouldn't you tell me?"

The hurt in Mum's voice left me ashamed.

"I intended to, but things got busy and to be honest I forgot all about it. But he was there in my dream, or should I say my memory. He was Dad's reaper. He remained with Dad after the crash and refused to let me stay." A small pink tear escaped at the memory of the respect Grandfather had shown my father. Swiping at the tear, I continued.

"But there's more. Dad didn't crash because of some dazed kangaroo jumping in front of him like the police suggested. He was murdered." I kept going in a rush; I needed to get the memory out in the open and out of my head before it began to fade. "I didn't notice him at first because I was too busy looking at Dad. He was singing completely off-key, like he used to." I smiled at Mum. "Then something caught my eye in the passenger seat, so I focused on the spot thinking I'd imagined it, and that's when I really saw him. Or maybe he materialised, I don't know…" Frowning at the memory, I tried to recall as many details as I could.

"Evanee, who materialised?"

Mum stood tense beside me, while Jordan made his way to her side and looked down at me too.

"I'm not sure. The dashboard light obscured his features. He was well dressed in a designer suite and tie. He looked as though he had black hair, but it was dark so it could have been dark brown." As I described him, the memory of him suddenly appearing and what that meant hit me.

"Shit, Mum! I think a reaper killed Dad." We stared at each other in horror, before my mother sat heavily at the edge of my bed.

"Why in the hell would a reaper want to kill Dad, Mum? I'd have thought reapers wouldn't be allowed to go around killing any old human they wanted too?"

Mum swallowed hard. "It's against our code to take a human before their time. We are there to observe and ferry the souls of the dead. Under no circumstances are we allowed to intervene or interact. To do so is punishable by death, by Grand-père himself. There are few things that will kill our kind, but one thing is consistent and that's having your essence removed. If you ended up in front of Grand-père, you knew you were in for a bad day. Why he let me live after I'd married your father is anyone's guess."

Because he thought you'd be the one to take over the kingdom he abandoned. I chose not to reveal this to my mother, who was already reeling from the thought one of her own people had killed her husband.

"So, I think the question here is which reaper would want Dad dead so badly he would defy Grandfather, and why?" I thought aloud.

Hands shaking, pure rage and savagery light my mother's eyes as she hissed her next words.

"I'm not sure baby girl, but I sure as hell intend to find out who it was. And when I do, not even my grand-père will be able to save him."

Watching my mother, I was glad I wouldn't be the once facing her. She was a fearsome sight to behold, but I didn't pity the bastard who'd be receiving all that wrath. After all, he'd murdered my father.

~

When I walked into the morgue that evening, my sombre mood weighed me down. Despite the three units of blood I'd devoured, I was still starving, and exhausted both emotionally and physically.

Erick had held me tightly to his chest after my mother and Jordan left. We'd lain wordlessly in the same position for what felt like ages, each of us digesting the new curve ball that'd been lobbed at us.

I'd reluctantly departed for work, with Erick kissing me on the cheek, muttering about some business he needed to attend to. In my distraction, I hadn't asked what, but I didn't think he'd minded too much.

I strode into Bob's office and sat in front of him, unaware of his hello. It wasn't until he came and sat beside me that I realised I'd been on autopilot.

"Sorry Bob, what did you say?" Finally registering the man beside me, my heart constricted at the lines creasing his face. He was aging right before me and I realised I'd be forced to lose him too one day.

"I asked what has you so distracted. You look, for a lack of a better word, haunted."

He placed a warm hand on my shoulder as he studied me in concern.

"Do you remember the nightmares I used to have as a teenager?" At his nod, I continued, "Well, they weren't all nightmares." I looked into his concerned eyes. "Uncle Bob,

some of those nightmares were suppressed memories…
Memories of the night Dad was murdered." The words were
out my mouth before I could censor them. The shock on
Bob's face echoed those of my mother, Jordan, and Erick just
hours before.

"John was murdered? How? Who killed him?"

Anger was quick to follow the shock, and I didn't
blame him, after all they reflected Mum's and my own
emotions.

"It appears to have been a reaper."

"Do you know which reaper, and can we do anything
about getting justice for John?"

I smiled sadly. It showed how much he trusted me,
that he hadn't asked if I'd been sure of what I'd just said. I
was glad I'd revealed the truth to him. He had been Dad's best
friend before he'd died, and he'd been there for me when I'd
needed him the most.

"Mum's on a warpath, while I haven't digested what
needs to be done or how. I only realised what the nightmare
was before I came in this evening."

Nodding in understanding, he asked, "Would you
mind keeping me posted on how things pan out?"

A quick nod from me, and he changed the topic,
satisfied with my answer.

"Oh, before I forget, I've found a replacement for the
day shift. She started this morning, and I think she'll fit in
nicely. She's fresh out of residency and has a good eye for the
finer details."

My eyebrows rose at the praise he'd bestowed upon this new young woman. "Wow, that's great. So, does this mean you'll be leaving soon?" Sadness at the thought our time together was ending before it'd really begun consumed me.

"At the end of the month which means you're stuck with this old fart for a bit longer."

Laughing at him, I reached over to clasp his hand tightly. He squeezed back before rising from his seat beside me.

"All right let's get to work. I'll go grab Mel and we can do a quick debrief," he said over his shoulder as he left the office.

I shook my head fondly, only to flinch at the sudden searing pain of my birthmark.

I was in reaper mode before I even realised what I was doing, searching for what had set off my internal alarm system. As my birth mark continued to sear a hole into my lower back as I shot up the corridor to check on Bob, who stood chatting animatedly to a laughing Mel. Turning, I was at the staff room door in the blink of an eye. When I couldn't detect a threat there, I turned towards the morgue as memories of the night I'd been attacked and infected raked at my mind.

My ghostly figure stepped through the shut door to the morgue. Stopping short, I stared at the empty room, my anxiety reaching its peak when I still couldn't pinpoint where the threat was coming from.

'Mic luptător, what's going on? I can feel your anxiety and stress.'

Erick's whisper within my mind did nothing to calm my impending anxiety attack barrelling towards me.

'Something's wrong, Erick. My birthmark... it's on fire like it... like it was the night I died.' Releasing my power with strict instructions to seek what sought to harm me, it blasted outwards, fog billowing and roiling, seeking an unknown target.

'Evanee, you need to calm down. I can see you've checked the facility and have come up empty-handed. Whatever you're sensing may be a forewarning. We've known an attack would come at some point, and perhaps it's closer than we thought. I'll leave now. You need to calm down, baby, and recall your power before it harms a human.'

Knowing what he said made sense, I inhaled deeply, and fought hard to centre myself. I painstakingly reeled the fog back, holding it tightly when it rebelled for a second.

The morgue door opening momentarily distracted me. In strolled Steve, who promptly paused at the sight before him.

He took in my transformed appearance before his eyes darted around the morgue in nervousness.

"Evanee, I thought I heard something down here. You okay?"

I nodded distractedly, all the while continuing to reel my powers in, and my talons exploded with the effort it took to control my power. Sharp fangs dug into my lower lip, piercing it as I scanned the room almost manically.

"Sweetheart, I think you're vamping out. Do you need me to get Erick or one of the others?"

Steve's calmness helped to ground me a little, yet the anxiety still clung to me.

"Erick's on his way," I panted. "Do I look normal, or am I full vamper mode?" My fangs scraped at my lower lip as I breathed in deeply trying to hold my power to me.

"What do you mean by vamper?" Steve asked, the usual smooth contours of his face bunched in confusion.

"It's vampire and reaper combined. Only name I could think of to describe myself," I ground out.

"You're in full vamper mode then. And sweetheart, I gotta be honest, you're terrifyingly beautiful. All that floating snowy hair and entrancing eyes."

"Steve, you're not helping. My birthmark's literally burning a hole through me and you're joking about my vamper looks. I'm barely holding it together, and the worst part is I'm absolutely starving. You need to leave and keep Uncle Bob and Mel out until Erick arrives. I can't have anyone in here when I'm like this." Clenching my jaw as hard as I could, my teeth ground together as the blood from my bitten lip trickled down my chin.

So hungry. Need more food.

"If you're starving, I could grab you some units of blood we stashed for emergencies like this?"

Steve stood at the door looking far too relaxed, which scared me more than anything. Did he not realise the only thing I wanted to do right now was rip his throat out? The images of warm liquid trapped beneath that thin layer of skin drew a long hiss from me; yet beneath it all a small voice whispered it wasn't enough.

I need more.

"Steve, I don't think blood will cut it. I haven't said anything to anyone because I'm scared of what they'll think, but the blood, it isn't enough. I've tried human food and threw it straight back up." I was scared, and the wobble in my voice gave it away.

"Okay, so the blood's not working. Let's think. You're technically only part vampire, aren't you?"

He continued at my abrupt nod.

"Right, and the other part of you is reaper. So, it's the reaper part of you that's hungry. What do reapers eat?"

"Souls!" I screeched. "Reapers feed on souls, Steve. I need to feed on a soul." My heightened emotions weren't helping contain the power fighting to escape my hold. It was hungry, and I feared what it craved—what I craved.

"Okay, so you need souls. Go find yourself a nice juicy soul and feed yourself."

Steve still hadn't moved, but I could hear Uncle Bob and Mel searching for me beyond the morgue doors.

"I can't," I wailed in despair.

"Why not?"

"Because then I'd be no better than the creature that infected me, or the monster that killed Tracy," I cried. "Not to mention, I have no idea how I'm supposed to consume a soul, I've never done it before."

"Think, Evanee. How do you normally get the souls out?" Steve barked, his tone demanding I think rationally.

"I do it one of two ways. I either go into my mind and release it in my morgue, or I pluck it from the body and think of Death before sending the soul to him. I assume he helps them to cross over to their afterlife."

I could hear Bob and Mel at the door to the change rooms beyond. They were nearly here.

"Okay, that wasn't all that helpful." After a brief pause, he clapped his hands. "I've got it. Try closing your eyes and let your instinct guide you. You know, like a predator and it's instinct to hunt and survive?"

"You're kidding me, right?" I said in astonishment.

When he raised his eyebrow at me, I shrugged. "I may as well give it a go."

Closing my eyes, I tried my best to calm my mind and allow my body to focus solely on what it needed—souls. A flash of something colourful popped into my mind before receding under my fear and disgust. Huffing with frustration I focused harder, the image re-surfacing sluggishly as my conscious fought my power and body. An image blazed to life, and my mind recoiled once again, the tiny orb disappearing.

"I'm scared, Steve. Erick already thinks I'm not ready to walk amongst humans. What the hell will he think when he finds out I need not just blood, but souls too?" Blood was one thing; but souls, that was a whole new level of a freak in need of an intervention.

Have I already turned into a monster? Am I destined to become nothing more than a supernatural mutation that views innocents as nothing more than a meal?

"Don't be scared, Evanee. Find what you need, sweetheart. We'll be here when you get back. Bob will understand you didn't want to hurt anyone, and I won't say anything about what you're feeding on."

At my look of horror, he smiled.

"You need to do something before you end up starving yourself or injuring someone close to you. Eventually you're gonna lose that tiny bit of control you have, and then what? Go now!"

Knowing he was speaking the truth, I summoned a portal, stepping through it. If I appeared in reaper mode no one would see me. No one would know my newest deadly secret.

~

Appearing in the ICU ward of Acrasin General Hospital, I stepped forward, allowing my power and instinct to guide me to whichever human was closest to death. Passing a room with a bed ridden elderly lady, I caught sight of a fellow reaper chatting animatedly to the apparition of what could only be a younger version of the old lady beside the bed. We stared at each other, each acknowledging the other's presence before I nodded and moved on. I was searching for something specific, but what, I couldn't tell. Then, at the end of the hall, I found it. A woman under police guard. Arriving at the side of the police detail I stood for a moment scenting the air whilst eavesdropping on their conversation.

"Do you really think she did it?" the tall male officer queried his partner.

"Hell, I don't know," the middle-aged woman replied. "How could any mother kill her babies? Forensics reckon she started with the kids first, and when the husband saw what she'd done, he attacked her. I'd probably have attacked the bitch too; except I'd have done more than break her arm and fracture a couple of ribs. Doctors reckon the stab wounds she inflicted on the poor guy are fatal. He's lost too much blood. Is it wrong that I want one of the ribs to pierce her cold, dark heart?"

Leaving them to their conversation, I disappeared inside. There, pale and drawn, lay a woman in her early 30's, her matted chocolate hair stark against the whiteness of the pillow. I said a silent prayer to whoever was listening I wouldn't be the one to autopsy her babies. I may not have thought of having kids, but that didn't mean I couldn't still feel protective and heartbroken for those gone too soon.

Stepping close, I took a moment to observe her before I placed my hand to that precious orb within her. There was no longer any pearl white left within that little orb. Instead, black, blood red and putrid yellow swirled chaotically within. Touching the orb gently, images of the life she'd led flashed before my eyes. I ignored her childhood and moved on to whether she'd murdered her family and why she'd done it.

Images of cherub babies with flaxen hair flashed before my eyes, their beautiful brown eyes haunting. She'd smothered them both during their afternoon naps, her husband walking in to find her hunched over their toddler, pillow still in hand. Searching her emotions and thought patterns, I detected no mental instability or drug induced haze, only the intense need to be with her newest lover and her unhappiness with the life she now lived. She'd never wanted the children to begin with; they were conceived primarily to keep her husband with her. The thought of leaving them hadn't even occurred to her, instead she'd intended on framing her husband for their deaths.

"Oh, you'll do perfectly. If you'd been innocent of the crime you're accused of, I'd have walked away, but all things considered, I think you'll make a perfect first meal."

Her soul shuddered in apprehension, as knowing what was about to come. Not wanting to cause any pain or draw this out any longer than I had to, I scooped the delicate orb out, staring at it for a moment. Shutting my eyes, I allowed my instincts to take over. I placed the soul to my lips hesitantly, sipping at it until it began to shrink, as the essence within drifted into my mouth and soothingly down my throat.

It had no flavour, but the feeling of fullness was a welcome relief from the constant hunger I'd felt until now. Finally, when the soul was no bigger than a blueberry, I popped it into my mouth, bursting it against my palate. The tingle across my tongue and cheeks reminded me of the pop rocks I used to eat as a child. Looking down at the shell before me, the woman's body continued to function, as though I hadn't just taken a vital part of her. A glance at my right hand and my scythe appeared, humming with the anticipation of reaping once again, only there would be no soul to see on its way.

I placed the curve of the blade near her heart, speaking clearly as I placed a tiny scratch to the area. "Die."

The piercing beep of the heart monitor flat lining sounded as I stepped through my portal and into the hallway just outside the morgue doors. I dismissed the lingering power cloaking my figure, composing myself before I pushed the doors open and smiled at the three figures gathered in the centre of the morgue.

"Evanee, there you are. We'd wondered where you'd gone off too," Bob greeted inquisitively.

"I was feeling a bit off, so I thought a snack might help."

"And did it help? Are you feeling better now?" Steve asked carefully.

Looking Steve in the eyes, I nodded pouring all the gratitude I had into my stare. "Much better. Thank you, Steve. It hit the spot perfectly."

"Glad to hear it. Now, since everything seems to be fine down this end, I think I'll carry on with my rounds."

With a quick wave goodbye, he was gone, leaving Mel, Bob and I to talk shop.

Chapter 9

I stepped out of my temporary office and made my way to the pathology lab down the hall intent on examining the substance Bob and I'd found on Tracy's body. Two weeks had passed since she'd appeared in our lives, and I was no closer to discovering what or who'd killed her.

We'd ruled rape out relatively quickly, with exsanguination determined as the official cause of death. The issue with the diagnosis of severe loss of blood, according to Detective Bernard, was forensic officers were having a lot of problems finding out where the rest of her blood had disappeared to. There'd been enough at the crime scene to determine she'd been murdered there, but not enough to account for just how drained her body was.

Sliding onto a vacant stool at the steel bench, I rubbed absentmindedly at my aching birthmark. Despite being blissfully quiet for the past two weeks, it'd played up once again.

Sighing heavily, I slipped a petri dish beneath the microscope, and focused on the collection of cells contained to the small culture dish. We'd removed the substance from the wounds at both Tracy's neck and her abdomen before sending it off to Brisbane. I'd retrieved a second sample for my own analysis.

Looking down through the microscope's lens, I frowned, perplexed by what I saw. The cells resembled deceased tissue one might expect to find in a patient who'd been suffering with a tuberculous pulmonary infection. The cottage cheese-like cells were soft yet granulated.

Lifting my head, I pulled the dish out and starred down at the sample when something caught my eye. I bent my head back to the microscope, replacing the dish with a frown as I refocused on the sample below. I adjusted both the magnification and resolution and saw nothing, so pulling my head back once more I stared hard at the sample, watching and waiting for whatever had happened before to happen again.

There! What the hell? Please tell me those black and blue lightening forks are not what I think they are. Please!

I recognised those lightening forks; I'd seen them come to life many times—on my clenched fists. My gut churned as the realisation of what I held in my hand hit me.

The consequences for my actions are rearing their ugly heads.

"What ya doing there, Evanee?"

I jumped, silently chastising myself for not paying attention to my surroundings. Jordan would be so pissed with me if he knew how distracted I'd become lately. He'd probably start hiding around corners just so he could jump out at me.

"Contemplating how one avoids karma and all her evil retributions." Smiling at Bob, I chuckled at his long whistle.

"That's some deep thinking going on for such a quiet evening. What has you thinking these kinds of thoughts?"

I placed the petri dish beneath the microscope once again, pushing back from the bench so he could look. "The tissue sample we collected from Tracy's body; it shows signs of what can only be caseous necrosis."

At the mention of my observation, Bob's eyebrows raised.

"How the hell did it get on the victim?" Bob removed his glasses before looking through the lens at the sample below.

"I have a theory, but I'm not sure I like the answer."

Looking up, he stepped back, crossing his arms as he waited for me to spit whatever I was really thinking out.

"I was chatting to Erick the other night about the possibility that I might know who Tracy's killer is. Before you say anything, we had to be sure the person I was thinking of wasn't involved. From the surveillance detail Erick has on said person's apartment, he feels that it isn't who I thought it was."

I was delaying I knew I was. I just wasn't as sure as Erick that this didn't have something to do with Brian.

"Okay, so who do you think it was?"

"Brian." When his jaw dropped, I spoke quickly. "It sounds insane considering the fact he is bedridden, but there are too many things lining up for my liking. For instance, Tracy's looks and their similarity to my own before I underwent my transformation. Then there was Mermaid Close, where they found her. The dates Brian and I went on were always in Mermaid Bay on the Gold Coast." Swallowing hard, I continued. "Not to mention the black and blue lightening I just caught lighting up the petri dish like Territory Day."

"Fair enough, I can see why you'd think Brian might have something to do with this. But sweetie it's only one murder, and truth be told, you've been extremely stressed lately."

The words were no sooner out of his mouth when the shrill of the portable hospital phone interrupted him. Dread twisted my gut as I looked from the phone to him.

"Bob here… Yep… Okay thanks Mel, we'll meet you inside."

I moved then, replacing the sample back inside the fridge. Shaking my head, we strolled out together.

"You should know better than to jinx us like that, Bob."

"Oh please, we don't know what we're receiving."

But deep down we both knew exactly what we were walking into.

~

Staring at the remains of the young female before me, nausea ate at my stomach while despair gripped my heart. I didn't need to see the young woman's photographic ID to know she'd been ash blonde with bright blue eyes. I could see an image of how she'd looked floating just above her body. It was disconcerting considering her throat was all but intact, while her stomach had been savaged by what we could only assume were claws.

"You were saying, Bob?"

Looking at Bob's pale complexion, I'd have been worried he was about to pass out, if I didn't already know he wasn't a fainter.

Hey, there's always a first time. But seriously, are we the only ones thinking this looks suspiciously like Brian's in cahoots with Aeternum? My inner teenager spoke from beneath a large fluffy blanket, her hunched posture radiating with the fear we all felt.

Oh honey, no one listens until it's too late. We should check for ourselves to make sure Brian is in fact bed ridden. It'd be best to set our own eyes on that sneaky little bastard.

Encased in a black cat suite, the bimbo's hair was set in a ponytail atop her head. She was ready for whatever was coming.

I'll think on the best course of action after I've helped this poor woman. I can't focus on anything else; although, you two should probably gear up for yet another fight for our lives—again.

I looked up as Bob croaked, "Detective Bernard, would you be so kind as to tell me where you found our young charge's body?"

"Brisbane Street. Her purse was untouched, the same as Tracy's. Some TAFE students found her on the way to their classes this morning."

At the mention of Brisbane Street, I looked at Bob before sighing in resignation. "You still think my theory's invalid?"

"What theory? Evanee, what aren't you telling me?"

I jumped at the bite in Detective Bernard's voice. I couldn't hold it back anymore, no matter how many people thought I was crazy. I trusted my gut, and it was yelling at me through a foghorn right at this moment.

"I think these killings may have something to do with me, but I have no evidence to support that. If you're okay with it, I'd like to examine this woman first before I give you any further details?"

At his curt, and less than happy nod, my attention went back to the woman before me. Looking at her with more than just my physical eyes, I gulped at the fractured thing that was her soul.

Why not drain the entire thing? Why is the killer leaving that pathetic thing still intact?

"I need to do my thing. You guys can either stay or leave. It's pretty bad inside, so I'm not sure how long I'll be."

No one spoke or left, and I shrugged, not caring who knew what I could do anymore. My only goal right now was to help what was left of this poor young woman find peace.

Beside Bob, Mel backed up to the seat in the corner of the room. Detective Bernard slumped into one of the viewing room chairs, leaving his female partner to stand looking between each of us, unsure of what was about to happen. Bob leaned against the table, patient as ever. My eyes drifted shut as I allowed my power to rise to the surface.

Drifting towards the pathetic thing that was this young woman's soul, I sighed forlornly. The soul was too far gone. The only thing I could hope for was releasing whatever was left to my grandfather in the hopes he'd be able to see her to her final resting place.

My transparent fingers grasped at the fragile thing and I slowly began to retract it from the chest cavity. Nearing the surface, images of blood, a star-laden night, and a blurred head appeared in my vision. I hunched against the pain her soul had felt in that moment—was still feeling.

At last the soul released from within the chest cavity, and my breath caught as it throbbed then disintegrated before my eyes. The floor rose to meet my knees as excruciating pain lanced every part of my body. I could have sworn red hot pokers had been driven through my gut, my brain and eyes receiving hundreds of needles simultaneously.

My hands landed against the cool polished floor, supporting me. In the distance a mobile phone jangled interrupting Bob as he yelled my name.

"Mel, answer this and tell him exactly what I'm telling you," Bob ordered.

I watched through blurred eyes as Bob raced around the table, dropping to his knees beside me.

"Evanee, talk to me. What's going on?"

Breathing through my pain, I prayed over and over for it to stop.

"Erick wants to know what's going on. He can't reach Evanee, whatever that means."

Mel was not enjoying whatever Erick was saying.

"I don't know. She can't talk yet."

At last the pain began to subside, the hot poker and needles piercing my body finally easing just a little with each passing minute.

"Evanee, you're scaring me and everyone else. Can you at least nod if you can understand what I'm saying?"

He sighed when I nodded.

"Good girl. Are you hurt?"

Not knowing how to answer, I opted to use my left hand, raising it from the floor to tilt it from one side to the other.

"She says yes and no to being in pain."

Bob's raised voice made me cringe, and I raised my hand to my ear to show it hurt.

"Bugger, sorry princess. Do you think you could try speaking? You have one concerned boyfriend who is threatening bodily harm if someone doesn't tell him what's going on."

Opening my mouth to speak, nothing came out. Clearing my throat, I tried again.

"Fine. Soul… disintegrated," I wheezed, not bothering to correct him about Erick being my boyfriend, and praying he'd understood what I'd just said. As Bob motioned for Mel to give him the phone, I sagged a little in relief he understood me.

"She says she's fine, but that the soul disintegrated."

Bob whispered conscious of my aching ears.

"Erick wants to know why he can't talk to you?"

I knew what he meant. Our psychic link was shut down tight, as was any connection to my round room of mirrors. My failsafe to protect not only myself, but those I treasured.

"In shut down … will reconnect soon. Protection… when... in pain." I spat the accumulating drool to the floor. I'd hose it down later.

"Hold on, I'll just put the phone to her ear. It might be a little easier. Don't yell though, her ears are sensitive."

Bob placed a warm phone at my ear as he sat beside me rubbing my back gently.

"Evanee, can you get to the mansion or do I need to come and get you?" Straight to the point.

A *man after my own heart.*

"Too tired and hungry. Need to sleep. Pain still there but lessening." My stomach clenched as I dry heaved.

Erick cursed at the sound before he ground out, "Evanee, listen to me, I'm on my way. I'm already in the car, and I'll be there as fast as I can. I couldn't reach your mother to teleport us. Can you put Bob on the phone again?"

Pushing at the phone, I indicated for Bob to put it to his ear.

"Uh huh. Okay, should I get her refreshments? Seriously? I have somewhere in mind, but she won't like it. I'll see you when you get here then." Disconnecting, Bob slipped the mobile phone into his breast pocket.

"Evanee, sweetheart, I need you to block your ears okay?"

I nodded, and his body angled away from me as I placed a hand over one ear, while putting the other ear to my shoulder.

"Bernard! Get in here, I need your help. Mel, I need you and the lovely detective to please watch over the body while I find somewhere for Evanee to recover."

Heavy black leather boots clomped into view moments later as Bernard came to a kneel at my other side.

"We need to get her into the freezer without your new partner seeing. Erick's on his way."

Bob whispered his plan, and I looked at him in confusion. Bernard must've been just as confused as I was because he asked the very question I'd been thinking.

"Why the hell are we putting her into the freezer, Bob?"

Yeah Bob, why am I going into the bloody freezer?

"Erick's concerned that her hunger may rise because of the pain. He's not sure just how much control over her hunger she has at the moment, so for her safety and ours he's suggested we put her somewhere secure and safe. The second freezer on the other side of the loading bay should suffice. There's only one door in and out, and the cold won't affect her all that much."

I nodded my assent through the twitches and spasms of my muscles, knowing what he said made sense. Together the two men pulled me to my feet. When my legs wouldn't support my spasming body, Bernard bent slightly, scooping me up beneath my knees.

Being this close to the detective, I could feel the fire I'd seen the other evening radiating off him. That fire cocooned me, soothing the worst of my pain, and I frowned at my body's reaction. We were polar opposites, yet there was something about Bernard and his power that felt right—felt familiar.

Together the three of us navigated our way through the walk-through freezer and out to the freezer at the back of the loading bay area. Hauling the door open, Bob stood back to allow Bernard and I to enter. The billowing mist from the freezer vents swirled around us. Stepping in a few moments later, Bob pushed an office chair in front of him.

"Here you go princess, I got you a throne."

He giggled at his own joke, and I smiled half-heartedly. Gingerly, Bernard placed me onto the chair, and I slumped slightly with relief and fatigue.

"I'll stand guard until Erick arrives. Bob, you carry on with the external examination in the meantime. We need to be as sure as we can be that our female was murdered by the same person or creature."

Bob stepped close placing a quick kiss to my forehead before he exited.

"Sorry Evanee, it's not the nicest of places to recuperate, but it's better than killing someone you love."

Giving me a sympathetic smile, Bernard retreated from the freezer, sealing the door shut behind him and taking with him the comforting heat that was his power. Light remained above me as I sat in the middle of the freezer, the dead surrounding me, yet offering no comfort.

~

The clank of the freezer door opening forced my weary eyes to open. The pain had finally subsided, but exhaustion had taken its place. Looking up at the figures towering above me, my lips quirked.

"Am I that special that I warranted both of you coming to collect me?" My body was thankfully healing from the psychic and mental effects of the backlash, and it seemed my humour had returned.

"Of course, but *mic luptător*, you really need to stop getting yourself into trouble. I'll end up getting that white knight complex you keep complaining about."

Dropping to his haunches, Erick looked me in the eyes as he assessed what sort of shape, I was in.

"Yeah, yeah. You'd have that complex even if I didn't keep getting sucker punched by invisible forces. Hey Jordan, you come all this way just for me?"

Jordan didn't smile, and it worried me.

"I felt the backlash Ev. it was brutal. It knocked me flat on my arse in the library. Needless to say, the old fella here freaked out. It's partially why he rang when he did; well, that and the fact he ended up with a spontaneous migraine. Just what the hell happened?"

Jordan didn't move from the entryway, instead he stood at the door, half in half out. Vigilant as always.

"We have a second victim, and her soul was left intact again, only this time the bastard drained it that much that when I went to release it, the thing disintegrated in my palm. I couldn't save her soul." Looking at Erick with misted eyes, I swallowed hard before continuing with my theory on what had happened. "The pain I experienced was the pain she felt or had felt during her death. It was the pain of a tortured soul."

"We'll talk to your mother about this when we get home. Apparently, she arrived not long after we left. She and Aunt Paige are planning an introductory party for when my father arrives. I believe they need to speak to us."

Oh great, another party. Let's hope this one doesn't end as miserably as the last one I went to.

'Mic luptător, I don't plan on having any sadistic stalkers or crazy scientists at this event. Well, not unless you include Brad and Ellie as crazy scientists.'

'No, you're right, instead we'll be surrounded by cranky stick up their arse royals from both our families. But

seeing as you met my mother, I guess it's only fair I meet yours.' Hesitating a moment, I looked at Erick, and a skitter of unease crawled up my back.

'*We haven't even been on an official first date and already the parents are being called in. Do you think she'll like me, your mother I mean?'* My stomach clenched in nervousness.

"Official date, hey? I think you're warming to me." Erick winked cheekily. "As for my mother, I'd say she's a tough nut to crack, but just be you. I've never introduced a woman to her before either, but my Aunt Paige seems to get along fine with you, so there's no reason she wouldn't like you. They're both similar."

Stroking at the errant strands of my snow-white hair, Erick smiled tenderly at me. Bending forward, our foreheads touched, and I closed my eyes, appreciating and embracing this rare moment of tenderness and intimacy.

"If you tell me you bought food, I'll pretend this is our official first date." I whispered hungrily.

Laughing, we pulled apart, and Erick responded huskily.

"I did bring food, but if you don't mind, I'd rather not count this as a date. If I'm going to take you out, I'd like to do it properly."

Jordan brought forward a dark blue esky.

"You have a choice between cold, and cold."

The graveness of Jordan's voice belied just how much our shared bond had freaked him out. He was my shield, my clipeum, and he'd failed to protect me when I'd needed it most. His anger and frustration at failing something so important beat at the door within my mind.

"Jordan, stop beating yourself up. I highly doubt you'd have been able to protect me even if you were standing right beside me. It was an unexpected side effect. Now you know how he feels whenever I go against his orders."

Erick shook his head wearily at my sassy smile.

"She has a point, mate. There is no stopping her once she sets her mind to something. She's stubborn that way."

Poking my tongue at him, I took the unit of blood Jordan proffered.

"Now I see why you two argue so much. I gotta say, Evanee, I think I might side with Erick more in the future."

I rolled my eyes at Jordan's melodramatic response, and I sipped at my cold blood.

"Can you walk yet?"

Erick indicated to my legs.

"Yeah, I can. I got some shut eye while I was waiting. I need to see what Bob's found first though, and then I promise I'll leave." At Erick's hesitation, I frowned.

"Erick, I need to take a quick look at her. I need to confirm if the same substance we found on Tracy is on this woman."

Erick murmured, "Does she look like Tracy?"

I gave a quick nod, and he rubbed at his dark spiked hair in consternation.

"Fine, but only ten minutes. I mean it, Evanee. You don't make for the exit by the ten-minute mark and I'll haul your arse out myself. Audience be damned."

Oh, for goodness' sake. How am I surrounded by so many overprotective males?

I grumbled. "Yeah, yeah. Let's get a move on, shall we? The night is slipping away, and I have so much to look forward to at home by the sounds of things."

Together we stood, following Jordan out the freezer. Bernard was nowhere in sight.

He must be in the viewing room.

Approaching the two-way freezer, I nodded to Erick and Jordan who disappeared in that direction. Walking through the freezer and into the morgue, Bob looked up from where he was studying the young female's sternum.

"What are you doing back in here, Dr. Sheperd?"

He was in professional mode, which was fine with me.

"I'll only be a minute. Just one quick look at... Do we have a name yet?"

Mel looked down at the chart in her hands, and said the name jotted down. "Miss Josephine Moss."

"Thanks Mel. I'm just here to take one quick peek at Miss Moss, and then I'll be on my way."

Bob looked towards the viewing room where Erick and Jordan now stood.

"Bob!" I snapped. "Don't look to Erick for confirmation. I'm my own woman, and I'm a professional. Have you ever known me to compromise a body in all the years I have worked here?" At the shake of his head, I barrelled on. "No, exactly. Now I promised to be out of here in ten minutes, so I really need to do this as fast as I can."

There was no way I was allowing him to treat me as though I didn't know my own limits. If I didn't think I could do it, I wouldn't compromise an investigation to satisfy my ego.

Stepping up to the body, I snapped on a pair of nitrile gloves before looking closely at the body with not only my new heightened eyesight, but with that part of me that was reaper. Taking in as much as I could, I bent close to where the claw marks perforated Josephine's abdomen. It didn't take long for me to find the yellowish substance I had been looking for. My gut clenched as I caught the quick and familiar flash of obsidian and electric blue.

"It looks as though we have the same yellow substance as on Tracy's body. Bob, if you could take a secondary sample for me to analyse, I'd really appreciate it. I'll be back in tomorrow evening." Looking up at Bob, he nodded.

"Right, well I think that's all I needed to see. I'll see you and Mel tomorrow night. Have a good evening everyone."

My gumboots clomped as I stomped towards the change room, I dumped my gloves in the sanitary bin before scrubbing my hands in the wash bay, all the while muttering profanities to myself. Wrenching the door open, I slammed it shut behind me, my anger getting the better of me. My handbag clutched tight, I marched towards the exit where Jordan and Erick now waited.

I couldn't look at either of them, my rage at tonight's events and yet another victim bubbling up as I snapped. "I'm ready. Let's go."

Chapter 10

Massaging my aching head, I fought the temptation to yell in frustration. I didn't think vampires could even get headaches, but apparently the circus performing around me was enough to induce one. Arguments of where the party would be held, and who would arrive when, bounced between my mother and Aunt Paige.

"We cannot neglect tradition, Reagan. Our laws dictate that the King and Queen enter last once all the guests are present. Your family, whilst royal in the Reaper community, aren't royalty in our community." Paige sat rigidly in the brown leather high-back chair.

"And I understand that, Paige, but my parents are just as important as your royals."

Mum's pacing was making me dizzy, and I wished not for the last time I was still stuck in the freezer at work.

'*Could you please lock me back in the freezer? It was so much quieter, with less bitching going on.*'

'*I feel your pain, mic luptător. There needs to be a happy medium though, or our species will never come together.*'

A long hiss from Paige followed by the soft glow of my mother's reaper form snapped me back to the room.

Oh, for crying out loud.

"Enough, you two. Sheath your claws, Paige, and Mum, snap the hell out of it." Standing, I looked between the two seething women. "I have better things to be doing right now than stand here watching you two have an all-out bitch fight." Shaking my head, I tried again. "Now I understand that this is supposed to be a party that introduces me to not only my mother's family, but Erick's as well. I get that traditions and customs have to be adhered to, but considering I'm a freak of nature…" I raised my hand to hush the protests from my mother and Erick. "Considering I'm a freak of nature and am now a vamper, I think it's time to ease away from some of the old customs."

"*Mic luptător*, that may be true, but we vampires are fickle creatures and we have survived this long thanks to our customs," Erick spoke carefully.

"I hear you Erick, but why risk offending one of our families when we can try something new and avoid an all-out war between us and them. I think in this particular situation I will be taking my grandfather's advice."

"What advice is that, sweetheart?"

My mother raised one delicate eyebrow.

"I am who I am, and I will not be what everyone expects or wants me to be. My great grandfather once ruled over all the species of death and according to some dumb prophecy I'm next in line. He thought it was you, Mum, but when you became pregnant with me to a human, he knew it would be me that finally united the species."

And boy am I wishing it was someone else right about now.

"Death seems to have said a lot during his visit with you."

Eyebrow rising at Erick's grumpiness, I stared hard at him.

"Look, I think it's time I put my big girl panties on and lived up to this so-called queen status. Erick, Jordan, and I will enter last. Your family and my family will enter all together, and there will be no special announcement as this party is not for them, it's for me to be announced or introduced." I sounded surer than I felt.

Being the centre of attention was not my idea of a good time, but I understood this was necessary. If I was going to unite the species of death, then I needed to show a backbone and authority. There'd be no respect if I pussy-footed around.

"It will also be about announcing you two as a couple. Future King and Queen."

Paige's soft reminder froze me in place.

"It is all right, *mic luptător*, don't stress. We aren't planning on rushing into anything, Aunt. Announcing us a future king and queen would imply we are intending on performing a commitment ceremony or that we already have. I doubt either of us is ready for that at this point in time."

I was grateful we were on the same page. Not that I didn't find being engaged to him appealing, it was more the fact we weren't in a fairy tale. We needed to know each other first, and he needed to know exactly what he was getting himself into. I hadn't been kidding about not wanting to drag him to hell with me.

"Well, if you're going to convince your parents not to sanction the death warrant looming over that head of hers, Erick," Paige said, "you need to decide what it is you want from each other, or part ways. At which point, Evanee, I would suggest you go into hiding somewhere no one would think to look for you. That includes your mother's family. Vampires won't be the only species demanding your head. You'll be considered an abomination."

Well hell, isn't she just full of sunshine and daisies? Remind me again why I decided to live, because so far, I'm not seeing an upside to this new life of mine.

"It's always encouraging to find out one has a death warrant hanging over their head." I looked at Erick. "Just when were you planning on sharing that little nugget of gold with me?"

Rubbing at the back of his neck, Erick huffed. "I'd meant to tell you sooner, but to be honest, there was no right time to tell you. It's why I've been absent so much since your conversion. I've been trying to put out the fire that was started when you executed one of the vampire survivors at Aeternum's lab. It raised questions about a new vampire that stole the life of another without removing the heart or head first."

"You should have still told me, Erick. I had a right to know." When he said nothing, I exhaled my frustration. "Right, I say let's skip the party and I'll just go straight into hiding. I've never performed well in social gatherings, and if I'm expected to make people like me to save my head, I'd best just skip to the end and make for the exit now." Not stopping, I merely observed Paige's raised eyebrow and her surprise at my confession. "I don't crave the acceptance of the hordes. I tried that once, and Erick will testify to just how badly it went. If I'm honest, I don't do politics and I straight up hate being lied to. I'd say those are not the qualities that make a good queen."

"You're also kind, loving, and protective of those you hold close to your heart. Don't short-change yourself, Evanee, just because you're scared of facing a large crowd," Mum whispered lovingly.

I poked my tongue at my mother's input before blowing her a kiss. "Love you too, Mum. Now, aside from the speed at which Erick's and my relationship is progressing, is there anything else you want to talk about? Paige, I get the impression you have something else on your mind."

She now stood beside the chair she'd been seated at not moments before. She seemed hesitant to move from the spot.

"You're right, Evanee, there is something I feel should be brought to everyone's attention. I've heard talk of your powers growing. There are some among the house who worry you're not in control of them. I feel that perhaps you should spend more time focusing on how to control the new powers as they present themselves, and less time focusing on your work away from the mansion."

I studied Paige's delicate appearance in her chic navy ensemble, not for one minute fooled by it. I'd silently observed her training one evening not long after she'd arrived back from Europe. The woman was lethal. She'd levelled Jordan in thirty seconds flat during their sword fight.

"Thank you for bringing that to my attention, Paige, but I will not be a financial burden on this household or its residents. I'm training for at least two hours a day with Erick and Jordan. I've also trained with you before you left. There's not much else I can do at this point in time." Looking around the room, I continued. "I wasn't raised to kiss people's arses. I was raised to not be a burden, and to pull my weight. Look, I've never aspired to a political position, and I'm learning as I go."

"Sweetheart, you'll eventually need to learn to manoeuvre through political situations, especially if you're to stand beside Erick one day." Mum spoke carefully, and I knew she was trying to reason with me, but I was losing what little patience I had.

The only person who thinks I can actually do this and still be me is Grandfather.

"I'm done for tonight. I've enough issues to deal with, and they seem to increase with each passing day. I have two dead girls who may or may not have been murdered by my sadist ex-boyfriend, an unidentifiable CEO hell-bent on killing me. Oh, wait, he succeeded there, my mistake," I said, sarcasm dripping from each word.

"To add to all this, I find out some wayward reaper murdered my dad. Let's not even touch on my emerging powers, and the fact that I'm supposed to take over my great grandfather's old job, which he seems to have ditched for some unknown reason." My voice rose the longer I spoke, panic at the enormity of what my life had become finally coming to a head. No one moved or said a word as I looked at each of them angrily.

Finally, I gave in to all that pent-up emotion, yelling at everyone and no one in particular.

"I will not change to pander to a bunch of ancient politicians. If no one likes me for who I am, they can go stick it where the sun doesn't shine. Funny how out of the people who pretend to know me so well, there's only one person who has faith that I will succeed just as I am. If Grandfather feels I'll handle the new title being jammed down my throat, then maybe you should all take notes."

Choking on raw emotions, I side-stepped a couch and stormed out of the library.

I made it as far as the giant mirror in the hallway before Erick's strong arms scooped me up. Tears of frustration and anger finally spilled down my cheeks, and I was powerless to stop them. Together, we were a blur as he rushed us through a set of open French doors and out into the cool night air. Placing me on my feet, Erick wiped my tears, but said nothing as he grabbed hold of my hand, his large one engulfing mine. With a soft tug, we set off toward the State Forest. We came to an abrupt stop, and I looked around me, grinning at where he'd bought me, despite my tears.

In front of me water fell from up high, hammering and pounding a steady rhythm against unyielding rocks below. Eucalyptus perfumed the air, while tall ghost gums and grevilleas shielded the bubbling pools that few locals knew about.

Sniffing indelicately, I wiped at the rest of my tears. "My father used to bring me here on our hikes during summer. We'd be pouring sweat by the time we got here, and by the time we got back to the car, but we'd always cool off here. He said it had been his thinking spot when he was younger," I said as I looked across at a large boulder at the edge of the natural pool. I could almost see him standing there looking out over the water.

"You still miss him, don't you?"

Erick gazed upon me as he spoke.

"Every single day. I'm grateful I got to be with him in some way before he died. He raised me to be strong and self-sufficient. 'I want my daughter to stand proud and tall. I want her to show kindness to those less fortunate and help those who cannot speak for themselves.' That's what he drilled into me every time we hiked. That, and how to wield a hammer and drill. His philosophical lessons are one reason I loved, and still love, working with the dead. They have no voice, and the murder victims had no kindness shown to them, so I give them that." I smiled sadly at the memories now floating through my father's door within my mind.

"No one is asking you to change who you are, *mic luptător*."

He moved closer yet didn't touch me.

"Aren't they, Erick? I wasn't raised to be a queen or a princess. I was raised to work hard, be kind and respectful, yet take no shit. Now people expect me to kiss the upper classes' arses and smile while I'm doing it."

"I see what you're saying Evanee, and I'd rather forgo the party altogether if I could, but protocol demands it. The truth is, the more time I spend in Australia and with you, the less inclined I am to take my seat on the council, or on the throne in Romania. I like the way things are here, the laid-back life we live in Murder Point Bay and Acrasin City. It's so different from Romania."

The bone-deep tiredness he harboured, seeped into his voice, with a sadness that clutched at my heart and throat.

"Would you have to leave Australia to do that?" I realised, that until now I hadn't known where he or his family were originally from. I knew *mic luptător* was Romanian, and that he'd converted Jordan in Romania, but otherwise, I'd never asked.

Ashamed at my selfishness, I asked. "Where exactly are you originally from, Erick?"

"The city of Sighisoara in Romania. That's where I was born and raised. Although, the council and my parents now reside in Bucharest for most of the year."

"Could you stay here in Australia if you chose too?" We stood listening the crickets and mosquitoes buzzing around us. Funnily, I hadn't been bitten by the little blood suckers yet. Another perk to being dead.

"I'd have to abdicate the throne. Technically, my oldest brother was meant to take it, but he married a human. She's since been converted. It seems, despite our many differences, my brother and I both have a thing for down-to-earth human women."

I laughed at his cheeky smile and put my arm around him. He hesitated for only a second, before his large arm engulfed my shoulders. Together we stared at the churning water before us.

"Okay, so here's the plan. You, me, and possibly Jordan fake our deaths, then start a new life somewhere no one would think to look for us," I said conspiratorially.

"Why Jordan too?"

His jealousy spiked at my having included the big fella into the plan.

"Because, silly, he'd find me no matter where I go. That little mark I put on him works both ways. Your family might order him to locate me, and thus you. So, we take Jordan, find him some nice girl and he can do whatever he wants from there."

Laughing at my mock grumpy retort, Erick hugged me closer.

"That would mean we would need to take Tristan. Tristan has a direct link to me, and if we took Tristan, we'd have to take Ellie too. I doubt he'd leave without her."

Hmmm, he has a point.

"Okay, fine. We take Jordan, Tristan, Ellie, and Brad. I can't leave Brad behind, he's family. Now, we could create a fire at the mansion. I'd try to get a hold of Grandfather, see if he could hold on to our souls until our families had seen our bodies. Hell, I'm sure he could work some mumbo jumbo to make it look as if we've all been fried extra crispy. Then, once our families see our remains, he returns our souls and summons a portal to a nice little village somewhere in some far-off country, and boom we assimilate and start over."

"It'll be that easy will it? What about work and money?"

Spoil sport. "I could work at the local funeral home, or hospital. Or I could become a GP. Do you have any qualifications, other than being fluent in politics and a fantastic fighter?"

"I have a few degrees, but here in Australia I hold a Law degree and a degree in Education."

"Hang on you're a qualified teacher? Wow, I did not pick that." It was a pleasant surprise. I'd expected him to be more inclined towards business or economics.

"I'm also a licensed lawyer."

"Okay, so we have some fantastic options. You could teach at a local school, and I'll be a general practitioner. Boom, new life plan all laid out. We could also start withdrawing our funds in small amounts, so as not to draw any suspicion. I'll sell my house, claiming I've changed my mind and relocate to the mansion permanently. I can use the excuse that all the warm-blooded bodies around me are just too tempting and I need to be closer to my man." I batted my eyelashes at him as I said the last part, and Erick threw his head back laughing uproariously at me.

"We could even give our plan a code name, how does 'destination uncomplicated' sound?" I added.

At last his laugh quietened and he turned to face me, my arms rising to encircle his neck as he drew us closer at the waist.

"While 'destination uncomplicated' sounds oh so tempting, I've a funny feeling you would struggle to not be helping the dead find justice or rest. It's in your genetics. I also think Fate might take offense to us running off on her big plans and would likely find some gruesome way of making us pay." Erick sighed.

I poked my tongue out at him, although I knew he had a point. "Spoil sport. But, you're probably right." My head dropped forward to rest on his chest as I muttered, "That crazy bitch would find some new and creative way of screwing up our lives. Oh well, it was worth a try."

Erick's chin rested gently atop of my head, moving as he spoke.

"It definitely was. Now game plans aside, would you like to take a dip?"

"That sounds like a wonderful idea." I sighed.

Stepping from his arms, I began to strip from my scrubs. The heat of his eyes tracking my every movement seared the bits of my already heated flesh. The scent of pheromones drifted towards me and I smiled slyly at just how effective a burgundy lace G-string could be. I loved my lingerie, even though no one beside myself ever got to see it. If Erick and I were giving us a go, I guess he'd see a few of these babies in the future.

Erick's throat cleared, before he asked with a strained voice, "You wear that to work?"

Turning to face him, I pretended to adjust a few straps, delighted when he hissed deeply. If the back was tempting, the front was mesmerising. Burgundy lace and mesh embraced my breasts, allowing my observer a sneak peek of what lay beneath. I'd completed the look with a matching G-string, its three burgundy straps embracing the curves of my hips.

"This is one of the tamer ones, but yes I wear this to work. Why, is there something wrong with it?" I knew there wasn't, but there was no harm in having a little fun with the delectable specimen of a man in front of me.

"Nope. Um… What I meant to say was no, there's definitely nothing wrong with it at all. Just curious."

He still hadn't moved, and neither had his clothing.

"Are you swimming in your jeans and shirt?" Folding my scrubs, I placed them on a rock nearby. Behind me came the sound of a zipper releasing, followed by the rustle of his shirt being pulled over his head. Turning back, I stopped blinking stupidly as every thought flew out of my head.

Oh damn. Holy hell, I forgot how bloody hot he is. Quick Evanee, think of something else.

Screw thinking of something else. Take that hotness in, woman. It's not every day a god of a man stands in front of us semi-naked. My inner teenager lay sprawled across a sun lounger, her glass of coke tilting to one side in danger of toppling over. Beside her was the bimbo, fanning herself with one hand, and clutching a Long Island Iced Tea in the other.

Would you hurry the hell up and handcuff that man to a bed? It's obvious the poor man is in desperate need of TLC. I mean look at all those curves, and edges; they're just begging to be kissed, licked and fu...

Crap, I can't think straight. Would you two shut up?

"You okay, Evanee?"

A shit-eating grin spread across Erick's gorgeous face as though he thought he had me.

"I'm fantastic, thanks. Just debating with the other two upstairs. The bimbo feels handcuffs and a bed are in order. Apparently you need to be licked and kissed." Turning at his stunned look, I thought I heard him mutter, 'I knew I liked those two', before I summoned a portal and stepped to the top of the waterfall. Looking down, I laughed merrily at Erick's grumpy reprimand.

'Hey, that's cheating.'

I grinned down at him. *'Is it? Well, not to worry, I'm sure you'll catch up—eventually. Or am I too much for you?'*

Launching upwards, he shot up into the night sky before landing solidly at my side a few seconds later. His strong hands gripped my waist, as his body came flush with mine. His low and deep growl into my ear commanded the hairs along my body to attention, and my abdomen tightened in anticipation.

"Are you challenging me?"

"Me, challenge you? Never." Laying my head against his bare chest, I smiled up at the stars above.

"Uh huh. Are you going to jump off or are you too chicken?"

His chest vibrated beneath my head as he spoke.

"I was thinking age before beauty." I yelped at the sharp slap he delivered to my backside; the sting not unpleasant.

"I'll show you what age can do."

Leaping from where he stood, he soared through the air, hurtling towards the broiling water below. He came to a sudden stop mid-air, flipping onto his back to wave up at me before he gently lowered himself into the embrace of the churning water beneath him.

Laughing at his antics, I clapped my hands. "Oh, this is going to be fun. Right, Evanee, let's show him what you've got." Calling to my power, I grasped it firmly, taking control.

Diving from where I stood at the edge of the waterfall, I sailed out into the air, arms out to my side. Plummeting downward, I brought my arms forward as I prepared to meet the water. As my fingertips touched the water, and my body exploded into a thick fog that coated the entire surface of the water.

Treading the water, Erick yelled out in worry. "Evanee? EVANEE!"

Reining the fog, and myself back into solid form, I grinned at Erick's open mouth as I lowered myself feet first into the water in front of him.

"I think beauty won."

"Come here."

He tugged me closer to him, drawing my arms up so they came to rest upon his shoulders. My nimble fingers found his hair as I ran them up the back of his scalp.

Studying his strong jawline, I wiped at stray droplets of water making their way towards his chin.

"That was impressive. You have been working on your powers, haven't you?"

Raising my legs to lock around his waist, I nodded. "I have."

Hesitating, I didn't want to ruin the mood, but there was a discussion we needed to have. "Erick, there's something I need to talk to you about later on; but, not now, I don't want to spoil the moment."

His wet hands cupped the back of my head, and I felt him tug gently at the hair band that had come partially loose during my dive. Soft snowy waves dropped around my face, weighted down by the wet ends.

"Tell me now. I'd rather know now, than wait until we are both tense and on guard. We'd only end up arguing."

He had a point, but the fear of how he would look at me when I told him I wasn't only feeding on blood made me hesitate.

"Promise me you'll keep holding me after I've told you."

Maybe if we stayed connected, it might lessen the disgust he'd feel towards me. Realising I was waiting on him to say he promised, he pushed my hair behind my ear.

"I promise, *mic luptător.*"

"Um, as you know since my conversion, I've been consuming a substantial amount of blood." At his nod, I continued. "We all thought it was a side effect of me being a fledgling, but it turns out it wasn't. You see… um… For the past few months I've been starving. I'm talking eating the arse off a low-flying duck, hungry."

"Okay, that's not something I've heard before, but why didn't you say anything?"

He searched my eyes as if hoping he'd find the answer in them.

"Because I was too scared you would all think I was a bigger problem than I already am. It wasn't until Grandfather came to see me after Brian's visit that I finally acknowledged the truth out loud." I whispered the last part.

"What did Death say, Evanee?"

"He reminded me I wasn't entirely vampire, and that I should remember I needed to nourish the reaper within too. It took a while for me to come to terms with what it was I needed to consume as a reaper, but the night my birth mark flared up I finally gave in."

Frightened, I didn't want to continue.

"What do reapers eat, Evanee?" he encouraged.

Judging by his expression, he already suspected.

"They… they eat souls. Erick, I eat souls." And there it was. I was a proper freak.

Erick's face remained purposely neutral, as he asked. "How many have you consumed?"

"Only two or three. The first one was a woman who killed her two young children, and husband. He died a few days after I consumed her soul. The second was an old man who'd not lived a very honest or good life. Oh, and I think there may have been an aged care worker who was abusing the residents of a local old age home in there somewhere." At his surprised expression, I quickly added, "I've only eaten those who've committed heinous crimes and are close to death. The aged care worker was in the emergency department after a resident finally clocked him with a walker around the head."

"So, let me just clarify a few things. You now require not only blood, but souls to survive. You've kept this a secret from me because you're obviously worried that I'll be disgusted and horrified. Oh, and you only consume the souls of the guilty. Am I leaving anything out?"

Thinking about what he said, I shook my head.

"*Mic luptător*, I really wish you'd told me you were so hungry. I'd have tried to help you. I know this is all new to you, and truth be told I'm experiencing certain changes too. If we don't communicate, we won't know what's going on."

His sigh of exasperation at my apparent foolishness, forced me to smile.

"What changes have you had?"

"Apparently, I've also got an extreme case of the munchies. I suspect you and I may have similar dietary requirements. I've also been waking up drenched in sweat and singe marks on my sheets."

His gentle strokes to my head were soothing, and my tense body finally relaxed despite the fear it'd held moments ago.

"I could take you with me the next time I go reaping. I should be able to shield you enough that we can sneak around without anyone knowing we were there." My eyes closed as he traced a thumb down the side of my face.

"I'd like that, thank you."

His breath tickled my lips, and I opened my eyes staring into the depths of his swirling ones. I knew he was being careful not to rush me. He was waiting to see if I'd meet him halfway.

Giving into the pull, I closed the gap. Our lips touched, and the world obliterated around us. The lightness of the kiss wasn't enough. I needed more. My nails dug deep into his back, so separation wasn't an option as I kissed him harder. His hiss of delight tickled at my swollen lips, and I grinned against his.

Erick surged from the water, clasping me to him as he approached the sandy embankment. Lowering us to the sand he nipped gently at my lower lip before he pressed a kiss to the spot encouraging me, asking me, to submit.

There were no more words to speak, no more arguments to have. It was the two of us, alone at last. I may have needed control in every other part of my life, but right now, right here, I would gladly give the reins over to Erick.

Chapter 11

Returning to work the next evening, a spring in my step, I hummed happily.

"My, my, aren't we in a good mood?"

Turning, I smiled at an amused Steve. "I am. I think Erick and I may finally be moving in the same direction." Waiting for Steve to catch up, we strolled towards the staff room. "We're getting to know each other as individuals, not as pawns in a game we never chose to participate in."

"That's great. Did you tell him about your new dietary requirements?" Steve spoke carefully.

I appreciated his attempt at diplomacy.

"Yep, we discussed that issue, and apparently I'm not the only one who's had a case of extreme hunger. We're going to see if he needs to consume the same things I do." I chose my words carefully in case other staff members might be around.

"I'm so glad to hear that, sweetheart. Well, I'll leave you to it then. Oh, and tell that boyfriend of yours he still owes me a carton of beer. He's been dodging payment."

I giggled at his mock sternness. "I will. Bye, Steve."

Waving to him, I changed direction, heading to the locker room. My handbag safely stowed in my locker, I approached Bob's office, looking forward to seeing him this evening. Knocking lightly at the ajar door, I saw Bob look up from where he was typing.

"Evening Evanee. How are you feeling?"

Looking me up and down, he checked to see that there was no physical damage from yesterday's fiasco.

"All good, boss. I'm fighting fit. In fact, things are damn good for a change." I knew I looked as though I were the cat that got the cream, but things had gone so well with Erick the night before, smiling was the only thing I could do.

"Really? That sounds promising. What's got you on cloud nine?" Bob sat back from his laptop, a quizzical expression creasing his features.

I was grateful I was no longer a human, or I'd have been blushing right down to the tips of my toes. There are some topics one should not discuss with their parental figures, and a mind-blowing make-out session is one of them.

"Nothing much. I had a nice evening with Erick, that's all. It was good getting to know him without having an entire nest of vampires or Fate breathing down my neck. Everyone seems hell-bent on having us married as soon as possible, just to fulfil a stupid prophecy or to spare my head when Erick's family rocks up."

"Oh Evanee, I'm sorry you're feeling so trapped. If I had my way, I'd keep you locked up in a tall castle, safe and sound from this big bad world. But then you'd never get to experience the highs and lows that are life. You should know that I truly believe your father would've been proud to have a man like Erick for a son-in-law one day. The man compliments you, despite how stubborn you are and how much you fight him."

Winking at me when he said the last part, I snorted at his observation.

"He's appears to be an intelligent, protective, and kind man," Bob continued. "I've known him a long time now, and I've watched the way he looks at you."

"How does he look at me?" I asked intrigued.

"As though you're something precious. He looks at you as though you might disappear at any moment, and the thought of losing you is too much to bear. Sometimes I caught him studying you during your teen years, but he never overstepped the boundaries, and was always very polite and professional. Honestly, I'd be proud to have him as a son-in-law. He is someone I know would love and protect you long after I've gone from this world."

An ache so intense I wanted to double over, took up residence in my heart at the mention of his inevitable death one day. I prayed I'd be the one to reap him, to help guide him through his death to beyond. I wanted to be there to say my final goodbyes when that day came long from now.

"Uncle Bob, do you think… do you think that you'd walk me down the aisle if I ever got married?"

Wringing my hands on my lap, it was the first time I'd mentioned marriage having reconciled myself to the fact I'd likely never marry or have kids.

Bob rose from his chair, his eyes glistening.

"Oh sweetheart, I'd be honoured to walk you down the aisle one day. You know Marg would demand that she make the wedding cake. I suspect she'd sabotage anyone else's attempts at the tastings."

Giggling at the image of his wife spiking cakes with salt and hot sauce, I rose to hug him tight.

"Thank you, Uncle Bob. You and Aunty Marg mean the world to me."

I pulled back pecking him on the cheek before I sat back down. He cleared his throat, and I watched as he subtly wiped at a tear on his cheek.

A knock at the door broke the moment as Mel popped her head around the door.

"Evening, Mel. How are you?" I smiled as she sat slowly and stiffly on the chair beside me, wincing as she did so.

"Sore as all hell. I started going back to the gym after fifteen years. The biggest mistake of my life. I had the devil himself as my trainer, I'm sure of it."

Giggling at her complaint, I shook my head in amazement. "Mel, why did you decide to re-join the gym after all these years? It's not like you need to shift any weight."

Raising her shoulder, she hesitated before answering my question.

"I've got my daughter's wedding coming up, and I was hoping to look a little more toned for it."

"Well, I think I speak for both of us when I say you look marvellous as you are, Mel. With all that gorgeous red hair and pale skin, you're a stunner. But I have to say, I'm still impressed you went back." I smiled as I tried to boost her lagging confidence. She did look stunning.

"As she said." Bob returned to his seat just as his mobile rang.

"Bob here."

We waited with bated breath as he ummed and ahhed. Hanging up, he stood again.

"Looks as though we have another victim on the way. Bernard's already contacted the coroner and got a rushed decision through based on the previous two victims. Evanee, you'll be taking this one. Mel, if you could kindly await delivery, I'd appreciate it. I'll join you as soon as the coroner's email comes through."

Understanding he was dismissing us, I rose and exited after Mel.

Pulling on my scrubs and hat, I changed quickly not wanting to waste time. Bending forwards to pull on a sock, the sudden stabbing pain of my birthmark made me topple head first into the floor.

"Shit!" Twisting sideways to preserve my face, I hit the smooth floor with an oomph, panting through the waves of pain that'd taken up residence in the middle of my lower back. Searching the room for a threat, golden sparks and flashes in my vision forced me to squint and wince. There was only one person who ever followed those golden flashes, and she was well and truly on the top of my shit list.

"You cannot escape me, Evanee Mors, for I am Fate. I alone can undo the prophecy, for it was I who set it in motion. Two will die tonight, and you'll not save them."

She sounded almost pissed, and I didn't understand why.

Finally, the pain settled to a dull throb, and realising what she'd said I immediately reached for Erick and Jordan. Could she have meant Jordan? What if she meant my mother, or Ellie and Brad? Question after question circled my mind as I waited for Erick and Jordan to respond.

At last I felt Erick's presence, and I breathed a sigh of relief, my body sagging. Jordan's presence followed soon after. There was no time to waste, I had an autopsy to perform.

'Fate just paid me a visit, and she sounded pissed. She's set her sights on at least two people, and I don't know who they are. Stay safe and be alert.'

'We've just reached the car and are making our way to you. She paid all three of us a visit. Jordan felt her presence through you, and she just appeared in my office seconds ago. Tristan is contacting Brad and Ellie as we speak, and Jordan's been trying to reach your mother. I understand now why you felt as though you were losing your mind that first time, I swear she fried my synapses. The crazy bitch.'

I smiled at Erick's spurt of anger towards Fate. Jordan didn't speak, but I felt his uneasiness through our link.

'We'll see you soon. Mic luptător, be safe please.'

I blew Erick a mental kiss as he left.

'Jordan, wait!' Noting his hesitation, I barrelled on. *'I need you to get my mother to accompany you two, she'll notice reapers before you guys do.'*

'Yes, my Queen.'

His formality was a dead giveaway at just how worried he was, and I didn't blame him. My stomach was in knots at the thought of possibly losing the people I cared so much about. Jordan's presence disappeared, and I crawled back onto the bench, my legs numb.

That cow really knew how to knock me for a six.

~

The body was already on the autopsy table when I finally entered, my legs still a little weak. Scrubbing in quickly, I slapped on my customary nitrile gloves. My gum boots clomped heavily on the smooth floor as I approached Detective Bernard and Bob, who were quietly talking at the freezer door. Mel stood beside our young blonde charge.

"Another victim, Detective? Where's your partner this evening?"

Bernard nodded his greeting before he pulled his notepad from his pocket. "Victim's name is Daisy Patterson. The same physical appearance as our previous two victims."

I looked back at the victim to see her true likeness hovering over her. He wasn't entirely wrong.

"Almost the same. Her true hair colour is brunette. She's had a dye done recently. Otherwise, height, eye colour and physical shape are very similar to the previous two. I think it's safe to say we definitely have a serial killer on the loose with a fetish for blonde twenty-year-old's with blue eyes. Good luck getting that out to the media. Where was she found?" The men shifted uncomfortably at my question, immediately raising my suspicions. "Where was she found, Detective?"

"Beside the Helipad out the front. My partner is out there canvasing as we speak."

The proximity to the hospital startled me. I said nothing, not knowing what I could say. I was yet to confirm Brian hadn't left his apartment with my own eyes, and until then I couldn't accuse him of being involved, especially considering the state I'd left him in.

I pushed my rising fear aside. I had a job to do, and a victim to help. "Right, well let's do the autopsy. Hopefully, the killer's slipped up this time and left a good chunk of evidence on the body."

Detective Bernard nodded, but the bleak look in his eyes told me what I already knew. We weren't going to find anything different from the others.

~

Daisy Patterson lay naked before me, her pale skin illuminated by the cold LED lighting overhead. Dark claw marks marred her once perfect stomach, the same as the previous two victims. Her body was fresh, as was the blood drying on her clothes. Hollow and unseeing eye sockets overshadowed the bloody mess that was her throat. Bending close to her chest cavity, terror and agony rolled from the fractured and mostly drained soul laying trapped and trembling within her. There was no getting it out in one piece, and I was wary of experiencing the pain that hit me the last time I'd removed a soul like this.

Absentmindedly I rubbed at my birthmark, not realising I was doing it until Bob asked if it was bothering me again.

"Yeah, it's killing me tonight. Death draws near, ready to reap those that have been chosen by Fate."

The words were out of my mouth before I realised what I'd said. Utter silence descended over the morgue, as the people within it shifted uncomfortably. The crunching metal sound of the loading bay's roller door being pried open broke the silence in the room.

Turning, I came face to face with my nightmare incarnate as there, in all his putrescent glory, stood Brian.

"Holy fuck!" My horrified yell, triggered Detective Bernard and Bob into action, the former sprinting from the viewing room, his gun already drawn. Bob appeared at my side milliseconds later.

"It can't be. How the fuck is that piece of shit out of bed?"

As though he'd heard Bob's question, Brian's head turned towards us. His eyes glowing red, he took a step, and his body became a blur before he came to a stop at the top of the loading bay steps.

Mel's scream pierced my eardrums, and I barely heard Bob's curse.

"Shit! He's been converted."

Brian approached a window overlooking the loading bay, a grin spread across his face. Fear dropped like a dead balloon to the bottom of my stomach as sheer terror gripped me. His fanged smile was at odds with the familiar power rolling from him. The reaper within me rose to greet that power as if it was an old friend.

"Bob, Mel get across the room, now. He's not just vampire. He's reaper too." I hissed.

Brian's smile broadened at my observation. A blur in my peripheral vision drew my attention, and I turned in time to see Bernard step around the corner, gun raised at the ready.

Yelling out to him in warning, his name barely left my lips before Brian was in front of him, snapping his wrist so the gun dropped uselessly to the ground. Bernard's body sailed through the air as Brian threw him across the loading bay, coming to a skidding halt at the base of the torn roller door. I prayed for him to roll to his feet, but he didn't move.

Backing away from the loading bay window, I held my arms out to either side of me in a pathetic attempt to guard the two humans behind me. We were nowhere near the locker room door, and I worried about sending them into the freezer with no thermal protection. Glancing quickly to the interview room window, I contemplated smashing it to get them out, when Brian stepped through the very freezer, I'd considered sending Bob and Mel into.

His ghostly appearance was all too familiar, as was his hair; whiter than freshly fallen snow. Forks of obsidian splintered his ruby red eyes as pearl lightening flashed intermittently across them. Coming to a stop in the middle of the room, he solidified once again. There, standing tall and proud before us was a shirtless Brian.

Bob's horrified whisper behind me sent shivers up my spine. "Evanee, is that what your curse did to him?"

I could only nod as it finally registered, I'd been right. The substance I'd found in the previous two women's wounds was in fact Brian's rotted skin.

I stared at Brian, my eyes wide; horrified that despite undergoing a conversion, he'd not healed as I had. The skin from his shoulders to his abdomen dropped off in chunks, hitting the floor with wet splats, and I stared at it in morbid fascination. His body was healing at a phenomenal rate so his skin no sooner hit the floor, then it was replaced by a new healthy piece of skin, which began to degenerate before our very eyes.

He's shirtless on purpose. This was his show, and I his audience. Behind me Mel retched, and the stench of vomit permeated the air.

I finally addressed him, my voice wobbling worse than an amateur in their first pair of heels. "Brian, I can't say it's a pleasure to see you. To what or whom do I owe a good punch to the head for converting you?"

If I found out who'd done this to him, I'd be delivering more than just a punch to their head; I'd be bringing my scythe with me, and together we'd indulge in its love of death and blood.

"Let's just say someone other than me is very much interested in seeing you dead," he said merrily, his handsome face still untouched by my original curse. "In fact, he's given me the honour of killing you myself. Tell me Evanee, did you enjoy my gifts?" He glanced towards the body on the table, lust sparkling in the depths of those hypnotic eyes.

"Oh, they were from you? I wondered what moron would do something so depraved and pointless." I was poking the bear, I knew it, but I needed his attention on me, and not on Uncle Bob and Mel shielded behind me.

"Tsk, tsk. You won't rile me up that easily, Evanee. I know what you're trying to do. You think I can't smell the sweet scent of all that delicious blood in those two meat sacks behind you?"

"Oh, I have no doubt you can smell them from where you're standing, just as I can smell the putrid stench of rot coming from you in waves. Turns out whoever changed you couldn't do something as simple as heal you."

Brian appeared before me in the time it took me to blink, his sharp rancid yellow claws digging into either side of my neck. Lifting me, he tossed me to one side as though I were nothing but a rag doll. My back met the viewing room window, the glass cracking around my torso as it connected. My head slammed back hard, cracking the glass further. Dropping to the ground uselessly, stars danced across my vision.

Uncle Bob's cry of outrage cut off suddenly as he slid beside my slumped over body. With a groan, he rolled onto his knees, and crawled towards me.

"Now Evanee, I think you're in desperate need of some discipline," Brian chortled. "That smart mouth of yours was a constant source of aggravation for me during our dates. I both dreaded and looked forward to the day I got to fuck you. You know I'd planned to handcuff you and duct tape those luscious lips of yours at some point, but we just never got to the bedroom. Not to worry, there are always other pleasures to be had." He turned slowly, his eyes landing on a petrified Mel, who'd been slowly stepping back in a bid to put distance between herself and the monster before her.

I pushed myself to my feet unsteadily to stall him.

"Fuck you Brian, and the putrescent hearse you rode in on!" I bellowed as I surged forward my nails lengthening and sharpening. Mel deserved better than what was coming.

My clawed hand slashed across Brian's rotted back; chunks of rotted flesh splashing to the floor, the blood coagulating instantly. Hissing in rage and pain, Brian's solid fist slammed into my chest, and I sailed across the room once again. This time instead of hitting glass, my body met the cold embrace of the metal freezer door. Dropping to my side, my back popped and cracked as my spine slowly realigned the fractures it'd sustained on impact.

Helpless in the precious seconds it took for my spine to heal, despair beat at me, there was nothing I could do to prevent the death I was about to witness.

I looked up as he stepped up to a cowering Mel, his rotted hands reached out to cup her face, and he looked back at me, glee lighting his face.

"Mel, look at me. Look at me, not at him," I wheezed past the pain. "Look at me, Mel!"

Her terror-stricken eyes swept to where I lay curled, willing my body to recover quicker. I held her eyes, not wanting Brian to be the last thing she saw before she left this world. Brian's eyes shone brighter as he bent slightly and snapped her neck with little effort. The sharp crunch of splintering bones jolted my body as though it was my neck under those hands. I refused to look away from her until her limp body dropped.

Chapter 12

"Noooo!" I screeched as Bob yelled hoarsely.

I sobbed, raging internally for my uselessness. Self-doubt crept in during the precious seconds I found myself hunched over, waiting to heal. Guilt for the pain I'd caused Brian for the past three years, and rage at the monster I'd helped to create, crept beneath my shields. I was supposed to help people, not condemn them to a life of pain and suffering. The consequences for my past actions were coming home to nest, leaving a bitter taste in my mouth.

"Oh Evanee, I warned you I'd seek my revenge." Brian turned back to face me, his cold smile taunting.

From the corner of my eye, I noticed Bob put his back against the wall beneath the cracked viewing room window. Shaking my head softly, I attempted to clear the fog of guilt from my mind.

I need to get Bob to safety. Brian can't have him too.

"Screw you, Brian. Everything that's happened to you, you brought on yourself, you wanker. Your condition isn't a reflection of that night, but a reflection of who you are on the inside. You're rotten to the core, and now the whole world gets to see you for who you truly are."

Brian was immediately in my face, snarling. His face was still as handsome as the day I'd met him; only this time, someone had given the beast laying beneath that beauty a new set of weapons to play with in the form of a set of sharp fangs and supernatural powers.

"My dick may not work, and I may not be able to fuck you, Evanee, but I will have those 'fuck me' eyes of yours as a trophy. It's never been just about the sex. No, no, no, it always been about the pain, the sweet cries of sorrow, and despair. I taught Desmond everything he knew; do you know that? Compared to me, he had a soft touch."

Motioning my fingers, I prayed Bob would catch my signals for him to make his escape. All the while I continued to stare at Brian, refusing to take the bait.

Jordan's words echoed within my mind. *If in doubt, fake it Evanee. Your opponent shouldn't know how much you're shitting yourself.*

"Too bad your twit of a cousin was going to screw you over to keep me all to himself." I smiled savagely at the astonishment that skittered across his face.

His rotted hand was a blur as he shackled my throat, his hand slipping slightly as rotted skin gave way. "You're lying. Desmond adored me. He'd have done anything for me."

Dragging me from my knees, I dangled limply from his grip, as he held me at arm's length. I gripped his putrid hands with mine for leverage.

Whispering hoarsely, I provoked Brian just a little more. "Evidently not. Not to worry though, I did us both a favour, and the rest of the world too. That sack of shit bit the dust squealing like the pig he was."

In a flash I raised my legs, kicking out hard. Connecting with his abdomen, Brian flew into the autopsy table, buckling it on impact. Daisy's corpse toppled over the edge, hitting the ground with a heavy thump.

I crumpled to the ground, with no time to retrieve Bob as Brian rose, once again hurtling towards me. I met him head on, relying on my supernatural strength and reflexes, and not that ancient power within me. Bob was too close to risk summoning it, especially when there was every chance I'd lose control and it would consume me.

I met Brian in a low tackle, grunting in satisfaction at the crack of his ribs. My satisfaction was short-lived as he lifted me at the waist and dropped me headfirst into the polished cement floor. Rolling my head in at the last second, my shoulder connected instead, snapping loudly. I screeched in agony, regretting it as Brian's delighted laughter erupted from above me.

Rolling to my back, I looked up in time to watch Bob drive the pair of garden shears we used as bone cutters through Brian's back. He shrieked in pain and swiped at Bob, just catching at his shoulder. Red streaks marred Bob's lab coat and he grimaced.

Using the precious seconds Bob brought me, I snapped my collar bone back into place, the pain washed away by the panic setting in. Seconds later, Brian reached for me once again, the garden shears—and Bob—forgotten.

Avoiding his reach, I rolled backwards into a crouch, but I was too slow. His large grotesque hands found me, slamming me up and into the dented fridge behind me. I kicked desperately; my training forgotten in my panic as Brian shackled me in place. Reaching behind him, Brian ripped at the shears and blood, gore, and more rotted tissue decorated the surrounding floor.

"These will do."

He drove the shears through my gut and into the fridge door behind me. The pain was agonizing as it reached through the links I shared with Erick and Jordan. Their yells of panic and fury pummelled my mind, but they were useless to me.

Blood sprayed in a frightening arc across the floor in front of me, and it took me a second to realise it was mine. It was strange how it glittered in the overhead lights, almost as though diamonds were caught within it.

"Now you wait right here, babe, while I go take care of your boss. After that, I think we might get better acquainted. We really didn't have enough time together in Brisbane."

"No," I pleaded, spitting a mouth full of blood to the side. "Leave him be. I'll go wherever you want, do whatever you want, just leave Bob alone. Please!" I begged brokenly.

I prayed then, prayed to God, Grandfather, and Fate they'd spare the man who'd been a father to me.

"Oh no Evanee, I think he needs to die. You need to be brought to heel, and I'll be the one to do it." Turning, he approached Bob, who was still slumped over, dazed from the wounds in his shoulder.

"BRIAN, DON'T YOU FUCKING TOUCH HIM. I'LL KILL YOU! DO YOU HEAR ME? I'LL RIP YOUR USELESS HEART OUT AND CRUSH IT AS YOU WATCH. LEAVE HIM THE HELL ALONE!" I jerked hard at the shears lodged within me, letting out a frustrated cry when they budged only slightly. With every jerk, Brian advanced on Bob.

I hung helpless and useless as Brian knelt beside Bob.

"Look at her, old man."

He spoke, loud enough for me to hear him over the pounding of my blood in my ears.

"Know she's the reason you're going to die tonight."

Bob stared defiantly into Brian's glowing eyes.

"I would die a thousand times over for her. She is and will always be the daughter I could never have. My love for her is unconditional, and she knows that. So, you go ahead and kill me, but know that woman will come for you. She has a strength and love you could never understand."

Tears tracked down my cheeks, dripping to mingle with the pool of blood at my dangling feet.

"In that case say your goodbyes. It'll only hurt her more knowing how helpless she is at this very moment."

Brian's amusement and glee at the pain he was causing sickened me, but not as much as the guilt and hurt that had my throat constricting and my gut squeezing around the blade.

"Evanee, sweetheart, don't cry." Bob was calm, his gaze gentle. "This isn't your fault. Tell Marg and Scott I love the…"

He gurgled the last part of his sentence as Brian latched onto his throat with an obscenely large jaw, ripping at his jugular like a mangy dog lost to rabies.

"NOOOOOO! BOB!" Tugging and jerking at the shears restraining me, they loosened, but not enough to release me fully.

Sobbing in agony and grief, I continued to struggle, all the while watching as Brian shredded Bob's abdomen. At last Bob stared at me with unseeing eyes, yet Brian still wasn't satisfied. Horror rose as his hand became transparent, reaching towards that place where Bob's beautiful soul rested, waiting to release. Realising his intent, I gave one final yank of the shears, grunting with relief when they finally released, and my wounds began to stitch together.

My aching knees hit the cement floor, but I had no time to recover. Instead, I reared back and hurled the shears I clutched with every ounce of strength I had at Brian, nailing him in his right shoulder, driving him backwards. I'd never been more grateful for the target practice Jordan had given me. Bob's body flopped lifeless to the ground.

For the first time in my pathetic life, I released that blind rage I kept at bay. A rage so primal, it triggered that ancient power that had nothing to do with the reaper or vampire within me, and everything to do with death and its place in the universe.

My bloodied scrubs and gumboots disintegrated to dust and liquid, settling atop of the blood beneath my bare feet. Fog exploded from my body, shrouding my nakedness as I stepped forward. Behind me massive translucent, shredded wings erupted, flaring out.

I risked a glance at Bob's body, and pain clawed viciously at my heart. My talons erupted from beneath my fingernails, joined by my lengthening canines. Brian knelt unaware, yanking on the shears still lodged in his shoulder. Up and up the pain and rage bubbled, seeking an exit, seeking control. And I let it.

I opened my mouth as my head dropped back and let loose a scream so intense it shook the room. Power exploded from me as glimpses of the people I called mine filtered through.

On a dark winding road, descending from the hills between Murder Point Bay and Acrasin City, Erick's power exploded ahead of him seeking its mate, his responding roar ancient and primal. Beside him, Jordan slammed on the brakes, swerving into the nearest emergency stopping bay as his power burst into the night seeking his mistress - his queen. Ellie dropped to her knees in a cottage somewhere in rural Ireland, her ear-splitting screech dulled by an icy afternoon storm that raged outside. Somewhere in a scorching hot desert, Mum's ghostly body stilled, her charge safely seen to his destination. Without a word, she summoned a portal, my battle cry heard and acknowledged. The trapped dead reached in agony from beneath me and around me, begging to be set free. Begging to be called to arms.

I appeared in front of Brian, hissing long and low as I fully merged with that ancient power flooding me, not caring about the consequences. I ripped the shears from Brian's shoulder, tossing them into the wall beside me. They landed in the wall, blades buried to the handle. My hand hurtled forward, smashing through Brian's rapidly healing tissue and bone.

His grunt of pain was sweet nectar, and I drank it in. Ripping my crimson hand from his shoulder, my other hand latched at his jugular. Forcing his neck to open up before me, I was on it before he had time to realise what I was about to do. I bit down hard, drinking down that heady mixture of genetically modified blood; tasting the vampire within him, the part of him that was miraculously still human, and the part that was reaper. Gulping heavily, blood dripped down the sides of my mouth and chin to lovingly caress my jugular and eventually my breasts.

His first punch to my abdomen dislodged my bite. The second hit tore my grip from his jugular. With a screech of rage, I swiped down across his chest with blood-soaked talons. Garnet drops sprayed hot and wet across the fog shrouding my body. My body drank it in, not allowing anything to go to waste.

Brian landed a punch to my jaw, and my head snapped to the side, allowing him to make his escape across the room. He reeked of fear as he wiped at the blood running down his neck. The wound refused to heal, and so did the one at his chest.

My scythe appeared in my outstretched hand as I stalked towards him.

I will rip his heart out before I decapitate him and dance amongst his entrails.

I smiled savagely, watching as he summoned a portal, my smile faltering. Frustration clawed at me when he stepped through it, all the while keeping his eyes focused on me as it began to shrink. Sprinting towards the portal, it closed just as I reached it, and I screeched in anger, the sound inhuman.

Turning to Bob's body, my eyes snagged on a dark hooded figure in the corner of the room. Before I could think, I leapt across the room, dropping in front of Bob, guarding him against the inevitable. I stood seething and growling, unwilling to give ground. I was more animal than human in that moment.

"You, my sweet child, are a thing of beauty and grace. I've not seen something as beautiful as you since my late love. You make an old man proud and humble," his voice echoed eerily.

"You cannot have him," I hissed.

"Evanee, I came to collect him and your assistant. I am paying them both a great deal of respect by being here." He stepped forward, and I bent low, ready to attack if I needed to. I felt his amusement and his sorrow for the pain I was in.

"You will sheath those talons, child, and I will collect their souls. It's their time. Do not force my hand, granddaughter. We are tasked with a great gift and an even greater burden; one we cannot escape."

Multiple faces flashed before my eyes, making it impossible for me to focus on any one face. The rage I'd felt before faded suddenly as I realised I was no match for the being in front of me. With its retreat came the pain and anguish. Releasing my scythe, it dissipated, returning to its place beside my bed at home.

Turning to Bob, I dropped to my knees, dragging his still warm body into my arms. Graceful wings surrounded us, shielding us. Replacing his fallen glasses carefully, I stared into his unseeing eyes. The pain was too much, and I lifted my head to the ceiling, releasing all that pain the only way I knew how.

My wail of despair perforated the windows, the glass shattering and exploding in a hail of shards as my pain sought the starry night outside. It went on and on until my vocal cords shredded under the effort. I didn't care, not anymore.

At last my head dropped, and I hunched forward, my forehead coming to a rest on Bob's. Sobs jerked my body, yet my wings stood firm, never budging. I protected him now, praying it would make up for my numerous failures.

A disturbance in the air drew my attention, and I watched my mother step through a portal, her ghostly figure ready for a battle that had long passed. Behind her, Erick followed, and I stared at the unfamiliar enormous leather-like wings protruding from behind him. Rage shook the earth with his every step. Jordan strode through next, his hands loose, a gleam in his eyes at the thought of an impending battle. His power crashed against the surrounding walls, and they groaned under the pressure.

He was too late, they all were, I'd chased Brian off. Just not in time.

I ignored them as my head dropped, once again keening quietly. I was drowning in the grief and unwilling to find my way to the shore.

"Grand-père? Has the danger passed?"

Mum looked around for the threat she'd felt through me.

"Yes child, it has. Your daughter drove him from here. She was elegance and strength during her battle once she got past her fear. You'd have been proud, granddaughter."

"I'm always proud of my sweet angel. Is this her true form then?"

They spoke as though nothing had happened, and it infuriated me. I hissed my displeasure at the blatant disrespect, but Grandfather continued as though he hadn't heard me.

"Part of it. I suspect there's more to come—for both of them."

He glided to where my mother stood, looking to Erick first, before he smiled down at me.

The wall crumbling beside me didn't faze me; the fiery presence of the being on the other side familiar. Brick and mortar erupted outwards, joining shattered glass as a fuming Bernard stepped through the hole. The fiery glow outlining him, halted the surrounding beings.

"What the fuck is he now?" Jordan asked.

"Beauty, life and love," was the only explanation my grandfather gave.

"Death."

Detective Bernard nodded towards my great grandfather.

"Good to see you again. Judging by age, I'd say it's long overdue." Bernard dismissed him then as he took in the sight before him.

"Evanee?"

Bernard turned his confused gaze to me.

When I didn't respond, he looked at my grandfather.

"Who is she holding?"

He stepped closer to me. Silence descended as the three newcomers finally noticed the body cradled in my arms. I continued to shield him, not willing to let go just yet.

Sighing sadly, Grandfather addressed me once more.

"Child, you must let him go. I will allow you one last chance to say goodbye, but that is all that can be done."

Shadows had begun to creep from beneath his cloak, and I knew I was out of time. Bob would travel to whatever awaited him on the other side, while I remained here lost in an ocean of agony and grief.

Finally, I nodded, spreading my wings open.

"Oh, Bob. Sweetheart, I had no idea. I only sensed Mel," Mum whispered, devastated at what she was now seeing.

I keened, blood red tears streaming down my face unchecked. In front of me Erick bristled, uncomfortable with my sorrow. Gently placing Bob on the ground, I stepped back; the fog shrouding my body swirling chaotically with my intense emotions. Grandfather stepped forward and bent towards Bob. My wings flared behind me, and the others stilled.

"Enough, Evanee. It is time."

His voice boomed, making me cower. Rising, he held in his hand Bob's soul. It was the only thing I'd save tonight, that and Mel's soul.

As I watched, Bob blossomed to life before me; a transparent and wavering vision, but still Bob.

He looked at Grandfather and laughed that deep-bellied laugh of his.

"Well, I'll be damned. Who'd have thought it was you of all people?"

Bob turned to me.

"Oh sweetheart, look at you. You really are beautiful. I love your new wings; they really suit you."

A sob escaped my lips, and I clenched my fists against the new wave of sorrow. Seeing my struggle, Bob stepped over his body, coming towards me.

"You'll always be my princess, Evanee. Never forget who you are and just how loved you are. I don't have a lot of time but know that I'm sorry I never got to walk you down the aisle."

I wanted to look away but knew this would be the last time I got to see him.

"Would you do me a small favour?"

"Anything," I whispered raggedly.

"Look after Scott and Marg and tell them how very much I love them. I know they will be safe in your hands, as will the grandchildren Scott will one day have. Be sure to tell Marg I'll be waiting for her sweet kisses on the other side."

His crooked smile broke my heart even more.

"I will guard them until my last breath. I promise. I'm sorry I failed you. I'm sorry knowing me ended your life. I'm so sorry." I clenched my jaw against the sob threatening to escape.

"Sweetheart, you've never once failed me, nor could you ever. I'm as proud of you as your father was. It's been a joy to watch you grow into the woman you are today. I've always loved you as though you were my own, and that will never stop just because I'm gone. I'm sure your father and I will chuck back a few on a deck somewhere watching over you. So, if you hear a few profanities through the veil, just ignore them. We'll be cheering for you all the way."

Stepping up to me, he slipped his translucent arms around me, and for just that second, he became solid. Solid enough for me to embrace him one last time. Stepping back, he pecked my forehead, his smile bright and happy before he turned back to the room, waving his final farewell.

"Righto, I'm ready. You'll continue to keep watch over our girl here?" Bob asked.

Grandfather's chuckle at Bob's question was eerie, and filled with not just one tone, but a thousand.

"Of course, I will." Grandfather nodded. "Be at peace, dear friend, and thank you for the life you have bestowed upon my granddaughter and great granddaughter. May you be rewarded beyond the veil."

With that, the vision of Bob faded, coalescing back into the orb of his soul. Opening his arms, my grandfather's cloak parted, revealing nothing but pure darkness beyond. Slipping the orb into that darkness, it was instantly engulfed.

Nobody moved or spoke, each paying their respects silently to the man we'd all known and loved.

"Kill me," I pleaded, and every head in the room swivelled toward me.

"Kill me, please! I can't do this anymore. I can't continue knowing everyone I love will die for knowing me. If I'm dead, Aeternum will no longer continue to create monstrosities, and everyone will be safe again." My shoulders slumped as I bowed my head in shame and defeat.

"I cannot and will not reap you, sweet child. This is a path you must walk, a morbid and sorrow filled path albeit, but one that will make you stronger in the end." My grandfather's words offered no comfort. Summoning my scythe once again, I held it loosely in my hands.

"It will not kill you Evanee, despite its power," he warned.

At the edge of my vision, I saw Erick step forward.

"*Mic luptător*, don't do this, please," Erick whispered. "Don't leave me. Who'll challenge my every word and decision? Who will keep me grounded when the world around me is going up in flames? I need you now more than ever. I can't lose you now that I've finally found you. Stay, let me get to know you better; let me love you."

His wings rustled at the last sentence. Behind him my mother cried silently, while Jordan held her. I hesitated, then a new wave of sorrow hit me like a sledgehammer.

Dropping to my knees, I sobbed openly, uncaring who saw. Dropping the scythe, my taloned nails rose to my face. Crimson lines appeared as I dragged the sharp talons down my face, the pain cathartic amidst so much sorrow.

Strong hands shackled my own, and I thought I heard Erick pleading with me. Opening my eyes against the trickles of blood drying on my face, I stared into the emerald depths of his eyes.

"Evanee, please don't do this. The pain will pass. You need to release it another way. Harming yourself won't help."

My sobs became louder, my world falling apart before my very eyes.

I've lost two fathers; I can't lose anyone else. If I end my life now, their pain will fade with time. They'll move on, and they'll be safe.

I struggled against Erick, growing frantic. Sorrow turning into anger as my sobs transformed into deep-bellied yells. Through the fog swirling around my naked form, hands reached up, voices crying out for release.

"She is summoning the dead. She is not ready for that yet. We need to calm her. Now!" Grandfather said, the urgency in his voice causing footsteps to race toward me.

"Forgive me for this, Evanee."

Looking up at Jordan, I had no time to prepare for the fist bearing down on me. It connected with my head, and the world melted into darkness.

Chapter 13

I stood, numb, amidst the throng of mourners who'd gathered at Murder Point Bay's local community hall to farewell Uncle Bob once last time. Their incessant murmurs buzzed around me, but I paid no heed to the questions and sympathies circling the room. My guilt wouldn't allow it.

Reaching out to touch the Australian Maple urn, my hand stalled, then dropped as inadequacy and worthlessness swirled within me. I bit down hard on the inside of my cheek forcing my tears into submission.

I searched the room for Erick and found him chatting quietly in the corner with some local businessman. Every now and again his eyes would flicker to mine, watching me closely as he'd done for the past three weeks. He'd become a constant presence within my mind, holding our connection open, as though to reassure himself he'd be able to save me if any new thoughts of suicide should arise.

Begging him to kill me in the morgue hadn't been my finest hour. If I was honest with myself there was a part of me that still longed to escape this life of sorrow I was trapped in. But my death wouldn't end Brian's rampage.

Brian's sole purpose was to cause me as much grief and sorrow as he could. Taking me out of the equation would see him go unchecked. I still hadn't told Erick and the others about my battle with Brian, and how my incompetency had resulted in Bob and Mel's death.

In amongst the swirling concoction of emotions was Erick's confession of love. I had feelings for my spunky sire, but just how deep they ran, even I wasn't sure. I mean, how was I supposed to tell the difference between Fate's interference and love? I didn't believe in love at first sight, but boy did I believe in lust at first sight.

My circuits may short out if or when we do finally hop in the sack.

May? Hell, you'll probably pass out. Do you even remember how to do the horizontal rap dance?

I could always count on my inner bimbo to pipe up where Erick was concerned.

Aunty Marg's familiar sweet rose perfume drifted up to embrace me, pulling my attention back to my surroundings. I hoped I'd smell that perfume for many years to come.

"I think the urn turned out well, don't you?" I spoke in a whisper, not really wanting the people congregating near us to hear our conversation.

"Superbly. Bob would've been so happy with it, as strange as that sounds. Australian Maple always was his favourite wood."

Out of the corner of my eye, I caught her sad smile.

"That doesn't sound strange at all. I'll admit though, I'm a little surprised you held the funeral here in Murder Point Bay. I thought you might have it in Brisbane."

Joined in grief, we stared at the urn, neither of us ready to look away from it.

"This was where his heart truly was. He grew up here, and we raised Scotty here. We'd intended to retire here in the next couple of years."

Nodding in understanding, I braced myself to deliver the message I knew I had to relay to her. "Aunty Marg, there's something I've been wanting to tell you, but I've not been sure how to say it." Turning to her, I needed to look her in the eyes as I delivered Bob's final message

"What is it, sweetheart? Just spit it out, that's usually the best way to say something." She gazed at me with her large brown eyes, unaware of exactly why or how her husband had died.

"You know how I have unusual abilities?" At her nod, I continued, "Well, you see, the thing is after Bob died, I got to see him one last time." I stopped, wanting to make sure Aunt Marg wasn't showing any signs of anger or extreme grief.

"Go on." A spark of hope flickered in her trusting gaze.

That trust left a bitter taste on my tongue as I spoke the next words. "Before his soul departed, he asked me to give you and Scotty a message. I don't know how much Scotty knows about me, so I thought it best to approach you first and you can choose how best to proceed from there."

She once again nodded at me to continue.

"Uncle Bob wanted you to know how much he loved you and Scott. He said to tell you that he'll be waiting for your sweet kisses on the other side." The corner of my mouth lifted at the last part.

"Oh, that silly fool. He always knew how to charm me or make me smile when I didn't think I could." Choking back a sob, Aunt Marg laughed softly at Bob's sentimental words.

"I also want you to know that Uncle Bob asked me to watch over you, Scotty and any future generations, and I gave him my word that I would. So, if there is anything you ever need, anything at all, just call me and I'll drop everything and come running. I've also set up a trust account for you and Scott, which thanks to a few donations, now has a sizable amount in it. It's yours to do with as you want." I didn't mention I was intending on selling my house to further top it up. She'd flip if she knew.

"Sweetheart, you don't need to go to that length. The money from Bob's superannuation and estate should be enough to see me comfortable during my retirement years. But I am grateful for the effort you've gone to."

I didn't care if she didn't want the money. Guilt ate away at my stomach that it was all my fault. The least I could do was provide monetary compensation. I wasn't taking no for an answer.

"I need to do this Aunty Marg. I need to know that you have everything you could need. Besides, the money is in the account already, all you and Scott have to do is sign a couple of documents and everything should be all set to go."

I was weighing whether to tell her the truth about who'd attacked Bob, when Erick's approach and gently spoken words distracted me.

"*Mic luptător*, you're looking fatigued. I think you might need to lie down."

'*Reading my mind again?*'

'*I didn't need to, the look of guilt in your beautiful eyes was all I needed to know that you were about to tell her what really happened to Bob.*'

Erick's soft murmur through our mental connection soothed my roiling mind, and I took comfort in the fact there was someone who could make it stop even if it was only for a moment.

'*You aren't wrong.*'

His arm came around my waist before he leaned down and placed a soft kiss to the top of my head.

"He's right darling, you do look exhausted. Are you getting enough blood?"

I smirked at Marg's question. "Only you could ask me something like that and make it sound like an everyday question. I'm getting enough blood by the way. I guess I must have pushed myself a little more than I thought this week. I'll be all right after I've slept for a bit. You and Scotty be sure to help yourself to whatever you want at home, okay?"

I'd made up the spare rooms and even baked Scott's favourite chocolate and pecan brownies. The fridge was fully stocked with wine, beer, and food, so they wouldn't have to leave the house unless they wanted to.

Taking up my hand, Aunt Marg patted it gently as she gave me a small smile. "I will sweetheart, and thanks again for lending us your house for the week. It's been a great help."

"If there is anything you need at all, please make sure you contact any one of us. I believe you have my mobile number?"

Erick's hushed tone lulled me into a false sense of security.

"I do. Thank you all so much for all your help. Reagan said she'll sort things out here, thank goodness. I don't know how I would go having to clean all this up."

"I believe she roped in Tristan and Ellie into helping with clean up duty. You should see Tristan, Aunt Marg, he's a master with the broom and cloth." I knew Tristan's ears had perked up at the sound of his name, and sure enough the scowl he was currently shooting me said he'd heard me. "I might be off now. Would you tell Scotty I said goodbye, and I'll try to catch up with you both before you leave, okay."

"Okay, sweetheart, that sounds like a good plan. I'll see you later."

Hugging Aunt Marg goodbye, Erick and I exited the building and into the harsh glare of the sun. I bent my head, as my energy drained even further. Technically, I should have been resting, regaining my energy and strength since the fight with Brian, but this had been too important to miss. I wouldn't go up in flames, but the sun's caress ached like all hell on the few bare spots of skin I had on display.

Rushing towards the car, Erick unlocked it as we reached it, and we both climbed in with sighs of relief.

"Thank goodness for extra dark tinting." My words rushed out of my mouth as my head hit the headrest.

"Yes. The perks of being rich is that no one asks why you need extra dark tinting on a Mercedes. Apparently, it adds to my mystique." He snorted as he revved the engine.

"They probably thought you'd be in the back seat, not in the front."

"True."

Pulling out of the parking lot, we drove sedately through town, and I stared at the blissfully unaware citizens going about their daily activities.

I felt the caress of his mind against mine, and I sighed. "You don't have to worry about me trying to kill myself you know. I won't do it, no matter how much it hurts right now." I kept staring out the window as we left the centre of town and headed out towards the valley.

"I'm glad to hear that, *mic luptător*."

He placed a gentle hand over my clenched one on my thigh, patting it soothingly before replacing his hand on the steering wheel.

"I know how much it hurts to lose someone you love so much. The hurt never truly ever leaves you, but it will lessen with time."

I knew what he said was true; the pain of my father's passing had dulled over time, but the longing to see him had never diminished.

"Jordan received a message just before, which is why he rushed off the way he did." Erick continued. "He's had word from Brad. Apparently, Brad believes he's found valuable information regarding Aeternum. Jordan's going to pick him up from the airport, and they should be at the mansion this evening."

Erick's hands tightened on the steering wheel as he spoke, and it groaned beneath his grip, threatening to bend. Reaching over, I gently extracted one of his fists, holding it in my tight grip. His grip lightened on the steering wheel once more. I could almost hear the leather thanking me.

"Hey, I'm the only one who's allowed to have temper tantrums. Someone has to be there to calm me down," I said as I rubbed his index finger lightly with my thumb.

He chuckled at my admission.

"Oh, is that right?"

Squeezing my hand lightly, we sat in silence for a moment longer.

"I need to feed properly tonight. It's been three weeks." Staring out the windscreen, I didn't have to elaborate, Erick was aware I wasn't referring to blood. I'd been managing on one soul a week before the attack, and had hoped to extend it to a fortnight, but Brian's attack had left me weak.

"We'll go hunting tonight before Brad's arrival. Is there any place in particular you want to hit?"

Withdrawing his hand from atop of mine, I felt the loss instantly, but pushed it aside as he navigated the car through the sharp corners.

"I was thinking the local prison. The back of my mind keeps shooting me images of the prison and multiple faces, so I'm guessing something big is about to happen there. I'll reap a few souls and ingest one or two to top me up. It might also be worthwhile you giving it a go. I usually drink them in, but I'm not exactly sure what will work with you." When he frowned, I rushed on, "You did say that blood no longer seemed to be the only thing you craved. Tonight, might be the chance to see if souls are what your body wants."

"True. I guess we could call it our first official date. Dinner and a show."

Taking his eyes off the road for a second, he grinned at me cheekily.

I couldn't help but giggle. "You really are a morbid weirdo, you know that?"

"I am, but that's what you love about me. My morbid weirdness matches your morbid weirdness."

And there's that word again - love. Do I really love this big hunk of a guy, or am I acting out Fate's little game? Maybe I can ask Uncle Bob about how he knew he was in love with Aunt Marg?

I'd no sooner finished that thought when I realised that was never going to happen, not anymore. Grief constricted my heart, uncaring that it no longer beat. I spent the remaining journey in silence, contemplating what my true feelings for Erick were.

Erick and I parted ways at the front door. He headed to his office, and I left him to his business too distracted by my own thoughts.

I turned towards the library. The doors sat open, overlooking the state forest and a section of the manicured lawns. Staring out over the gardens, a cool sensation brushed across my birthmark warning me I was no longer alone.

"I can feel your presence, Great Grandfather. You may as well come out."

Turning towards the desk against the opposite wall, Grandfather revealed himself. Shadows shrouded the corner of the room where he stood, skeletal hand of the condemned reaching through the veil of the dead towards the living seeking release.

"Evanee. I wanted to see how you were doing. Did you get my message?" His voice whispered through the room with a depth and lightness that contradicted each other.

"What message was that?" Sighing, I approached the leather lounge, sitting in exhaustion.

"The deaths that will take place at the prison this evening."

He sat opposite me in the second lounge chair.

"Ah, so that was from you then? Yes, thank you, I received it. Erick and I plan to go together. He's calling it a date. Dinner and a show I believe were his words." My small smile only just registered on my lips.

"Now that's good thinking. I knew that man had potential."

Looking around the room as though his surroundings interested him, I suddenly realised I'd not given him Fate's message from my conversion. "Oh, by the way Fate said to say hi and to tell you how hot she looked. She also said to be sure to mention just how *helpful* she'd been during my infection and conversion period."

A flicker of annoyance flashed across the multiple faces his features seemed to swap between.

"That woman doesn't know when to quit. I thought the events that played out had her unique signature of madness."

At my confused look, Grandfather elaborated.

"You could say we've had a love-hate relationship for centuries now. When they say don't date someone you work with, I'd listen to that advice. She's a pretty woman, with a vengeful streak a mile long. Our last relationship did not end well, and that's when she must have concocted this little prophecy you now find yourself in."

"Hang on. Are you telling me that because she's pissed at you for leaving her, she decided it'd be fun to make one of your relatives fulfil some shitty prophecy? Are you bloody kidding me?"

Indignation consumed me, as I tried to come to terms with the fact that some stupid cow had ruined my life all because she'd thrown a tantrum.

"I'm sorry, sweet child. She's had a habit of making me pay dearly because of her jealousy. I lost the love of my life to one of her many tantrums, and I regret it dearly every day."

My heart twinged at the sadness in his voice, and my indignation dimmed.

"Judging by her message, I'd say not even she realised just how far her prophecy would go. She's sidling up in the hopes I don't seek her out and remind her that not even she can escape me. Everything dies, even those who think themselves above death."

Trying to wrap my mind around everything he'd said, Erick's power drifted into the library as he sought me out, which reminded me. "Before Erick arrives, I need to ask you a question. Is what Erick feeling for me and vice versa a result of the prophecy, or is it real?" I brought my hands together on my lap and twisted them.

"Ah, I see. I'm guessing you're worried that the prophecy is in some way making you feel what you think are fake emotions, and that it's effecting Erick in the same way? A logical assumption, but let me ask you this, what happened the first time you touched each other?"

Leaning back against the chair, he crossed his leg over what I could only assume was his knee. I wasn't sure if he even had a body beneath that flowing robe.

"It felt as though the world stopped around us, as though it took a breath and let it out in one giant shuddering breath. It sounds stupid, but it was as though I'd found a home, I truly belonged to for the first time." The moment flashed before my eyes as I recalled that night all those months ago at Desmond's house when my vision had been blinded by the kaleidoscope of colours.

Grandfather's husky laughter drew me back to the present.

"What you're feeling is indeed real. That poor bugger has no idea what he's gotten himself into, just as your father had no idea what kind of woman had stolen his heart the day he met your mother. Fate may have brought you together, but that sensation you felt when you touched him, that's our species' way of knowing we've connected with our mates, the loves of our lives, our soul mates." Laughing joyously, he shook his head. "I still remember the day I bumped into your great grandmother. The world shook to its very foundations. It's why part of the earth flooded. You know the whole Noah's ark incident and all that. Now in that case, I had no idea what I was in for. There was no other woman in history who could pull me into line like she could."

The door opened as Erick entered, pausing only briefly as he noticed the hooded figure on the couch before him.

"Death, welcome," Erick said with a casualness his mind didn't hold.

Erick sat beside me. He looked from my shell-shocked face to Grandfather's ever-changing one.

"What did I miss?"

"I think I shocked our dear Evanee here into silence. Tell me something Erick, when you first touched Evanee, what was it you experienced?"

I watched Erick carefully as he mulled the question over.

"It's hard to explain. It was as if every connection I had with my people melted away, so that I could think clearly for once. There were no knocks on the door to my mind, just silence and peace. Oddly enough, I felt as though I'd arrived home at last, as though every other place I'd ever lived had never truly been home. It was as though I'd been searching my whole life and I'd finally found what I hadn't known I was looking for." Erick rubbed the back of his neck embarrassed.

"You poor, poor bastard. You have no idea what you're in for. My dear boy, you have now experienced how we reapers identify our other halves—our mates. She will be your greatest happiness, and your greatest sorrow. What she feels, you will feel tenfold. The same could be said for you too, Evanee. You'll know a love that not even you could've imagined, but that's not to say that there won't be times you won't want to do him through with your scythe." His glee was unsettling.

"If that's the case, then why the hell didn't I fall instantly in love with him? I've spent more time butting heads with him and clashing over who gets to wear the pants than anything else. Surely that's not love?"

Grandfather's soft chuckle raised my eyebrow.

"Not everyone experiences love the same way, Evanee. For some it starts as mutual respect and then evolves. For others it's love at first sight, whilst others feel an intense lust that evolves into love. There are so many ways humans and supernatural beings experience love. Which one are you, Evanee?"

I am not touching that one. Hell freaking no. There is no way I'm admitting it was the latter. I'd look so shallow. Those beautiful eyes and dark brooding looks are enough to make any grown woman drop to her knees.

"Can I call a friend?" I asked.

Beside me Erick laughed hard, his arm coming around me as he placed a hard kiss to my head.

"I have no idea what that means, but I suspect you want to change the topic, do you not?"

Grandfather surprised me with just how at ease he looked. I'd have thought he had places to be.

"You would assume correct."

Laughter light Erick's grinning face.

"My advice to you, Erick, would be to hold on tight. She has a lot of her great grandmother in her. Chava was always so full of life and fun, but I couldn't control her. Her temper was similar to Evanee and Reagan. To control her would be to drain the very life from her. I tried once and only once to command her obedience, and let's say I felt a wrath such as nothing I'd ever experienced."

"Chava, so that was her name. It's a beautiful name. What did she look like? Do any of the family resemble her in any way?" I felt sad I'd never be able to look upon a photo of my great grandmother, but considering how old my family was, I could understand there being a lack of cameras during their youth.

"In human form she appeared as a Hebrew. You and your mother have her nose and eye shape. I'd say your figure is close to hers, and that of your father's family. My daughters looked similar to her in their facial appearances, while my sons took on her skin tone and her flaming hair colour. She always did have trouble keeping her hair hidden. Try as she might, it was the one feature she couldn't change or dampen. It was as though the very life she represented needed to be witnessed by all. It was a mission to keep her and the babies safe during her pregnancies. Which is why I created the reapers, so that I could take the time to be with her and distract other beings with fears I was amassing an army. With each pregnancy, I created more reapers." Grandfather sighed at the memories of what must have been very trying times.

My curiosity reared its head once again. "How did she die? Mom doesn't seem to know, and apparently the family won't discuss it." Sitting forward out of Erick's arms I waited for what I was sure would be a tale of epic proportions.

"That is because not even they know what happened to their mother. I will tell you about it one day, but now is not the time for a tale as gloomy as that one. I have something else I needed to talk to you about. The other night I noticed you both had a new addition added to your anatomy."

I looked at him in confusion.

He elaborated. "Your wings."

"Oh, yes those. Technically mine weren't new, they erupted the night I left Brian's apartment. I didn't know you had wings too. Is it a vampire thing?" I looked at Erick.

He shook his head in bewilderment. "No, it's definitely not a vampire thing. It shocked the hell out of me when they erupted. I've not really had the time to think about them."

Grandfather chuckled, drawing my attention away from a fidgeting Erick.

"No, it's a 'me' thing. I'm the only one in this family aside from Chava who has a set. They were a sight to behold. Seeing your beauties was a bit of a surprise, not to mention Erick's. If this means what I think it means, you will find in coming months you will both undergo some rather extreme changes. Erick, I'm not sure just how much you will undergo. But Evanee you need to prepare yourself for the possibility your reaper form will evolve and scare a lot of the elder vampires and my family. I have a strong feeling your ancestry will soon be on full display." He spoke cautiously, but calmly.

"Is this to do with the fact that you once ruled over all the species of death?" I wasn't sure if Erick was meant to know that, but he did now.

"Yes. It will be a reminder that I live on. Not everyone will be happy with that reminder. You have allies, the both of you, so use them when the time comes. Once you show your true form, the attacks will come at you from every direction. Show no mercy. Most of the elders have grown complacent in the positions I tasked them. Sadly, my people have been left to do their own thing for far too long, and as a result a divide has grown that shouldn't have existed. There was a time when they co-existed in harmony."

Grandfather stood gracefully signalling our time had ended.

"I don't have any allies, other than humans." I shrugged.

"Your best friend is a banshee. She is destined to be chief of her clan, help her achieve her full potential. Erick, rally those you trust and start now. I wouldn't rely on your family, rather those you've sired. I must say, Evanee, I was rather proud of you for choosing a vampire for a shield. That was a great choice. Jordan has proven over the years to be efficient during wartime, am I not correct?"

Addressing Erick, the shadows beneath Grandfather began to grow.

"He has. Jordan's saved my life more times than I care to remember. He's as ruthless and savage as I am when the time is called for, but also strategic and even-tempered."

Together Erick, and I stood to bid farewell to my great grandfather.

"He will be an asset to Evanee and yourself, but especially Evanee. Her temper can sometimes get the better of her."

He chuckled as my hackles rose.

"That is not a critique, but an observation, sweet child. Now, I must be off. You two have an enjoyable evening. I dare say you will leave with your bellies full."

I stepped forward, surprising him by raising my arms up to hug him.

Embracing my great grandfather was odd. His coat was solid, yet not. I'd not expected to scent anything on him, but there were so many smells, and there beneath them all, I thought I detected someone familiar. Before I could identify who, he pulled back.

Stepping back silently, large wings shot out of his back and he grinned cheekily. They were magnificent, raven-coloured wings of an eagle, that spanned the width of the room. Golden tips stood out against the inky darkness of the flared-out feathers. Beating them once, he hovered an inch off the ground before disintegrating into a fine mist.

"Show off!" He met my yell with faint masculine laughter, before the room descended into silence.

"Well, that was interesting. Is it just me or do you get queasy looking at his face?" Erick asked.

"You'll get used to it," I said as we sat on the couch. "Did you want to talk about anything Grandfather brought up?"

Erick stared across the library distracted by his thoughts, and I wondered if he'd heard me.

Finally, he shook his head, and I clapped my hands with exaggerated delight. "So, you ready for a night in prison? They'll have shanks and full on fist fights."

I waggled my eyebrows at him when he looked back at me, his deep chuckle drawing a grin from me.

Chapter 14

We stepped through the portal I'd summoned and straight into the chaos consuming the dining hall at the local maximum prison facility. Cloaked by my power, Erick and I stood bewildered by the sheer mayhem surrounding us.

A body hurtled through the air. I gripped Erick's hand tightly to anchor him to my side as the man disappeared through our invisible bodies, landing on the floor behind us.

"Only those close to death should be able to see us. Both humans and supernatural creatures will be unaware we're here unless I will it." When he looked at me in confusion, I enlightened him, "Grandfather once said that he could stand right in front of me and I'd never know it. He can bend reality to his will, and to some extent so can his creations and descendants."

"Being a reaper does have perks then," Erick drawled.

"I guess it does. Another perk is knowing who's going to bite the dust next, which just so happens to be the lanky blond guy cowering in the corner." I tilted my head toward the scared man then looked to Erick. "You ready for this?"

Erick nodded, then squeezed my hand. Squaring my shoulders, we approached our target, conscious of the broad-shouldered inmate doing the same thing from the other side. I observed the advancing inmate who searched for something he couldn't find.

"He has no weapon," I yelled over the grunts and yells of pain.

"I'd say he's going for a good old-fashioned beating. He'll either beat him to death or break his neck," Erick responded.

I cringed.

The blond man shook violently as his harbinger of death came closer. His eyes darted around the room, searching for someone to save him. The cowering man's fear vanished momentarily as he caught sight of us standing undisturbed despite the violence surrounding us. Then it was gone, his face obscured by the shoulders of the advancing inmate.

My hand squeezed Erick's harder with each passing second, the surrounding chaos driven further from my mind with the thud of each punch delivered by the inmate. Relief washed over me when a fluttering sensation finally took up residence in the back of my mind.

It's time.

Sighing, I clicked my tingling fingers, and the room slowed to a crawl.

I gave into the fluttering at the back of my mind and with a small shudder, my reaper rose to the surface. The jeans and t-shirt I wore disappeared, replaced by a tattered white dress. An unfelt breeze lifted the strands of my hair, and the soft glow from my transformed eyes and body cast shadows around me.

"Come on, it's time," I whispered sadly.

With Erick's hand still in mine, we approached our target. His face was a bloody mess, but I ignored it as I leant over, my free translucent hand reaching forward and into his chest cavity. Scooping the tiny orb within, I ignored the images of his life trying their best to flash before my eye as I extracted the soul. I had no interest in how this man lived his life.

Rising, I faced Erick, never releasing his hand. His heated gaze drew a shiver of anticipation from deep within.

"Don't look at me like that, Erick. You're making it difficult for me to concentrate," I admonished.

With a cheeky grin, his fangs peeked from beneath his slightly parted lips.

"I'd never dream of interrupting your concentration, *mic luptător*," he murmured huskily.

He drew closer to me and the soul in my loose fist.

"Ah huh, sure you wouldn't. Now be a good student and pay attention."

"Yes, ma'am," Erick drawled. "Do I get disciplined if I don't behave?"

I snorted in disbelief. "I'd say yes, but that'd probably make your day. Now shush, we need to move quickly." When he nodded, I continued, "You can put your fangs away. You won't need them. Now, I'm going to raise the soul to your mouth. I need you to tell me if you can see it, okay?"

"Okay."

My free hand came up, and I slowly opened my fist to reveal the glowing orb within.

Wonder lit Erick's face, his awed whisper making me smile,

"Wow, so this is what a soul looks like? The colours are beautiful."

"Good, you can see it. Now, comes the tricky part—ingesting the thing. When I consume a soul, I sip it down or inhale it. Does that make sense?" I explained.

Erick frowned. "I think so."

"All right. Well, give it a go then," I encouraged.

Bending forward slightly at the waist, Erick studied the orb for a second before his free hand rose to cup my outstretched one. His index finger caressed the side of my wrist. His eyes connected with mine eliciting a shiver of excitement from deep within me.

My body tightened, lust now my master, and I, its willing student.

Pursing his lips, Erick's eyes never left mine as he slowly sucked in a breath, taking with him the essence swirling within the orb.

When at last the soul was no bigger than a blueberry, I whispered, "Stop."

Rising to his full height, I closed the distance between us. My breasts met his chest and his arm circled my waist securing me to him. Releasing his hand, I plucked the orb from my palm, bringing it to his parted lips.

"Open," I whispered.

Placing the orb on his tongue, my fingers caressed his jaw. My eyes never leaving his heated gaze, I rose to my toes placing my tingling lips to his top lip. Erick's groan spurred me on, giving me the courage to explore.

My tongue darted out, tasting the lip I'd just caressed. Strong fingers speared through my hair as Erick lost what little patience he had left. His lips met mine, our tongues tangling so the orb burst, popping and crackling over our taste buds. We drank down the remainder of the soul, our groans unheard by those around us.

Pulling back softly, I grinned, "How was that for your first soul?"

"I'm sure that was the best damn meal of my life. I think I may have to demand we eat like that every night."

Laughing at him, my arms circled his neck.

"I need to finish reaping him," I grumbled, disappointed my work wasn't done yet.

"How do you plan on doing that?"

"Like this."

I slipped from Erick's arms, my hand travelling down to take his. With a thought I summoned my scythe, its comforting weight settling in my hand.

I bent beside the blond inmate and placed a small scratch just beneath his ear as I breathed, "Die."

Rising, I clicked my fingers the sounds of chaos once again assaulting us.

"Who's next?" Erick yelled.

I pointed across the room. "Let's start there."

~

Staring up at the beautiful wooden roof, I lay supine on Erick's lap, listening to him as he spoke on his mobile phone to one of his people.

He'd taken what Grandfather had said seriously and had begun rallying his people in anticipation of the fast approaching party. I was yet to speak to Ellie, but I would once Brad had rested. What I had to ask needed to be said to the both of them and in person.

My gaze drifted to his face, and I watched as his lips pursed ever so slightly. I smirked at the slight puckering, reminded of our date earlier this evening. Bringing my phone to eye level, I sent off a text to my mother, asking her to be here in roughly half an hour. Her confirmation came seconds later. Lifting the message up to Erick, he read it before nodding. He continued to stroke at my hair absentmindedly, and I let him. I mean, what girl didn't love that? I was in heaven and could have remained there for all eternity.

The door to the library burst open, shattering our peace as Ellie and Brad strode in arguing about the latest outbreak of Ebola. Smiling at the familiar sound, the world felt right once again. I might not have Bob here to guide me, to walk me down the aisle if I ever got married, but I had these two and that would be enough. Behind them followed an arguing Tristan and Jordan, and last, a silent Paige.

"I need to go. I'm trusting you to take care of the necessary arrangements with the rest of the family." Ending his call, Erick smiled down at me as my mother's portal appeared behind the desk.

Ignoring our guests, I whispered to Erick. "Did you get what you needed done?"

Erick nodded as Tristan got straight to the point. "What problem has you summoning an urgent meeting, Erick?"

'Wow, he really is direct, isn't he?'

'He's good that way. It keeps my meetings on track and on time.'

Erick's grin made me snort with laughter.

'He's like a take no shit personal assistant. Gotcha.'

Shaking his head at my needling, he addressed those present in the room.

"There are a few things I would like to discuss, and they are confidential."

As Erick spoke, I sat up, trying to look a little more professional.

'The only time you're professional is when there's a corpse in front of you.'

Jordan's deep laughter rumbled through my mind.

'Well, if you want to get technical, I see at least six dead people in this room, and that's not including myself.'

'Hey, we are the living dead. Get it right. I take offense to such off handedness; but then again, come to think of it, Tristan probably could be classed as dead.'

Coughing loudly to hide my laugh, Erick looked between the two of us before rolling his eyes.

"We have an issue, and it's a big issue; but I will get to that in a second. First, Brad please update us on what you discovered during your travels."

"There was a lot of sorting through shell companies, false leads, etcetera, but I still couldn't find information about who had or owns Aeternum. Finally, I was able to track upper management back to Paris, with the help of your delightful children, Erick. Lovely bunch by the way; a little on the torture-torture side, but very accommodating none the less."

Shaking his head at what could only be a gruesome memory, Brad continued.

"Anyway, we were able to get to one of the big wigs, and let's just say he wasn't very resistant to torture methods. He couldn't give us much, other than it had been in the same family for generations. He mentioned someone's poured a lot of equity into the Australian branches recently, more specifically into Acrasin City and Brisbane. Apparently, Brisbane has seen a lot of activity in the last few months."

I surged to my feet and made my way towards the closed French doors.

'*Mic luptător, what is it?*' Erick's concern whispered through my mind.

"Brad's information isn't a surprise to me. In fact, it only confirms what I already know." I didn't turn around. Instead I chose to focus on the tree line ahead. They wouldn't have any trouble hearing me. I didn't have the emotional strength to reveal what happened the night Bob, and I were attacked, and still make eye contact with the people in this room.

I can't look at their faces when they realise how badly I failed Bob. I can't bear to see their disappointment at just how pathetic I was.

"I know you've all been waiting for me to talk about that night; and, can I say how grateful I am that none of you pushed me to reveal anything until I was ready. I understand it's been frustrating for each of you. Most of you knew Bob personally, and his death has been monumental to say the least." Standing silently for a time, I organised my chaotic thoughts.

"It makes sense that Brisbane's headquarters have seen more action in the past few months because that's where they would have found their test subject," I said finally.

"What are you saying, Evanee?"

I could tell by my mother's tone she already suspected what I was about to reveal.

"I'm saying Mum, that Aeternum plucked its newest experiment from beneath our noses. Brian, as it turns out, made top of the list for their newest guinea pig."

Erick cursed before I heard him stand. Jordan's profanities were muttered, but he didn't move from where he stood.

"Hang on. Who the hell is Brian, and what's so important about him that they'd select him?"

This came from a perplexed Brad, while Ellie, Tristan, and Paige's confusion scratched at my back.

Tension tightened my shoulders, and I moved my neck from side to side, the click of my vertebra loud in the still room. I owed them the truth. If not because they were my friends, then because they'd all risked so much despite the danger they now found themselves in.

"Brian's the man who tried to rape me in my final year of residency. We'd gone on a few dates beforehand. Long story short, I realised on the final date the night before my attack that he wasn't for me. I guess he wasn't a fan of rejection." Rubbing hard at my face, I fought the images that threatened to overcome me once again.

Strong arms circling my waist proved to be the perfect distraction as the thoughts ebbed away. Patting Erick's arm in thanks, I allowed my head to drop back and my eyes to carry on staring unseeing out the windows. No one spoke, obviously stunned by my confession.

Just wait until they hear the rest.

'You did nothing wrong, mic luptător. Don't you dare feel guilty for what he deserved and more.'

'Thank you. It just went against my very nature at the time, but things have changed… or at least, I've changed.'

Bracing myself, I continued with my story. "The night he attacked me my power surged forward to protect me, and I ended up laying a whammy of a curse on him. I left him to rot slowly from the outside in. You could say his outsides eventually reflected his true nature. I wasn't the first and I wouldn't have been the last girl he raped or tortured. Him and Desmond were rich boys with sadism hiding beneath all that pretty boy charm. That's what Desmond meant when he said he was avenging his cousin. Brian was his cousin." Leaning forward, I felt incredibly tired all of a sudden; the happy glow I'd held inside for such a small time was beginning to ice over.

Pulling away from Erick, I surprised him when I reached for his hand, taking him with me towards the couch. Settling back into where I'd been seated previously, Erick dropped down gracefully beside me. Gripping his hand, I stared down at it, not ready to look at anyone.

"When Desmond revealed Brian had continued to rot, I went to see him. I don't know what I expected, but I went there ready to grant him peace and to reap him; instead I found him unrepentant. I don't know if it was a power rush, me being a spiteful bitch, or the anger, but I sat there and told him I wouldn't reap him. I tormented him with the fact that he would continue to rot until eventually his heart gave out or one of his other organs." Tears of shame clogged my throat, but I pushed them down.

"I suspected Brian was responsible for the deaths of those women when the location of their bodies started ringing bells. Then we found cells that resembled those you'd find in someone suffering with caseous necrosis, and I knew without a doubt that Brian was in some way responsible, but I had no proof."

"When the third body appeared, I'd only started to examine her when her attacker showed up. Brian ripped a hole in the roller doors before he tossed Bernard across the loading bay." Clenching Erick's hand, I struggled to get the rest of the events to line up. That night had been chaos and pure hell combined into one big crappy concoction.

"If you're not ready, don't continue, sweetheart." My mother could sense my internal struggle and judging by the intense emotions roiling off Erick, so could he.

"No, no I need to do this. You all deserve to know what happened that night. You need to know what we're up against."

Squeezing Erick's hand, I unlocked the new door that had appeared the night Bob had died, allowing it to burst open within my round room. I shoved Erick and Jordan's doors open allowing the images to flow through to them.

Images of Brian materialising through the freezer door echoed in the minds of Erick and Jordan as I forced words past my dry lips. I could still hear the sound of Brian's skin hitting the floor with a little wet splat.

Pausing, I croaked, "He presented no bite marks traditionally associated with a human converted, yet I sensed the vampire within him. I also sensed the reaper lurking just beneath the surface. From what Death mentioned, he is the only one with the ability to create reapers, or at least he was."

"You're not wrong there, Evanee," Mum confirmed.

"It wouldn't be unreasonable to assume that Aeternum mastered DNA splicing to some degree," Brad reasoned. "From what you've described so far, I'd say that the splicing wasn't one hundred percent effective, or he'd have fully healed."

"I concur, Brad. However, we should stop and consider the possibility that Evanee's curse was too powerful," Paige suggested. "Please continue, Evanee."

Jordan and Erick remained silent as I sat staring at the ground as my conversation with Brian circled around my mind.

The weight of Erick stare turned my head to him.

"You tried to distract him, *mic luptător*. You tried to have him focus on you instead of Mel and Bob."

Nodding at Erick, he pulled me closer in comfort.

At everyone's confused look, Jordan enlightened them. "The events from that night are being relayed through our shared link. Tristan, you should be able to see them through Erick, if you connect now."

Tristan nodded.

I knew the moment he was seeing what the other two men were seeing, because he flinched.

"Is that what he did to his victims? Shit me, Evanee, I'm sorry. I had no idea."

Tristan's harsh whisper gave little reprieve from the memory, but I appreciated the sentiment none the less.

The three men winced as my head hit the viewing room window. "Evanee fought well."

Jordan addressed the room before looking toward me.

"That hit you took would've left even me feeling dazed."

I nodded, not believing a word of what he was saying. He was larger than life, just as Erick was. I couldn't imagine a crack to the head rendering him useless.

Long low hisses of pain erupted from Jordan, Erick, and Tristan. It was then that I realised that they were feeling the pain of my spine snapping.

"Baby, he broke your spine." Erick looked at Mum, dazed by the pain he felt in that moment. "The arsehole broke her spine."

"Your healing capabilities are phenomenal, Evanee. I can feel her spine popping back into place. How the hell am I feeling what happened to her?" Tristan asked bewildered.

Jordan shrugged. "I feel the pain too, which didn't happen when we were last in your mind."

"It would appear your powers have amplified, *mic luptător*."

Erick pressed a kiss to the crown of my head as he spoke.

He sounded proud, but there would be no more pride once he saw what came next.

"Brian killed Mel while my spine was healing. I physically couldn't get to her," I choked.

Tristan scrubbed at his restrained hair, silver blond strands escaping his hair tie, as Brian snapped Mel's neck. He approached me, bending so that he looked up at me.

"What you gave to Mel in her final moments, by forcing her to look at you so that her last sight wouldn't be that of a monster, was… You gave her as much peace as you could in her final moments," Tristan said in earnest.

I bit the inside of my lip, not willing to speak at that moment. As if understanding, Tristan squeezed the tops of my knees before resuming his place beside Ellie.

My throat was too tight to continue, thankfully Erick understood.

"She's taunting Brian, in the hopes he won't turn on Bob. You tried hard to get Bob to go, baby, but he refused to leave you," Erick said.

"She's fighting him again."

I could feel Jordan analysing my fight as he spoke distractedly.

"You delivered some brutal kicks. Remind me to up our close quarter defence lessons during our next session."

Yeah, I wouldn't be doing that. The man would have my neck snapped more times than I could count.

"The old man had fight in him. He shoved a pair of garden shears into Brian's back."

Tristan smiled at the image, only to jerk back as Brian shoved the shears through my gut.

Jordan stumbled before falling flat on his backside, while Erick jerked back in the chair beside me.

"I begged him. I said I'd do anything, even go with him, if he'd only spare Bob." I looked at my mother, tears coursing down my cheeks. "Do you know what he told me?"

Mum shook her head, her eyes reflecting the heartbreak I once again felt.

"He told me I needed to be *brought to heel,* and that *he'd be the one to do it.* Uncle Bob died because I wouldn't bow down to the arsehole who tried to rape me," I spat.

"Oh sweetheart, I'm so sorry." Mum sniffed sadly.

Her sorrow was forgotten when Tristan stilled, his look of awe confusing those not privy to the memory he was witnessing.

"Care to share what you're seeing?" Ellie snapped impatiently.

"She transformed. I've never seen anything like her," Tristan whispered.

"She looked beautiful. They both were." Mum smiled, remembering mine and Erick's appearance from that night.

"That they were," Jordan agreed.

Ignoring the room, Erick gripped my face before kissing me hard.

"I am so incredibly proud of you. I think even Tristan might be a bit in awe of just how well you did in your first battle. As I recall, his first battle saw him sleep the sleep of the dead for a month, and that was against a regular vampire."

I giggled lightly at Erick's confession.

"I heard that. What he's not telling you is that the guy I faced was a trained mercenary and had a good few inches on me in height and weight. Why not tell her about your first battle, Erick? I'm sure she'd love to hear about how you only lasted one minute before being knocked out and rescued by your older brother."

I laughed a bit harder at the embarrassment in Erick's eyes.

"I knew I should never have shared that story with him."

Shaking his head, his soft lips caressed my forehead.

"Not to be rude, but there are those of us who did not have the privilege of witnessing what some of you so obviously did," Paige groused.

Erick reluctantly released my face, but dropped his arm around me, unwilling to break our contact.

"My apologies, Aunt. Perhaps Tristan, Jordan and Reagan could explain what they witnessed," Erick suggested uncomfortably.

"I think we need to do one better, Erick, don't you?" At his blank stare, I addressed Paige, Ellie and Brad. "We'll show you what the others saw."

I pushed to my feet as I shoved the door to that ancient power within me open. A sigh of relief escaped my lips as that power washed over me, disintegrating my clothes, and moulding to my body. Talons replaced my fingernails, and my fangs lengthened in anticipation. The wings I held such fierce control over, erupted behind me, flaring out happy to be free once again.

I looked down at my body, sparkling in the soft light, and smiled.

"Okay, why can't I have your powers? All I can do is screech people's heads off, and maybe float if I'm lucky," Ellie huffed.

Chapter 15

My wings rustled softly behind me as though they had a mind of their own. Behind me, I heard Erick shift uncomfortably. Twisting around slightly, I looked pointedly at him.

"Don't look at me like that, *mic luptător*."

"Look at you like what, Erick? I'm not the only one who transformed that night. Why are you hesitating? They deserve to know." I questioned the stony-faced vampire.

My eyebrow rose in challenge and Erick cursed shoving to his feet. The anger shinning in the depths of his astonished me. I'd never seen him angry before, but it was there in the rigid set of his shoulders, and the white knuckles clench of his hands.

Erick's clenched fists burst open, talons now in place of his human fingers. Mesmerised, I watched as an orange and gold flame erupted within those talons before it shot up his arm and over his body, his clothes turning to ash in the blink of an eye. Giant wings burst from between his shoulder blades, and his flame raced to cover them before settling into the wings to form a translucent golden coat over the top of them.

I smiled dreamily as Erick's flames settled over his body, providing cover where his clothing had once been. The flames danced enticingly over his six-pack, and I almost wished they were on display—almost.

"Wow, I'd say you look hot, but that might feel a bit too cliché." I grinned at Erick whose only response was a grunt.

My talons twitched with the need to feel that flame and what lay beneath. Looking out at the room, I frowned at the looks of fear rolling from our audience.

I held up my taloned hand to calm those present. "It's all right guys, don't be afraid. Erick is still a vampire, well mostly anyway." I looked over to my mother.

"Mum, you mentioned that a few of you had noted some odd things during my transformation, isn't that right?"

She nodded. "That's right. Every person in this room noted the odd distortions within the glass you two were protected by."

"Right. First, what do you see when you look at Great Grandfather?"

"His face shifts constantly, as does his voice. I could swear though that I've seen both human and animal forms. Once I was sure I noted something other, not human or animal."

Mum shifted in agitation, and I didn't blame her. It was disconcerting.

"Jordan, Erick, would you agree with my mother's description?" Looking between the two men, they nodded.

"What does that have to do with these monstrosities?" Paige gestured angrily towards us.

She was scared, and I didn't blame her. Erick was her favourite nephew, and the fear of him no longer being what he once was, frightened her.

"I believe *my* wings are a manifestation of the gifts my Great Grandfather bestowed upon me not long after my birth as is customary in our family. The wings' appearance likely has more to do with my increasing powers, and my body adjusting to them."

I flexed my wings again, and the room stood transfixed.

Interesting. I wonder if it's the fact I have wings protruding from my back, or if the wings themselves are holding them captive?

Tucking my wings tightly behind me, I concentrated hard, drawing them in so they would once again become a part of my back. The glittering mist swirled gently, parting to allow the wings to settle on my back once more. Beside me, Erick's leathery wings rustled, and I placed a hand on his glowing forearm, drawing his attention.

His flame didn't burn my hand. Instead, it crept along my talons, warming them. I wanted very much to step into his arms to see whether that flame would warm my entire body, but now wasn't the time.

'Wait. I want to test a theory.'

'What theory?'

'I'll tell you in a minute.' He frowned at my request but complied.

"That still doesn't explain why Erick has inherited wings. Vampires do not have wings," Paige hissed.

"If I'm not mistaken, I would say he has inherited some of my abilities, as I have inherited his. The conversion requires him to take my blood and part of my very soul into himself. The same can be said for me. Because he's taken on a part of me, he now has reaper DNA and essence swirling within him." At the confused look on everyone's face, I explained.

"When a vampire converts a fledgling, they take in their blood, right?" The vampires present nodded in agreement. "They also, to some extent, take in the mortal's soul. I understand you never take the last drop when you feed, but essentially the soul is infused with every part of the human body. Each being, human or not, has some form of a soul. This may be their own, or one placed within them to animate them." The last bit of information came from deep within me, and I was once again reminded of that ancient power housed within me.

"Are you talking about zombies?" Brad asked.

Trust Brad to think of zombies.

"Yes, zombies are one creature that require animation by a necromancer. In each of your cases, I can see your essence or souls trapped within your flesh. When I see souls in humans, they resemble orbs. These orbs have certain colours, which indicate what kind of life they lived. Erick, that is what you saw this evening," I reminded him. "With vampires, well, yours are no longer orbs. They look like this."

Extending my arm, my power trickled forward to produce a swirling mass of colours. Garnet, multiple shades of blue, and a tiny speak of black chased each other endlessly. The slightest hint of gold appeared and then disappeared again as we watched.

"This is what your soul looks like, Erick." Surprise registered on his face, and I smiled warmly.

"Ellie, yours has purples, blues and white in it." I grinned happily at her.

"And you can see this in every being?" Tristan asked wondrously.

"I can. Even in you." I winked cheekily at him, and he shook his head.

"Erick, when we met with Grandfather you mentioned you could converse with every single one of your children telepathically, isn't that right?"

"Yes, that's right."

"Did none of you ever stop to consider why that was?" I asked.

"I believe we all assumed it was part of our powers as the living dead," Paige responded quietly.

"I see. Well it is, and it isn't. When Erick converted me, he ingested a part of my soul, and a great deal of my DNA." His raised eyebrow suggested he was following what I was saying but wasn't sure where I was going with it. "By doing so, Erick, you inadvertently took on my genetic composition. Essentially, you have a significant part of me floating around you permanently, and I'm the same. As a result, you now possess reaper DNA, which is fusing with your power and genetic makeup. You were converted just as I was."

"Okay, so why doesn't it affect us when we consume human blood? I mean none of the people I've feasted on over the years have psychic connections to me." Jordan said.

"Doesn't it though? You aren't truly immortal, and a stake to the heart would render you useless, not to mention decapitation. Look, at the moment all I can assume is that it's because you are *feeding* on your primary food source, and not actually taking their life."

"Then by that assumption that would mean we would become closer to human in DNA structure each time we converted someone." Erick's giant leathery wings rustled, and around the room, our guests fidgeted in worry.

Intriguing.

"Fair point; but, what if supernatural DNA is more parasitic or viral in nature? If I recall correctly, prior to my death there was much debate in favour of us not exchanging blood. Could it be that your elders suspected or feared they'd create a new species each time they attempted a conversion?"

By the shocked looks throughout the room, it was evident no one had thought of the issue from this angle.

"What do you think, Erick? Could it be that the elders were more concerned about being bred out than fulfilling the prophecy?" Tristan sat at the edge of the lounge, his fingers clasped beneath his chin.

"I'd go so far to say that they're the same. I don't believe they were necessarily scared of me coming, but that others would find out it was possible to share blood between the different species of death, or potentially even complete a successful conversion. Yes, there are consequences, but are they as bad as most have feared?" Silence met my query, as we all took in the conundrum we now faced.

'Erick, I would like to test that theory I mentioned before I mention your wings again. Could you please open your wings for me?'

'Why?' Suspicion crept into my mind, and I smirked at him.

'You chicken?'

'No, but I'd like to know what's coming at me before I take part in your little test.'

'That's why they ask for test subjects, so they can determine the outcome before rolling out the finished product. How can I tell you what's going to happen when even I'm not sure?'

'Yes, but you have an inkling, don't you?'

"Oh, for goodness' sake you ninny, just open the damn things before I do it for you."

My temper sparked as my patience hit a brick wall. With a frustrated sigh, Erick flared his wings, and I stared, admiring their shimmering beauty.

I'd believed they were closer to leather texture that night in the morgue, but I'd been wrong, they were so much more.

I caressed the one closest to me and it shuddered beneath my touch, glowing a soft emerald where I'd touched. They were softer than any leather I'd ever touched. Open, they resembled a raw, uncut blue sapphire, the colour changing beneath the fiery power coating the wings earlier. In some places it appeared almost black, whilst others were a Burmese blue. I bent closer, observing the thousands of little gold veins.

Pulling back with a smile, I stopped short as I noted the look of fear on everyone else's faces.

I cleared my throat. "Jordan, how are you feeling right now?"

"I'm not sure. If I didn't know any better, I'd have to say I feel extremely uncomfortable." Jordan moved to take a step back, only to stop when he realised what he was doing. With a subtle shake of his head, he tried to clear his mind.

"And you, Tristan and Paige?" I asked.

"Fear, I feel fear." The tremble in Paige's voice was notable despite her attempt to control it.

"As she said." Tristan gripped Ellie's hand tightly.

"So, does everyone feel the same way as Tristan and Paige?" I inquired, noting Brad and Ellie's nods.

"I'd have to echo Jordan's statement. I'm not afraid, but rather uncomfortable. It gets stronger the longer I look at the wings," Mum confessed quietly.

"Okay, Erick we're done."

His large wings flared once more before they slowly starting to shrink and flatten to form a tattoo on his back, just as mine had.

"What's going on, Evanee?" Erick snapped.

"Calm down, Erick. I'm not sure what's gotten into you, but to answer your question, I believe our wings have an emotional and mental impact on those observing them. I noticed it when all of you were staring at mine just before. You seemed transfixed, like my wings held a kind of magnetism. It seems yours has a different effect, Erick. They induce fear."

"So, what do we do about it? Because I can't go around scaring the hell out of my people every time I open my wings."

I struggled to understand why Erick was so angry. I hadn't thought it'd be that upsetting to him.

"I don't think there is anything we can do about it."

At his thunderous look, I continued, "What do you want me to say Erick? I had no idea this would happen, and you heard what my Grandfather said about the extreme changes that would be coming our way. You have an issue with them, take it up with him."

"Perhaps this is a topic better discussed in private."

His fists clenched tight, and my anger rose.

How was I to know this would happen? It's not like I have a bloody manual with chapters outlining each milestone. How the hell am I the bad person all of a sudden?

Darling he's probably scared; did you ever think of that?

The bimbo snorted; a coffee martini poised at her lips.

Looking at Erick with new eyes, shock jolted through me as I realised the bimbo was right. Erick was masking his fear with anger.

He's a damn immortal, how has he not been blindsided by unexpected side effects before now?

Honey, he was born a vampire, not created. He wouldn't have an ever-loving clue what it means or feels like to transform from all you've ever known into something entirely new.

"Right, so we've covered what happened to you at the morgue, and that Erick is essentially a butterfly emerging from his cocoon," Jordan said cheekily, grinning at Erick. "By the way, you're looking so pretty there, mate."

Erick's one finger salute elicited a not-so-subtle clearing of Paige's throat.

"What else did you two need to discuss?" Jordan asked.

"Thank you for reminding me. Death recently paid us a visit and imparted some valid and important advice that we both feel we need to act on," Erick responded, seemingly glad for the change in subject.

"What advice did my grand-père give you?" Mum sat forward, bracing herself to be ready to deal with whatever Erick was about to say.

"He suggested we tighten our ranks and start surrounding ourselves with allies and those we trust. He believes there would be those amongst the elders who would not be so happy at Evanee's appearance."

Erick resumed the seat we'd both been nestled in before all the drama had once again invaded.

"Surely it's not as bad as that? Do you really think there will be assassination attempts from within one of the royal households?"

Mum stood and began to pace.

"If you were in a position of power for the last few centuries, wouldn't you try to kill the being who'd reunite the species of death? I dare say there are those among each species who are comfortable with the power they hold over their subjects. If Evanee assumes the throne Death sat on all those centuries ago, I dare say there would be a lot of misplaced pride," Erick pointed out. "Reagan, your father would no longer hold the head of house as he has since your grandfather left. My father and the council will have dented egos knowing they no longer have the final say over how the living dead are ruled. I can only imagine how Ellie's mother will react, being a general."

The power encasing my body swirled faster, giving away my agitation of the conversation.

"I'd say the only reason no one's come after Evanee yet is because people aren't fully aware of her powers, or the fact that she's the preordained queen," Tristan added.

"How do you know they don't already know?" Brad frowned.

"Because my father would be here already had he known. Unless, someone in this room has said something, and they are biding their time?"

He looked hard at each person, waiting to see if anyone would break.

"I think it's safe to say no one in this room has given this secret away, despite the threats my brother has thrown at me," Paige murmured.

"Thank you, Aunt."

I began to pace, trying and failing to find a way to ask the people I loved most to risk themselves to help me. "Well, that's all sorted, now on to the business of solidifying our ranks."

I hate this. Why the hell can't I just disappear like Grandfather did, and pop in every now and again to say hello.

Because you love these goofballs and would never leave them unprotected. Don't forget, there is someone after you, and he's not likely to take it easy on your loved ones because you disappear.

Damn it, I hated when my teenage-self pulled her logical crap on me.

Clearing my throat, I finally spoke. "I'm not bringing much to this table. The only thing I can offer any of you is a fierce loyalty, undying love, and rather faulty protection. I'm sorry I can't offer more, I truly am," I entreated each of them. "I don't have an amassed fortune or fledglings. I respect the hell out of each being present here tonight." Looking at Ellie, Brad, and Jordan, I asked what I wished I didn't have to.

"Will you stand beside me? Will you align yourselves with me, knowing that this is life and death? Think carefully, because once you're in there's no going back. I can understand if you might like to have a little more time to think on this." I rushed, wanting nothing more than to escape this room.

I ached for the solitude of the mountains or to be elbow deep in a corpse.

"You know me, Evanee, I'm always keen for a fight. I've been at your side since the day I first laid eyes on you at that pathetic excuse of a party Desmond and Jared threw. Not to mention I am your one and only shield."

Snorting at Jordan's boast, I was grateful someone still had a sense of humour in this room.

"Hey, you know me princess, I'm with you all the way," came Brad's response, loud and clear. "In all honesty I've thought of you as more of a sister than a friend anyway. I haven't had a family since my mother died, and I'll be damned if I'm letting go of the one I've found now."

I bit the inside of my cheek to stop the tears threatening to spill, nodding my thanks to him.

"Mother will be so pleased to see I'm finally embracing my heritage. I'm not so sure how happy she will be once she discovers I've made the executive decision to side with the soon to be Queen of the Dead," Ellie said, the laughed. "Having said that, I'm looking forward to seeing her face when I tell her." Savagery lit Ellie's usual bubbly demeanour.

"You're scary, you know that? Scary, but entirely lovable," I said, grinning at her.

"I know. It's pure talent of course."

Inspecting her nails, Ellie faked the confidence I knew she'd struggled to attain for most of her life.

"Mum?" I needed to ask her, because it would likely mean losing the family she had just reacquainted with, and I owed it to her.

"That is not a question a daughter should ask her mother, and it breaks my heart that you have." She sat rigid in the chair.

"Mum, I'm not asking to be a cow. I'm asking because I am fully aware that this will likely put you in a position that will alienate you from your family again. There is no way your father will be happy with me assuming a ruling position. I was asking out of respect."

"I see. But, just to be clear, you are my daughter and there is nothing I wouldn't do to protect you. I would never have wished this life on you, but Fate had other plans," she spoke quietly.

"Thank you, Mum. There you go Erick; my allies are all sorted. I'm sorry it's not much more. Now, if you'll all excuse me, I have a few things to sort out. Thank you all for your support. I really appreciate it."

The tension, fear, and anger radiating from Erick was getting to be too much for me. I knew this was all new to him, and that he need time to process what was happening. If I stayed, we'd end up having an argument over something inconsequential because we were both stressed.

I'll bow out now before we both say something neither of us means.

My power responded instantly, pulsing gently over my skin. I stepped forward towards the library doors and watched in amazement as my foot disintegrated as it touched the ground. My lower body dissolved right before my eyes, followed quickly by my upper body. A weightlessness took over, and I drifted across the room seeping beneath the crack of the door.

Chapter 16

Drifting free and amorphous was exhilarating. There were no threats to my life, no brooding Erick I needed to soothe, or loved ones I needed to protect. There was just me exploring this new world. Time became irrelevant and so too did everything around me as I drifted through the house, peeking curiously into every nook and cranny. Hidden passages and rooms revealed themselves to me and I cherished these seemingly forgotten areas of the mansion. I allowed my curiosity the freedom it so rarely got.

I flowed through the mirrored hall connecting to the training room. The mat stood empty, and I touched my foot to it, at last solidifying so I stood naked, observing the silent dark room around me. A deep masculine clearing of a throat came from behind me, and I sheathed myself in power once more.

"Now that was cool. Well, except for the naked part. That I wish I could scrub from my mind."

Turning to where Jordan stood at the doorway, I smiled ecstatically.

"I know, right? I've done it once before, but only in Erick's mind."

I observed all my fingers and toes, making sure I hadn't lost or forgotten to reform any of them. When I was sure nothing was missing, I looked to where Jordan still stood.

"Are you going to just stand there, or are you going to tell me why you followed me?" I challenged.

"I wasn't following you," Jordan argued.

When my eyebrow rose, he conceded.

"Fine I was, but only because I wanted to talk to you about working on your self-defence."

Sighing heavily, I rubbed at my temples. "Not tonight, Jordan. It's been a long day, and I seriously don't feel like having my neck broken repeatedly."

"What if I promise not to break your neck?" he compromised as he approached the mat.

"Jordan, cut the crap. What's really bothering you?"

"Honestly? I failed you. I should have been able to get to you quicker the night Brian attacked you. I should have been there guarding you, like I'm meant to." Jordan huffed as he rubbed the back of his neck.

"How in the world were you meant to do that? You don't have the ability to summon a portal like reapers do. Even if you'd worked your vampire mojo and flown to me, you'd have only reached me when Grandfather did."

Stepping up to the big guy, I placed both my hands on his chest.

"You did what you could, and that's all anyone could ask for. You can't be by my side every second of the day. Hell, even Erick can't pull that off and he's supposed to be my mate and future King," I reasoned.

"I know that, Evanee. That's why I want to work on your self-defence. So the next time that arsehole comes at you, you're at least better prepared," he fumed.

"Jordan, the arse-kicking I received had nothing to do with a lack of training, and everything to do with me freezing up. My fear killed Bob and Mel." Jordan made to argue, but I held up my hand. "But if it makes you feel any better, I would be happy to work on more moves with you this evening."

"Good, now get on the mat. We have work to do."

Gripping my shoulders, Jordan directed me back towards the centre of the mat. Positioning myself, I squealed when Jordan leapt at me, his claws reaching for my throat.

Falling flat on my back, I rolled as his fist bore down on me only to encounter his leg. Reaching down, claws gripped my throat, and I prayed he'd stay true to his word and not break my neck.

"Too slow, Evanee. No one fights fair, you know that," Jordan hissed.

He shackled my arm and yanked it hard, snapping my collar bone.

"Ow! Shit, Jordan. You said you wouldn't break anything," I yowled.

"No, I said I wouldn't break you neck, I never said anything about your other appendages. Now, get up and fight me before I break another bone."

Rolling to my knees, I snapped my collar bone back into place. A movement in the corner of my eye caught my attention and I blurred to the corner of the mat avoiding Jordan's next attack.

For the next hour we played cat and mouse, with me as the mouse. My arms ached from the repeated breaks and dislocations.

"I've had enough for the evening, Jordan," I warned him wearily.

"I don't think so, Evanee. You're done when you best me, and so far, you haven't come close," he spat angrily.

"Jordan, I'm tired and sore. I said I'm done, and I meant it," I ground out.

"Is that what you said to Brian? Do you think him or anyone else is going to back off because you're *tired*?" Jordan taunted. "Dig deep, woman, because you're not done until you break something of mine; and by the looks of things, it's going to be a while."

I said nothing, my temper boiling just below the surface. What was this really about? Was he angry at himself for not being able to protect me, or angry at me for failing to protect myself?

"Now, are you going to put your big girl panties on, or are you going wimp out because you're scared?"

And just like that, my temper snapped. "You want big girl panties, Jordan? I'll cram them so far down your throat, you'll be choking on them for the next bloody month."

I leapt, knowing he was ready and waiting, but I was one step ahead. Baring down, I dissipated into a fine mist as

I had in the library only to reappear behind Jordan. Shackling his wrist, I slammed his elbow down over my raised knee. The loud crack of Jordan's elbow breaking never registered as I released his arm once again disappearing as he swung at me.

Reappearing in a crouch, my taloned hand swiped at his calf, and above me Jordan grunted in pain. Not pausing, I smashed my clenched fist into the side of his knee, dislodging the knee cap. Jordan dropped like a ton of bricks, but I was already moving, my talons latching onto his throat as I emerged above him. My knee dug into his chest, pinning him to the floor.

"Do I get deadly powers like that?"

Jordan's pain-filled question niggled at my mind and my power rose, reaching out for him.

"Clipeum, your power was gifted to you the day I marked you." Jordan's eyes widened at the slight shift in my voice and power.

Ignoring his hesitancy, I released him and stood waiting for him to heal. Popping his knee back into place, the wound on his calf had healed enough it only wept slightly.

Rising, Jordan cradled his arm. "It was? I don't feel any different."

"Think, Clipeum. Think back to the night you came to wake me from my sleep. The night you showed your loyalty to me, by standing against your King and Sire."

Images of Jordan standing before me in that round room within my mind flashed before my eyes. The room darkened, so it became oppressive and cold as though it had trapped us deep beneath the earth where the soil lay undisturbed.

"I remember that night. Erick went into a rage for a reason not even he would tell. As I recall, the room within your mind went dark, but I assumed that was you."

"Clipeum," I smiled savagely, "if I wanted to plunge a room into darkness it would look like this."

The light evaporated from the room, leaving the two of us facing each other. Unearthly cries of the damned and forsaken keened for release around us. Jordan stood before me clear as daylight, and it was because I allowed it he could see me. Clicking my fingers, the room was once again visible, soft light flickering from the chandeliers above.

"Holy shit. Who were all those people crying out?" A sheen of sweat coated his forehead, belying his calm exterior.

"They are the forsaken, the damned. Forever trapped in purgatory for their sins. They are not the souls of humans, but the souls of those supernatural creatures we ferry to their final resting place. They are my army to call. I may not be Death, Clipeum, but I am his descendant and chosen heir, and I will rule what was once his. I will unite what has been fractured. There will be order again."

Inhaling deeply, the room flexed, the walls groaning under the pressure as that ancient part within me stretched. It settled once more, allowing my consciousness to once again step to the forefront.

Arm forgotten, Jordan dropped to one knee, and I frowned.

"I may be your queen, Jordan, but you are as much my friend as you are my clipeum. Please stand up."

"Sorry, it's a habit," Jordan mumbled as he rose.

"I see." I smiled at him. "I'm all for following customs, Jordan, but not if it forces me to change who I am, and not if it forces me into a box. I'm once again straddling two worlds, only this time I'm fully dead. I may not be as old as the beings I'll soon be facing, but there is a part of me Jordan, a part that is as old as Grandfather himself."

Sighing, I cracked my neck in tiredness. The weight of my power and obligations weighing heavily on my exhausted shoulders.

Is this why Grandfather left his subjects to fracture?

"What do you mean?" Together Jordan and I walked towards the sparring mat, sitting on its edge.

"It's hard to explain verbally. The only way I can help you understand is for you to see it and feel it for yourself. You up for a little trip psychically?" Receiving a nod, I closed my eyes and trusted he'd do the same thing.

It didn't take much to enter that round room within my mind, like it used to when I'd been part human. Materialising in the centre of the room, I turned towards Jordan's door. It had finally settled on a gorgeous ebony African Blackwood with a giant wrought iron handle.

The door whooshed open quietly, and in stepped Jordan. He paused for a minute staring at the surrounding room before he turned towards where he'd entered.

'Now this is a serious door. What wood is this?'

Closing the door, he touched it gently, running his palm up and down.

'I believe it's an African Blackwood. From what I remember it is extremely hard to work with by hand or machine. It's strong and stubborn, just like you.'

'Huh, you got me there. It's also gorgeous just like me.'

I rolled my eyes at him as he turned to face me, clapping his hands, a glint of mischief in his eyes.

"So, tell Uncle Jordan all about this power that's got you twisted into a pretzel."

'Pretzel? Seriously? I'd say it's got me stretched out on a rack more than twisted.' At his raised eyebrow, I threw up my hands in defeat. *'Okay, fine you have me. Yes, I am a little worried, maybe even still scared of it.'*

'That's perfectly okay. You're only getting used to it. You need to remember you're still a fledgling.'

I watched him looking around at all the doors within my mind. Brian's door was locked securely, and I had no intention of opening it. I wasn't scared he would appear, rather I wanted no part of the memories on the other side of it.

'You are not understanding me, Jordan, but you will. Come here.'

Doing as I asked, we stood shoulder to shoulder, facing that black door that had once kept my powers at bay. Flicking my wrist lightly, the door crept open, inch by inch.

'The door is there out of habit. My powers are free to come and go as they have done since I was converted. But there's a part of those powers that is ancient. It was my gift from Grandfather after I was born.'

I was whispering, and I had no idea why. It wasn't as if talking normally would affect what was coming through that door.

Jordan responded in a whisper of his own.

'So the gift from Death is what has you worried?'

'Yes.'

The fog coating my body in reality barrelled through the door. Obsidian lightening forked sporadically within that fog as it crashed into my and Jordan's legs. I watched him flinch slightly whenever a lightning bolt touched him.

'Is it hurting you?' I asked.

'Not so much hurting, it's more of a sting.'

I nodded, understanding. *'Do you remember when you and Erick first came into my mind while I was recovering in hospital?'*

'I couldn't forget that day, even if I tried.' He flinched again, but only slightly.

'When Erick touched me and freaked out, it wasn't entirely his fault.' I swallowed hard at the memory.

'Yeah, he told me. He said he worried how you would awaken after being subjected to so much pain. Your mother hadn't been certain what he was talking about, but I think she suspected.'

'Mmm, Mum wouldn't have said anything, she keeps her cards close to her chest. The black abyss Erick saw and the pain he experienced was this power. The pain you are feeling is a fraction of the pain I experienced while I was in a coma.'

Two armchairs appeared before us, and I motioned for him to take a seat. When he was seated comfortably, I proceeded.

'With every death there is a moment of pain before that oblivion takes over. I experienced that pain during my entrapment within my mind. It was constant, never ending. It was also this.' I motioned towards the settling fog. *'It was a way of prepping my mind and in many ways my body for when I would fully come into all my powers.'*

'That was when Erick sped you to the forest after you awoke in the hospital.' Jordan recalled.

'Yes, but it was more than just coming into some funky new powers. It was living with a foreign entity, one that had its own memories, its own thoughts and instincts.'

'Can you show me?' Jordan asked intently, sitting up straighter.

'I'm not really sure, to be honest. There are two of us inhabiting my body, while one of us is an actual physical being, the other is more power than anything else.'

Thinking for a moment, I considered how best to show Jordan what I meant. Looking down at the fog, and how it flowed into me and through me, an idea flickered to life.

'This will be uncomfortable, but don't fight it, okay?'

Jordan nodded slowly, wary of what was about to happen, and for a good reason. With a thought, I directed the fog to enter Jordan.

The fog gathered around Jordan's feet, clawing its way up his legs and torso until it finally reached his chin. His eyes widened with fear as the fog settled and began to seep into his pores, his body forced to absorb every bit of that power. Jordan stiffened against the foreign entity, his heavy pants loud.

'Do you feel that? Can you feel the millions of thoughts running through your mind? Knowledge that you never acquired yet is there floating freely.'

He nodded stiffly.

'Now feel that strange power; how ancient it is. That power that has seen the rise of man and will see its fall.'

'This is what you've felt since you came into your powers, that night in the forest?'

Jordan's pained voice revealed the strain he was under.

'Not since the forest—since I first came into my powers. I contained it behind that door.' I pointed towards the door the power had barrelled through.

The power slowly bled from Jordan, settling to the floor before drifting back towards me as though it were a dog seeking its master.

'Shit Evanee, I had no idea. I'm sorry. Does Erick know?'

His enormous shoulders sagged as he slouched into the chair, relieved to be rid of my power.

'I haven't discussed it with him, yet. We've had other more important issues to deal with lately. We've been working on our relationship, despite my reservations. Some days I feel as though there's this large gap between us, and I don't know if we can ever truly meet in the middle.'

I motioned towards his door, wanting to get back to reality. Understanding what I meant, he made his way towards his door.

'It sounds as though you've lost confidence in yourself and others, Evanee. You both have your own pasts and coming into a relationship with as much baggage as the two of you have probably isn't helping either of you."

With that last statement he exited my mind.

'Well, he's not wrong,' I murmured.

Blinking my eyes open, I looked around the gym not focusing on anything in particular. Swatting at the errand strands of hair tickling my face, I stared at Jordan beside me.

"You're not wrong, Jordan. I've lost who I was so many times some days it feels as though I'll never be reacquainted with the person I used to be,' I whispered, exhausted.

"The way I see it, you can look at this situation in one of two ways. You can backtrack to find your old self, and risk losing even more confidence in yourself if you fail, which is likely to happen. Or, you could embrace the changes and shit that's been thrown at you, take it all and be a better version of yourself."

Flopping backwards onto the training mat, I stared up at one of the many chandeliers, admiring the wrought iron and wood tones, while I thought on what Jordan said.

"As for you and Erick as a couple, you have to remember you two grew up in different worlds—hell different times. He's lost those close to him just as you have; but where you would rather push everyone to one side so you can't be hurt if they die."

Jordan held up his hand, stalling my rebuttal.

"Don't bother debating it, Evanee. I wasn't born yesterday. You push those you love away, whereas Erick would rather lock them in a windowless room and stand guard at the only entrance."

"You're not wrong. You're pretty tuned into this stuff?" I looked at him suspiciously as I jabbed him in the ribs playfully.

"It's called common sense, thank you very much."

I snorted at his haughty response.

Jordan dropped back lightly, lying beside me as we stared up at the roof together. Silence settled between us, as we listened to the signs of life within the house.

"I found some nifty hiding spots in the house while I was drifting around." I lifted my arm distractedly, watching the fog glitter in the soft light from above.

"Seriously? Any of them have hidden coffins with some hot women in them, because you know I could rescue them? They'd be my adoring fans forever." A wistfulness crept into his voice as he joked.

"Sorry, no women, just hidey spots. If you're really nice to me, I'll show you the one with the weapons in it. There were some old-looking weapons in there. Some of which I'd like to get my hands on," I commented.

"I like the sound of that. So, are we planning on lying on this mat all night, or are you gonna go have a chit chat with Erick? Cause I gotta be honest, I don't like it when Mummy and Daddy are fighting."

"Seriously, you had to add that last bit in? You realise that would make you my overgrown stepson, who probably should have left home, but got too comfortable with the perks and is now freeloading."

"Hey, I happen to like all the fast cars Dad lets me drive and all the weapons he lets me play with."

Laughing as he finished his sentence, it struck me as odd I'd somehow allowed myself to relax and laugh properly since Bob's death. It was in some ways a relief, yet the guilt still sat waiting to pierce me with its sharpened claws.

"I might have to talk to your *father* about setting up some restrictions. I can't have the kiddies playing with weapons or driving fancy cars, now can I?" I laughed.

"You two are seriously deranged, you know that?" Erick's amused drawl from in front of us. We raised our heads from the mat.

"Apparently dating you means I inherited a bunch of deranged and possibly clingy kids. You really need to think of giving them restrictions on the toys they get to play with and saying no every once in a while." I smiled at Erick, rising to my elbows.

Beside me Jordan stood, now fully healed. "I take it back. I don't want Mum and Dad to make up. Mothers are no fun at all."

I giggled at his petulant tone.

"I've tried saying no, but some are more difficult than others." Erick looked pointedly at Jordan, who shrugged.

"I see. I read somewhere time outs work effectively. You could always start by taking away their favourite toys."

"That's it, I'm leaving before *Mother Dearest* here tries to take away my new knife set I just bought."

Waving goodbye, I laughed as he walked out of the room.

"What the hell just happened? And why is there blood all over the mat?"

Sitting up fully, Erick extended his arm to help me stand.

Taking hold of it, a zing tingled down my arm.

"Just getting some relationship advice. The man has some serious words of wisdom. Oh, and that's Jordan's blood. He felt I needed more self-defence training." Together we walked from the gym, wondering the halls in no particular hurry to be anywhere.

"I see. So, what great advice did Jordan give you?" Erick inquired.

"Only that I should probably talk to you instead of pushing you away. Apparently, we both brought a hell of a lot of baggage into this relationship, and we probably need to unpack or chuck out some of the old things so we can make room for the new."

"Uh huh, well I have one smart offspring if he's giving advice like that. I guess there is a lot from our pasts that we've brought into our relationship, not to mention the added stress of interfering deities and impending doom at every corner."

I looked at him then. He was gazing down at me with those kind eyes of his, and a smile in place of the anger that had tightened his lips when I'd last seen him.

"True. I'll admit there are a few things that you might not understand, and that I probably haven't explained very clearly or even tried to explain to you. But if you're open to it, I'd like to at least try."

Erick responded tenderly, "I'd like that a lot, *mic luptător*."

"Do you want to know what I found during my exploration earlier?" I grinned at him.

"Does it involve any damsels in coffins in distress?"

"Are you kidding me? Jordan asked the same thing. What is it with you two and vampire females needing rescuing from coffins? It's not a fetish, is it?" I asked exasperated.

Erick roared with laughter and pulled me closer.

When he could speak again, he said, "It's an inside joke. That and I heard the last part of your conversation with Jordan."

"Cheeky bugger." I stuck my tongue out at him.

"But, in all seriousness, after I redress in the clothing that seems to have found its way back and tell you all about my adventure, there are a few things we need to talk about," I murmured.

"That sounds good, *mic luptător*. Let's go to my room, it's more private."

Erick's hand dropped to mine and we strolled towards his room hand in hand.

"Oh, and the clothes in my room are new pieces I had your mother pick out in case you stayed here from time to time. But don't feel obliged to get dressed, I'm completely happy with how you're dressed now."

His cheekiness spoke volumes about the tension between us.

"Hey, focus. Talk first and then we can negotiate sex later. It depends on how nice you are to me. And how are you dressed, and I'm cloaked in nothing but power?"

I stared straight ahead, and found his doors looming up ahead a lot quicker than I'd anticipated.

"I dressed after I left the library. Also, I'm always nice to you."

I snorted at his retort, false bravado my only defence against the nerves tightening my gut.

Chapter 17

I studied Erick's broad shoulders as he pushed open the door to his suite, my nerves reaching new levels.

Sex is supposed to be like riding a bike, right? Once you've learned, you never forget.

My inner bimbo stepped out of her changing room, a scarlet teddy hugging her hips.

Honey, in your case I'd say you have amnesia. You may as well take this gift horse by the reins and learn all over again, but with someone who cares, and who probably knows what he's doing.

The bimbo's sage advice wasn't lost on me, and neither was the fact that tonight would be yet another step in my search for absolution from my past.

What if I can't give him what he needs or wants? I haven't looked at another man in over three years.

Oh, sweetie. Has Erick ever pushed you for more in this relationship? The bimbo sympathised.

No, he hasn't.

There you go. Tell the man you're nervous, and it's been forever since you did the horizontal rap dance. He won't know unless you tell him, she asserted, looking into a mirror as she applied a delectable plum lipstick to pouting lips.

She was right. Erick wouldn't know unless I opened my mouth and told him.

The fragrant night air drifted in from the open French doors, playfully tugging at the curtains before rushing into the room. I inhaled, filling my lungs with the soothing scents of eucalyptus and night jasmine as I took my place beside Erick in the love seat in front of the dark fireplace. The power still clinging to me, swirled with lazy contentment.

"You're nervous, *mic luptător*. Why's that?"

"Probably because I'm about to discuss something with you that had you flipping out the last time you came into contact with it. Or, it might be the fact I haven't been with a man for the past three years," I blurted out before I could censor my words.

"First things first, Evanee, nothing will happen tonight unless you want it to. You say no, I back the hell off. I might come across as controlling with matters of safety, but with sex, I'd rather it to be a shared experience," Erick reassured. "Second, I admit I didn't handle your powers well after the hospital, but things have changed since then, wouldn't you agree?"

"Yes, they have." I nodded.

"I understand things have progressed relatively quick since you came into your powers, and that you're doing your best to control them."

I interrupted him before he could say anything more. "It's more than getting control of it, Erick. I don't think this is something I could ever fully control. This is something other. Something as old as my Grandfather."

When Erick said nothing, I huffed in frustration. "Look, the only way you'll probably understand is if I just show you. I can't explain it, because there aren't really any words that adequately describe it. Would you be up for a trip to my round room?"

"Of course, *mic luptător*. Let's lie on the bed and get comfortable first," he suggested.

I nodded, and we moved towards the giant king bed at the far side of the room. Lying side by side, my eyes drifted shut, only to reopen in my round room of doors. Seconds later, Erick stepped through his door and onto the carpeted floor.

Motioning towards the large black door, we approached it together. I took a deep breath and whispered, "You ready for this?"

"Show me, Evanee," was all he said.

With a flick of my wrist, the door flew open and that ancient power barrelled into the room, zapping at Erick's legs as it had with Jordan. Erick stood still, never flinching despite the fact that it was winding itself around him like a cat might upon finding a living statue made entirely of catnip.

I watched, stunned, as it settled over Erick, his body absorbing the power without any resistance. Just as quickly as he absorbed it, his body expelled it. I frowned when it continued to wind itself around his body.

"That's enough," I commanded.

I grew impatient when it refused to leave Erick and I stamped my foot.

"I said enough," I growled.

Erick smiled, amused when that ancient power still wouldn't depart, and I resorted to threatening it. "If you don't retreat, I will lock that damned door and put a solid brick wall in front of it. Don't test me."

My threat worked and the power grudgingly retreated.

"That is not what it did with Jordan," I murmured distractedly.

"I should bloody hope not. I'm your mate, and it recognises that."

The edge in Erick's voice drew a frown from me. "I know that Erick, but that was not what I expected. Did you feel anything?"

"I felt a lot of different sensations. Some painful and others pleasurable," Erick responded thoughtfully.

"Did you feel its age?" I whispered.

Erick frowned. "I did. It's nothing like the power we vampires inherit or are born with. It felt almost as though it was an entirely different entity, as though there is a living being trapped within all that power."

"Let's return before it comes back for seconds, and I have to build that brick wall."

My eyes blinked open, and I rolled to face Erick. His eyes blinked open seconds later, and he turned his head to stare at me before he rolled to face me.

"You're not freaked out by what I showed you?" I asked, concern pulling at my forehead.

"I'm not weirded out by that part of you, Evanee. It's a part of you and always has been. I'm more wary of just how much the two of you are melding together. I've noticed it taking over your body more often lately, and I'm not entirely sure how much of you it leaves once it takes over."

He had a point, especially considering my departure from the library the night before.

"You're not wrong, Erick, and I understand your concerns because I share them. The thing is, there really isn't much I can do to solve this problem. I can't worry any more than I have been about this, Erick. There's so much to deal with as it is." Sighing, I placed a hand to his soft cheek. "I wanted you to understand what it feels like, and what I'm dealing with. I'm trying to communicate better."

Erick's large hand enveloped my much smaller one, sliding the palm of my hand to his lips, where he pressed a soft kiss at its centre.

Speaking into my palm he mumbled what sounded like "Thank you."

I stared into Erick's eyes, watching as his pupils dilated. My hand still at his lips, I drew in a shuddering breath when his teeth scraped lightly through the middle.

Lifting my hand from his mouth, my cry of frustration was at my lips when Erick murmured in a silken tone.

"I meant what I said, Evanee. If you're not comfortable at any point, we can stop."

I nodded past the lump in my throat.

"What if we dropped our mental barriers so if you're even in the slightest bit in distress, I'll know and stop?" Erick suggested.

"I'd like that. Thank you," I whispered.

"Anything for you, *mic luptător*. Now can I kiss you, because if I don't I'm sure I'll die a slow and painful death just looking at your lips?"

I laughed as he tried his best to pout, not pulling it off.

"Mmm, I don't know. I'm not getting that desperate vibe you're talking about," I said thoughtfully. "Maybe I should go and give you some time to think about whether you really want me?"

I rolled to my back, moving to sit when Erick's arm shot out, his long fingers gripping my hip as he growled.

"Woman, there are only so many cold showers I can take. I've had more since I met you than I have in my long life and that's including my teenage years."

Laughing at his admission, his head appeared in my vision, and I smiled happily at the laughter in his eyes.

Lifting my arms to circle his neck, I whispered huskily, "Well, what are you waiting for? Kiss me, silly man."

Erick's head descended, his lips brushing softly across mine.

"Relax your mind, baby," Erick whispered.

His fingers met my bare flesh beneath the power still clinging to me.

My hands drifted down from around his neck to cup his face as I did as he asked. The barrier I kept in place dropped and so did the power clinging to my body. The fine mist slid from my body and down to the floor bursting outward to coat the floor and entries to the room.

Information and images drifted through my mind as my power relayed its discoveries. Lifting his head, Erick looked around the room and back to me.

I smiled cheekily at his surprise. "You told me to relax my mind."

"That I did," he murmured as his head dipped once more, his kiss deeper than before.

My hands wandered to his shoulders skimming down to his lower back, and I groaned at the soft material that stood between me and the supple skin beneath. Understanding my frustration, Erick pulled back, divesting himself of the annoying garment, only to stop short at the sight before him.

His eyes widened at the sight of my bare body, and I caught at my lower lip. My teeth scraped at it as I worried whether he liked what he saw.

My worry drifted between our link, and he groaned.

"Trust me, baby. I'm loving everything I'm seeing. I'm trying to regain some control of myself. I want this to be good for you. I need this first time to be what you want."

"And what if I said I just want you," I responded.

"Evanee."

He groaned as my fingers splayed across his lower abdomen.

I watched, fascinated as his stomach clenched beneath my fingers, the bulge in his jeans evident despite the thick material. My eyes never left him as he stepped from the bed and out of his jeans. Sitting, my legs hung off the edge of the mattress as I studied Erick, my eyes drinking in every inch of him.

I itched to scrape my nails along the ridges of his taut stomach and further down. My eyes dropped lower taking in the sight of his hard length before they darted back up to him.

My inner bimbo all but fainted at the sight of him, with her yelled, 'Get in me big boy' screaming between our link.

"I told you I liked her."

Erick stepped forward until his thigh's brushed at my knees, his chest heaving with barely contained laughter.

Emboldened by his ease and laughter, I scooted to the middle of the bed as I beckoned him. "Well if you want her to shut up, you'd better kiss me and hope she faints from the sheer bliss."

His laughter ceased instantly. "I don't need to hope she faints, because when I'm done kissing you, she won't be appearing for the rest of the night," Erick purred seductively.

Breathing in deeply, I clutched at the bed cover watching Erick crawl onto the bed. A shiver skittered through me when he gently grasped one of my legs and pulled it down, followed by the other.

"I'm going to kiss you now Evanee, but it won't be on your lips. Remember, if you need me to stop, you just say stop or think it and we are done for the night. Okay?"

"Yes," I breathed.

Erick's head dipped to my ankle, and he placed a soft flutter of a kiss on the inside, while his fingers massaged gently at my calves. My head dropped back, my eyes drifting shut as I gave myself up to the pleasure. His next kiss pressed to the inside of the opposite leg's knee, my breath hitching when his teeth scrapped where he'd just kissed.

The gentle pressure of his hands parting my legs tightened my stomach in anticipation and I groaned at the kisses he pressed along the inside of my thighs. My hands found his shoulders, and I gripped them, my fingers digging deep when his mouth found my clenched core.

The first brush of his lips and I wondered if I would survive the blinding pleasure that came next. A swipe of his tongue and I knew I wasn't. His kisses were soft, his tongue enticing, bringing me closer to the edge with each pass. When I thought I would tumble over that delicious precipice, Erick pulled away and I cried out in frustration.

Trailing kisses up my abdomen and across my breasts, Erick nipped at my chin gently.

"You'll have your release, *mic luptător*, but it won't be until I'm inside you."

His words of seduction fluttered against my lips.

Two can play that game.

Reaching down between us, I took him in my hand and stroked downward. Erick shuddered above me, his hands bunching on either side of my head.

Another two deep strokes and he reached down, gripping my wrist as he hissed, "That's enough."

I'd felt his pleasure through our link, and it was a heady feeling knowing I'd been the one to give it to him. It emboldened me to lift my legs and wrap them around his waist, my hips tilting up to entice him further. There was no hesitation, only need to feel him within me.

Tiny stars danced throughout my vision when at last he pushed slowly into my soft folds. Beneath my fingers, his muscles bunched as static filled his mind, his rapture matching my own.

Our groans and sighs drifted through the room, trapped by the shimmering mist around us. Erick's body moved within mine, rebuilding that blinding pleasure from before. I could feel him within my mind, that reassuring presence caressing me—loving me.

Erick's trust and devotion to us filtered through our link followed closely by his fear of losing me. My heart clenched with the beginnings of hope when I detected in the corner of his mind, the first blossom of love. I let myself free-fall then, my orgasm shaking me to my very soul.

~

An annoying ringing broke through the pleasure haze luxuriously swirling around Erick and I as we snuggled naked together in the middle of his giant bed. Breaking apart, we both looked dazedly around the room for the offending object. The bright screen of my phone glared at me from the bedside table.

Looking at the screen, I mumbled, "It's work calling." I grinned up at Erick. "Let me answer it, and we can get back to where we… umm… left off."

I grabbed it, and hit the green button, switching it to speaker.

"Dr Evanee Sheperd speaking, how can I help you?"

"Dr Sheperd, this is Dr Richard Denver." I paused, shocked to be receiving a call from the new head of the Pathology Department in Brisbane.

It took me a second to respond. "Dr Denver, how are you? What can I do for you…" Looking at the time on my phone I noticed it was past 9am. "This morning?"

"I have what I hope is good news. I've just finished speaking with the director of Acrasin General, and the morgue has finally been repaired. We have installed all new security measures and are at last ready to get back to business.”

Wow, that was quick. They must be getting good at fixing damages to the morgue. At the rate I've been destroying the place, the local tradesmen will make a fortune for many years to come.

“That's fantastic news. When is the first shift scheduled?” I squirmed as Erick traced my birth mark, resisting the urge to giggle.

“The first shift is tomorrow evening. I was hoping you would check that everything is in order? You've been there the longest and are familiar with the layout and stock.”

Fair point.

“I'm sure I can make it in this evening.” Beneath me Erick tensed.

Lifting his head, he whispered into my ear.

“Ask him to hold.”

Nodding, I reached forward ready to hit the mute button.

“Richard, will you give me one second please?”

“Certainly.”

Hitting the mute button, I straightened back up. *Please don't fight me on this, please don't.* I chanted to myself. We'd come so far.

“I have one small request if you're returning to the morgue. I'd like for you to take a guard.”

Before I could open my mouth, Erick continued.

"It will allow me to get on with my business, without having to stress that I've left you unprotected. Please."

We stared at each other for a second before he squeezed my arse cheek.

How am I supposed to resist when he asks so nicely?

"That's cheating, but okay, I'll ask Richard about a guard on site. There's no guarantee he'll let me though."

I hit the mute button popping the phone on speaker. "Richard, are you still there?"

"I'm here, Evanee," he responded distractedly.

"I'd be happy to come in this evening and check things over before we open back up officially. My partner has made one small request. In light of the recent attacks I've suffered, Erick feels it'd be best that I have a security guard with me at all times."

I waited with bated breath. Had I pushed for too much too soon?

"I'd love to put a security detail in the morgue 24/7, Evanee. Truth is, we can't afford it."

Okay, well on the plus side he didn't say no to the guard.

"Dr Denver, this is Erick Tenebris. Evanee's boyfriend."

Holy crap, he just said boyfriend. Breathe Evanee, breathe. You're not a teenager anymore.

Butterflies fluttered merrily away in my stomach as the teenage me stilled for a second before whooping and doing a crazy, happy dance in my mind.

"Mr Tenebris, I remember you. You helped Bob on a few of his more difficult cases, if I'm not mistaken."

"That's correct. I understand how inconvenient it might be for Evanee to have a security detail assigned to her during her shifts, but I would be more than happy to cover the expenses. In fact, I'd prefer she had someone from my security detail with her. I trust and know them, and I'm sure we could find someone who'd satisfy your department."

Erick was all politeness and diplomacy as he spoke.

"I can understand your concern for her safety, especially considering she has now been attacked at work twice. I'm assuming you'd want them around Evanee while she's performing autopsies?"

Richard tapped away at his computer the keystrokes click clacking down the line.

"That's correct, Mr Denver. Both times she's been attacked she was performing autopsies. I think it would be wise to put someone in the room with her."

"Mmm, very true. Okay, I'll see what I can do. If you have someone in mind, have them fill out the paperwork I'm sending through now. Evanee, you'll be on pathology work and general admin until we can sort something out guard wise. I'd also like you to take over as head forensic pathologist at the morgue. I can't be there as often as Bob was, so I need someone trustworthy there to run meetings and oversee the necessary day-to-day management of the place."

Hang on, was he promoting me?

"Richard, are you suggesting what I think you're suggesting?"

I waited with bated breath, not even realising this was something I'd even wanted.

"I believe I am asking you to step into the head forensic pathologist role. There will be the obligatory pay rise, and I can't say there will be any new perks, unfortunately. Are you willing to move into the new position?"

Richard sounded bored, whereas I was doing a happy squirm against an amused Erick. "Um, I'm happy to move into the position. I'll keep an eye out for my new contract."

I needed to see the evidence, I wanted to see it on paper. I'd probably print the first page of my contract out and frame it just so I could stare at it for at least an hour each day.

"Right, well I've just sent the standard contract through, and the necessary forms Mr Tenebris' people will need to fill out. Please get them both back to me as soon as possible."

"Will do, Mr Denver."

"I think that's all I needed to discuss. I will speak to you later. Oh, and congratulations on the promotion Dr. Sheperd. I believe this is something Bob would've approved of, and the rest of us aren't far behind him." He hung up, ending the conversation.

Rolling off Erick, I forgot about him for a second as my feet stamped happily against the mattress, my fists pumping into the air.

"I got it, I got it. Holy crap, I got a promotion."

His laughter trickled over me, reminding me he was still lying beside me.

Pushing up onto his knees, Erick smiled down at me before bending to place his luscious lips to my smiling ones. Linking my arms behind his neck, I pulled him to me, fitting all that glorious naked body over the top of mine.

Happiness tingled through my body, quickly replaced by desire as Erick's kiss deepened, his supple hands resting either side of my face moving to stroke my hair. I nipped at his lip, and his husky chuckle breathed across my lips.

Pulling his head back, his brilliant smile matched my own.

"I'm thrilled for you, *mic luptător*. I know how much your career means to you."

His words murmured in between his soft kisses to my face.

"Thank you, and it does. Now enough talking, more kissing. " I batted my eyelashes knowing they'd do the trick.

With a husky laugh, he murmured into my parted lips.

"Who am I to say no to you? Especially when you've asked so nicely."

Grinning, his lips touched mine softly at first before he took control, deepening the kiss once more.

We parted, and I panted. "Wow. I should get a promotion more often."

Erick chuckled as he lay back, and I rested my head on his chest. My hand reached for his tousled hair and I ran my fingers through it before they trailed down his face. He caught at my hand, kissing it gently.

"That tickles."

I smiled cheekily, knowing I'd found one of his weaknesses.

My man's ticklish.

"Oh, really? I might store that little nugget away for the next time I need to win an argument." I smiled sensually at him.

"You use that to win an argument, and we'll never be leaving this bedroom," he grinned.

"I could live with that," I muttered as thoughts of returning to work and what it might mean finally registered.

My 'to- be- worried' about list was lengthening by the day. As it was, it included: *Hunt and somehow kill the serial killer Brian; find a way of carrying my scythe around without freaking people out; get over my anxiety and PTSD so that my stupid mind won't freeze up at the sight of aforementioned serial killer.*

"Evanee, I can see that mind of yours turning things over, and I'm trying hard not to read it right now. You need to meet me half-way and verbalise what you're thinking."

His soft fingertips traced the line of my nose and down to my lips.

"I was thinking I need to find a way of carrying my scythe around with me without it scaring the hell out of any law enforcement officials and the general human and supernatural population. I want to be ready the next time Brian shows his face. I need him gone, Erick, and I can't afford to lose again because I freeze up at the sight of him. Carrying the scythe on me might help channel that ancient part within me."

My fist clenched against the pain that arose at the memory of the night I'd frozen and failed to protect those I cared about most.

"Perhaps we could ask Death or your mother? I'm sure one of them would be able to help us out with disguising the scythe. As for Brian's impending death, I completely agree with you." He paused in thought before he continued. "There is one thing that struck me as beneficial from the fight you showed us last night though."

"Really? What?"

"It took him longer to heal from a wound inflicted by your hands and mouth than from the shears you threw at him. He's also afraid of dying, even considering that he is an immortal. This gives us an advantage. That and his desire to subdue you. I believe there's a part of him that wants you dead, while the other part of him wants you very much alive and by his side."

"Well, that's not half confusing. Although come to think of it, his actions were at odds with someone who supposedly wanted me dead. His comments were contradictory in nature." My mind turned this new information over, dissecting it from every angle.

"If we could get you trained to wound him where it counts, it might slow him enough for you to extract his heart or decapitate him with the scythe."

Rolling to his back, Erick took me with him, so I lay against his chest. His fingertips drew lazy circles against my back.

"Well, personally I'm all for ripping out his heart as he watches before I decapitate him. I feel like it's important to do both. I can't have the little cretin resurrecting. Supernatural taught me that much. Hell, I might even light his body on fire and salt it, before washing the ashes down the drain with a drum of holy water."

"Mmm, extreme, but you're right. One can never be too careful especially where exes are concerned. I really need to watch this Supernatural series."

"You'd probably like it. Do I need to be concerned about any of your exes rearing their ugly heads?" My hand stalled on his chest as I fought a surge of jealousy that reared its green head at the thought of Erick with another woman.

"None that I'm aware of. They all seemed to be fairly level-headed."

I could hear the smile in his voice. I returned to tracing pictures on his chest as I murmured sullenly, "Ah huh, so you think. The next thing you know, they've found some witch to put some curse on me so that every time you look at me you see some grotesque hag."

"*Mic Luptător*, no one could ever change the way I feel for you. The feelings I have continue to grow the better I get to know you. Besides, even if they did put a curse on you, you'd only have to open that delectable mouth of yours and ignore my well-intentioned orders. I'd know exactly who was hidden beneath the spell."

My palm slapped his chest at his jibe.

"I need some alone time with Supernatural. I believe I'm long overdue for a date day with my TV boyfriends. They're always so devoted and are never mean to me." Raising my head, I stuck my tongue out at him.

"That's it, teleport me to your house right now so I can burn every single one of those DVDs. I can't have these men taking up any of your attention."

He made to get up, and I held him down laughing hard at his antics.

"Don't you dare touch my TV series, Erick."

Dropping back to the bed, he let out a burst of laughter as I tickled his ribs.

"We could spend the day watching Supernatural in the theatre room. That is, if you don't have any urgent matters to attend to?" Smiling shyly at him, I hoped this would be another thing we could share together.

"I'm sure I could manage that."

Erick smiled, placing a quick kiss to my lips.

Chapter 18

The ringing of a mobile in the darkened room drew a chorus of groans from around me. The last episode of season one of Arrow had just started, and no one had any interest in knowing what was going on in the outside world. I'd settled on the superhero TV series fearing Erick would follow through on his threat to make my beloved Supernatural disappear.

Looking down at my lit screen Steve's grinning face stared back at me.

"Who is it?" Erick whispered into my ear.

Adjusting the screen so he could see it, I whispered, "Steve. I need to get this. I'll just go out."

Erick stalled me. "Hit pause on the TV please, Ellie."

Ellie did as Erick requested.

"Hey Steve?"

"Hey sweetheart, are you home?"

"No, I'm at Erick's place. Why?" My internal warning system began to tingle, and I tensed, waiting on his response.

"Thought so. Look, I don't wanna scare you or anything, but I can see someone moving around inside. Lights are flicking on and off in each room, but I can't see Marg's car out the front. Does your mother still stay at the house?"

My posture grew more rigid the longer he spoke. The whole room had stilled every vampire picking up on our conversation. I may as well have had the damn thing on speaker.

"I doubt it's her. She's travelling overseas." Looking at Erick, his arched eyebrow echoed my thoughts.

Just who the hell was making their way through my house?

"I see. Well, perhaps I should call the police in case it's some bloody mongrel thief trying to make off with your goods," Steve offered.

"No, Steve, don't worry about it. I'll deal with it. Thanks for calling me. Are you working tonight?" I hoped my change of direction would stop him from taking it upon himself to go over there and confront whoever was in my house.

"Not tonight, I'm having dinner at the pub with the boys. The cricket's playing."

"That sounds great. Make sure you order steamed veg or salad with your meal, please." I grinned at Steve's soft grunt into the phone.

"Yeah, yeah Bossy Boots. I'll eat a *balanced meal.*"

Just because I was dead, didn't mean I'd stopped caring about making Steve's heart stay on track.

"I'll deal with my visitor, so don't worry about calling the police. Oh, and Steve, thanks for calling me to let me know."

Saying our goodbyes, I ended the call.

"I'm going."

Was all I said as I stood, Erick following suit. Just then Erick's phone rang, eliciting a series of curses to tumble out of his mouth when he saw who it was.

"Tristan, I need you to deal with my father. I don't give a shit what he wants, he can wait. Jordan, you're with us. Ellie, no watching episodes while we are gone."

Ellie giggled at him.

He'd eased the rising tension in the room with one simple request, and I was grateful.

"No promises," Ellie said with a devilish grin.

Turning to me, Erick grasped my hand, while Jordan picked his way over strewn pillows to stand beside us. Summoning a portal, I glimpsed my backyard patio, and hoped it would give us an advantage.

~

Closing the portal behind me, I took a second to look around at the looming shadows on my neglected backyard. I'd had so many grand plans, but they had gone up in flames as I recovered after my sudden death.

I stilled at the sudden pulse of power that came from within the house. That part of me that was reaper rose to the front in response. Foreboding washed over me. I knew exactly who was in my house.

'It's Brian, and he knows I'm here.' I spoke telepathically, knowing the men would hear me, but Brian wouldn't.

Both men tensed before they each gave a short nod in understanding.

Approaching the door, I reached up above the door frame, finding the spare key for the back door. There had been no time to grab my set of keys from Erick's room. Sliding the key in as carefully as I could, I cringed at the squeak of the door handle. I waited a few seconds, pulling the door open slowly and silently. When no attack came, I breathed a sigh of relief.

'Brian's power seems to be coming from the direction of the lounge room.'

I stepped back from the door, extending my arm so my scythe appeared in my outstretched hand. Its weight was comforting and reassuring, as was the little zing it sent up my arm.

Erick nodded with a smile as though he was proud I'd remembered to summon the blade. I'd have been slightly insulted if it wasn't for the fact I'd told him how much of a state Brian put me in every time I saw him.

Hell, who am I kidding? I'm proud of myself for being able to think at all right now.

The three of us made our way cautiously into the kitchen and my muscles tensed more with each step I took. The rancid stench of decay forced pink tears to our eyes. That's when I heard him, the voice that haunted my nightmares.

"I know you're there, Evanee, just as I know you've brought company."

There was a cockiness to his statement, and it set my teeth on edge.

Together the three of us glided through the kitchen, and the scene that greeted me in my lounge room stopped me dead. Brian reclined casually in my favourite couch, his legs extended and crossed at the ankles as he wiped at the corners of his mouth with his index finger and thumb, licking at the crimson smear colouring them.

My focus shifted. There, positioned carefully against him, as though they had been cuddling as they watched TV, was a girl who looked no older than seventeen. She had the trademark blonde hair, slim figure and what would have been blue eyes before Brian had gouged them out. Her soul was in the same condition the others had been, and I wondered again why he hadn't consumed the whole thing. Looking at the young girl, it dawned on me, I knew who she was.

My broken whisper cut through the tension in the house. "Brian, what have you done?"

I made to step forward, but Erick's tense arm held me back, securing me to his side. Brian's thunderous expression at our contact didn't go unnoticed, but I ignored it. Beside him, a young and beautiful Abigail's bleak eye sockets sat staring into nothing, and my heart broke at the loss of such a bright girl.

The two of us had talked a couple of times as she'd been coming come from school and I'd been on my way to work. She'd dreamed of being a midwife when she graduated. The idea of ushering new life into this world had excited and amazed her all at once.

"I got bored waiting for you. So, I thought I'd leave you a little present for when you came home. Then I heard your neighbour call you, and thought I'd just wait right here for you instead."

Picking at a strand of Abby's matted hair, he twirled it between his nimble and decaying fingers.

"I'm here now. What the hell do you want?"

Fear slithered through my body, rendering it immobile. Around us the sounds of families settling in for the afternoon breached the windows and doors. Kids played in their yards after a long day of school, the odd yell coming from frazzled parents trying to separate arguing siblings. It occurred to me that escalating the situation with so many innocent people surrounding the house would only end with disastrous repercussions. There was no way of knowing if Brian would target one of those innocent children in retaliation.

"I've missed you. You haven't been at work, and I can't get a lock on where you have been hiding. Judging by present company I'm beginning to understand exactly where you've been. Are you planning on introducing us?" When I remained silent, Brian sighed. "Here, let me start. Hi, I'm Brian and you are?"

No one spoke for a second, stunned at his callousness.

Malice lacing his growl, Erick addressed Brian, his face remaining neutral yet calculating.

"I am Prince Erick Tenebris, King and Mate to the future Queen of the People of Death. I head the Australian coven and have done so since 1770. I know very well who you are."

"And I'm Jordan, no last name. I am *paznic onorat* to the heir of the Romanian throne, and Clipeum to the future Queen of the People of Death."

'*You could've just told him you were an honoured guard to the prince and my shield; you know,*' I thought at Jordan.

'*I could've, but this idiot needs to learn his place in our society, and he's sitting right at the very bottom.*'

There was no arguing with that logic.

"I have no idea what any of that meant, other than the fact that you, Evanee, seem to have lowered your standards. As I recall, you mentioned on one of our many dates that you would never date or fuck a married man, and here you are with a man sworn to some queen."

"It was a handful of dates Brian, and my stance on married men hasn't changed." My voice was steadier than I felt.

The tension and adrenaline were not doing me any favours, neither was the drying blood staining my beloved couch.

"It hasn't? Because he just said he was some sort of mate to some que…"

I could see the moment he finally cottoned on to what Erick and I had said, and I wasn't entirely sure it was a good thing.

"Wait … nooo. You're this queen they're harping on about?" He laughed.

"Queen of the People of Death. Your memory getting rusty there, Brian?"

Would you stop baiting the idiot? There are innocent people he could abduct at any moment.

"Don't get smart with me, Evanee," Brian hissed.

"You're right, Brian, I just can't seem to help it. Stooping down to your level of understanding is just so much work, and frankly I can't be bothered exerting that much effort.'

Again? Seriously, someone tape my mouth shut.

Before I could blink Brian materialised before me. The room blurred as I sailed across the room, slamming into my island counter. The ominous crack from behind me hurt more than my actual landing.

Oh, he's going to pay for that. My beautiful kitchen.

I hissed at Brian, who now had Erick's arm sticking out from where it had impaled his gut. With a malicious grin, Brian gripped Erick's forearm, his body dissolving around

Erick's hand and wrist. Brian ripped hard at Erick's forearm dislodging him in one swift move.

Not waiting for Brian's next move, I surged up and rushed forward, my body a blur as my talons extended. Deep crimson lines peeked through Brian's black t-shirt as I slashed at his chest. I mourned my cream carpet now decorated with not only bits of his decaying flesh trailed throughout the house like Hansel and Gretel's breadcrumbs, but his clotted blood as well.

Brian swung at me, connecting only slightly with my shoulder. It was then I felt the giant arm circling my waist. Jordan unhooked his arm from around me, shoving me unceremoniously behind him and into a seething Erick.

'Are you okay, mic luptător?'

'I am. Thank you.'

'What were you thinking, responding like that?'

He wasn't as furious as I thought he'd be. Jordan stood shielding us waiting for Brian's next move.

'Strategy. Watch how long it takes for the marks on his chest to heal. Jordan, you need to move to the side slightly, please.'

"You stupid whore. You're lucky I don't rip your fucking heart out right here and now." Brian spat, fury lighting his ruby eyes.

"What's stopping you Brian? I'm right here. Come and get me."

The four claw marks still hadn't healed fully and neither had the hole Erick had made, but they were showing signs of slow regeneration. The blood now seeped lethargically through cuts and a hole half the size they'd originally been.

A sweet tingle hit the back of my tongue and I recognised the familiar scent. Enticed by that smell, the ancient power within me unfurled itself.

'You guys, he's dying,' I whispered telepathically, my hunger rising with each second.

'What do you mean he's dying? He's already dead.' Jordan asked.

'I can smell the sweet scent of death on him. It's similar to the night I visited him in his apartment.'

Pushing my power through our connection, two sets of eyes focused on Brian as they scented the air with delicate sniffs. My power latched onto that familiar scent and relayed the information.

'I'll be damned. You're right. How the hell is this even possible?'

Erick and Jordan's delighted, devilish grins went unnoticed by Brian.

"No, no. We have something very special planned for you. Right now, it's about me having fun. It's been so boring all these years stuck in that forsaken bed, day in and day out. You know my folks still think I'm stuck in that room."

His cackle drew the hairs from my arms.

"My creator is one talented bugger, wouldn't you say?"

Got you, you cocky twit.

Brian had just unknowingly given me a vital clue.

The owner of Aeternum, and mastermind behind the attacks on me was in fact a reaper. How else would his parents still think he was stuck in his bed in his apartment? Surely someone would've noticed his absence by now if a reaper hadn't been involved.

Behind Brian, the remains of Abby's fractured soul pulsed once, distracting me. She'd slumped over since Brian's departure from the couch, as though she were a bloodied doll.

I need to release that soul now, before it's lost completely.

Without a thought, I threw my scythe handle first at Erick, who caught it in surprise. Lunging at Brian, I drove my fist through his right shoulder, bloodied talons erupting out the back. I needed to get to that soul. The reaper in me ached to see that soul complete its journey to the other side. Every fibre of my body burnt with the need to get to Abigail.

"Urgggh."

Brian's pained yell barely registered as I gave myself over to the power riding me.

My talons latched onto Brian's shoulder blade as he tried and failed to extract my hand. There was no point in him dissipating. I knew his little trick now and would match it with my own powers. Realising his predicament, Brian fought dirty, his clawed hand slashing deep across my abdomen. I shoved the pain to one side, my sights set on the task ahead of me.

Drawing Brian closer to me, I snarled into his stunned face. "Is that all you have, you pathetic excuse for a mutant? I am the queen of all those who are dead and will be dead. I have suffered a million deaths and will suffer a million more. You're genetically enhanced manicure is nothing more than annoying splinters. Annoying little pricks until you dig them out, just like you."

I shoved Brian hard, my talons releasing at the last second so my wrist ripped upwards and outwards, snapping his collar bone and shredding the skin and muscle from the sheer force of the throw.

Flying over the back of the couch, Brian landed atop my wooden coffee table, shattering it beyond repair. Splinters and chunks of wood catapulted into my television while the couches took on the brunt of the shrapnel.

An eerie fog seeped from beneath my bare feet, creeping along the wooden floorboards to seek that which belonged to the land of the damned.

"Know this, Brian Turner, the next time we meet will be your last. You have taken something precious from us, and there will be retribution." My mouth remained shut, yet my whisper echoed from the shadows creeping into the room and the fog roiling around our feet.

"Who are you? I can't sense Evanee anymore."

The heady scent of fear drifted along the air, and I sniffed appreciatively at it as I had with Desmond all those months ago.

"Evanee is here, within this body, shielded for her protection. Where there were two, there will soon be one. You will survive this day because I wish it, and I have a task for you." Pausing, I stared hard at him. "You will deliver a message to your master, and if you won't I will carve it into your chest with my talons."

My hand shot out and the scythe Erick clutched, appeared in my hand. Brian nodded, petrified.

"Tell your creator the Queen has risen, and he is in my sights."

I strode across the room, never taking my eyes from his now cowering form. My form wavered and solidified as I walked through the couch. Looking down at Brian, I grinned. Whatever he saw in that smile drove him backwards into the couch. I reached down with deathly white taloned hands and grabbed a hold of his damp, tattered shirt. Hoisting him up, Brian dangled centimetres above my ruined mat, his diseased skin escaping from beneath his shirt to fall with little splats.

"You're staining my floors with that sewage of blood and rotted flesh. Now open a portal to your master and get the fuck out of my house." I sneered and was pleased to see a portal open near my dining table.

Scenting the air, my power extended analysing the portal and what lay beyond. I was careful, hiding behind Brian's power and scent, so as not to give myself away.

"Good boy. Don't forget to deliver my message to your master."

I threw him then, already dismissing him as his body sailed through the portal. With a flick of my wrist the portal splintered, then shattered. Brian would never step foot in this house again unless he walked up to the front door.

I turned towards the poor degenerating soul on my couch.

"Evanee?"

I silenced Erick's whisper with a hand as I approached Abigail's corpse.

Dropping lightly beside the couch, I cooed softly to that broken thing that had been her soul, my attention wholly focused on the girl before me.

"He is gone, sweet angel. You have nothing left to fear. Peace awaits you now. May the loved ones who paved the way for you guide you home."

Reaching my hand into that place where her soul cowered, I extracted it carefully. A part of me breathed a sigh of relief when it came away and didn't disintegrate as the others had previously.

With a gentle breath of air, I released the soul to my grandfather, who would guide her to her resting place. Sitting back, a bone-deep sadness enveloped me as my power receded, and I mourned the loss of such a bright life lost to a sick and depraved creature.

Erick rounded the couch, approaching me with a cautiousness I'd noticed whenever my power rose. "Evanee?"

"I'm here, I never really left. The power pushed me to the back and took control so my fear of Brian couldn't. I found some clues as to where Brian is staying."

I didn't move, too emotionally drained to do much else.

I don't think I'll be going to work after all this.

"What did you find?" Jordan came to a rest on his haunches beside me.

"It's a lab as we suspected. The scent of cleaning products was strong, and I could hear lab assistants in the background. They're Aussie, with the distinct Queenslander accent. I'd say Brad is right in assuming Aeternum's Brisbane laboratory is where Brian is being housed. The reaper wasn't there, and if he was, he did a good job of hiding his presence."

Erick gently drew me towards him before we stood together. He drew me towards the couch opposite to where Abby lay—finally at peace.

Scooping me into his lap, I lay there, my emotions overwhelming, but unable to release them. I didn't want to feel anything just yet. I had too much to do.

"Jordan, call Detective Bernard. Tell him we have another victim, and that it's at Evanee's address," Erick ordered.

Chapter 19

Candles flickered merrily around me, but my heart was empty, fractured and incapable of experiencing any joy. The organ was nothing more than a weight, burdened with the knowledge I'd purposely released a serial killer back into the world. I'd had him in my grasp, and I'd let him walk. At the time it'd felt like the right thing to do, but now I was questioning my judgment.

The bath's warm water sloshed around my hunched figure as I lay back and slipped beneath the surface. The world grew silent once again, interrupted only by my sombre thoughts. Enormous wooden beams bore the weight of the vaulted ceiling above me, and I wondered if they would've collapsed under the weight that now sat on my shoulders. Time ticked by.

Erick's blurred solemn face appeared above me, and I surfaced at last. He waited patiently as I wiped my eyes dry, pushing my hair back from my face before he finally spoke.

"Detective Bernard just called. Abigail's parents have identified her body at the local hospital."

I nodded my thanks. I had no words as self-doubt crept its way back into my heart and head.

"Please talk to me, Evanee," Erick beseeched.

He knelt beside the tub, and I stared, memorising his features as though this was the last time I'd see him.

My fingers traced little zigzags in the water beside me as I whispered the questions that had been bothering me. "Why'd I let him go, Erick? I let a serial killer escape when I had him within my grasp. Did I do the right thing? Because it sure as hell doesn't feel like it."

"It's strategy, *mic luptător*. You did what you had to do to catch another killer. Sometimes we have to look at the bigger picture. There will come a time when you will confront him, but yesterday was not meant to be that day. I thought what you did was brave and wise. You're going to make a wise and powerful queen one day."

His long fingers stroked at my head, and I pulled my knees up, resting my chin on them.

"You know she wanted to be a midwife?" I croaked. "Abigail. She thought there was nothing more special than helping families usher in a new life into the world. We'd sit on my front patio and talk about what it would take to get into med school, what the best schools were, and where she wanted to do her placement."

I allowed a tear to escape, but there was no time to shed any more. I had a serial killer to track down and hang out to dry.

"She sounds like she was a kind girl. She was obviously smart, considering she consulted you about her future in medicine. I don't think I've ever met a sixteen-year-old who wanted to be a midwife. That's extraordinary."

Erick spoke softly as he stroked my neck.

I tried to smile, but it never reached my eyes.

"She had an older sister who she helped during her labour. That's what sparked the passion for her." Sighing, I stood, water dripping from me.

I accepted the towel Erick wrapped around me, grateful I wasn't alone right in this moment. Stepping into his arms, I rested my head against his broad chest, hoping and praying he could handle the weight of my emotions this morning.

"You need to rest. It's been a crap morning, and you need time to recuperate. I've rung Dr Denver and informed of the situation."

He pressed a firm kiss onto the crown of my head, lingering there as we stood together in silence.

Sighing, I spoke into his chest. "Thanks. I can't rest now though, there's too much to plan. I need to speak to Ellie and Brad about the layout of Aeternum's Brisbane laboratory. I need to speak to my great grandfather somehow, and I need to train for what's coming—"

I was cut off as Erick lifted my face to his, kissing me firmly.

"What you need is to sleep. I won't let you sleep too long. I promise. You can sleep as the humans do, and I will wake you when Brad and Ellie return. As for figuring out how to find or speak to Death, perhaps you could go into your mind and figure out if there is a connection in there between the two of you. But for now, I want you to rest."

He was right, even if I didn't want to admit it. I couldn't think when my mind was crowded with thoughts of innocent lives lost to Brian's need for vengeance and torture.

"Okay, fine, you win. I need my pyjamas if I'm going to sleep then. There are way too many people in this mansion for me to sleep naked."

"You sleep naked when I'm not around?"

Erick's inquisitive question came from behind me as we made our way into the bedroom, and I smiled.

"There is nothing better than the feeling of fresh sheets against your bare skin when you finally lie down at the end of a long day."

Draping the towel over the top of a teal love seat, I sauntered towards the bed feeling his eyes on my body.

"Why is this the first time I'm hearing about this?"

"Because you never asked. I also have a thing for lingerie but prefer naked when I'm exhausted. Now where are my pyjamas?"

The rip of cloth being shredded came from behind me, and I turned in time to see bits of material floating to the floor.

"What the hell did you just shred?" I frowned, then blinked in astonishment as I recognised the colours lying in strips around him.

"Nothing. Just a shirt I didn't like anymore. You know how temperamental I can be."

"Those were my pyjamas, weren't they? Really? You had to shred them? You couldn't have just hidden them beneath a pillow or something?" Hands on my hips, I gave up trying to be stern and giggled instead.

"You didn't need them anymore. There's really no need to hold on to such material things."

He had that cheeky grin that did things to me, and if I wasn't careful, there would be no sleeping for me and no work for him.

"Fine. I'll sleep naked, but if anyone walks in on me…."

"I will cut their eyes out and feed them to the dogs." He crossed his heart as if he were some saint.

"Erick, you don't have dogs."

"I'm sure I could find a dingo somewhere. Now go to sleep."

"Yeah, yeah, bossy pants. You'll contact Ellie and Brad?" I asked climbing into bed.

"I'll do it as soon as I walk out of here. Now go to sleep." I blew him a kiss, and I snuggled down, shutting my eyes, and praying there would be no dreams.

~

Ellie, Tristan, Jordan, Brad, Aunt Paige and Mum were all once again congregated in the library, arguments about the suitability of Aeternum's Laboratory in Brisbane being the place to confront Brian bouncing between each person.

"Will you all shut the hell up!" Erick hollered. "*Mic Luptător*, what are your thoughts?"

"I don't know Erick, this is your area of expertise, not mine. If you say it's a bad idea, fine we choose another location." I stood overlooking the garden, the air cooling. Autumn would soon be upon us.

"I have to agree with Brad, the laboratory doesn't sound like it would be a good place to lay siege. We need somewhere we are familiar with, somewhere open where casualties will be kept to a minimum."

As Erick spoke, I thought of Brian's patterns and behaviour.

"I think I know where he will dump his next victim," I spoke up, turning towards the library. "Initially Brian wanted to get my attention, to announce his presence, which he did with the first victim's body in Mermaid Close. Aside from Abigail, he's always placed the bodies in specific locations reminiscent of the time we spent together or places he associates with us."

"I believe the helipad outside Acrasin General Hospital was supposed to be the second to last location he placed a body, a nod to our time as residents together. He wouldn't risk killing someone in such a confined space with so many people around."

"Where do you think he'll leave the final body before he comes for you?" Ellie asked.

"The car park," Erick ground out.

Jordan stood and began to pace.

"What car park? There are about a thousand different car parks in Acrasin City alone, Evanee, you'll need to be a bit more specific," Tristan exclaimed.

"The hospital car park, Tristan. That's where it all began. It'd be a rather poetic ending, don't you think?" I spoke evenly.

"Evanee, that's a highly emotional location for you to confront him. I'm not sure given the location's significance and previous panic attacks that it would be wise to ambush him there."

Erick stood and approached me.

"Think about it, Erick. He's been reliving our short relationship through his killings. The street names have correlated with places we visited together. This was always going to end in a car park whether it was in Acrasin City or Brisbane, so let's just skip to the end of the book and close this fucking story."

"She has a point there, Erick," Jordan reasoned. "We all know Brian has been building up to this. He's obsessed with everything Evanee and is in some ways reliving the past few weeks before she cursed him. Yes, there is a part of him that wants her alive, but the rest of him and his master very much want her dead."

Jordan had once again taken a seat, his feet resting on the wrought iron and silky oak coffee table.

"I know that, Jordan, but we're not taking into account how Evanee will react emotionally," Erick retorted.

"And you're thinking of the situation from the angle of a concerned lover, not as the strategist that you are." Tristan's response was risky, but it was the truth.

"I love that you're concerned about my emotional well-being, but it has to end somewhere. We have bigger fish to fry, and this needs to happen before he progresses to killing any women he sees at random. The question is how are we going to get him to appear at the car park at a time and day of our choosing?"

Brad dropped his head forward as he spoke almost helplessly at the floorboards beneath his feet. "That might be tricky. I mean Evanee can't exactly camp out in the parking lot in a tent until he rocks up. It could take weeks before he shows up, especially after your last confrontation."

"I believe the man has a point," a new voice whispered through the room.

The library vibrated with power before a darkness so dense and pure nobody moved for fear of being lost to it forever, took over. The soft lighting of the library blinked back to life seconds later to reveal Grandfather standing at the back of the room.

Long low hisses of fear erupted from the vampires who had not yet met my great grandfather, while a petrified Ellie turned deathly white. Her hair rose to float around her head as her eyes bled to pitch black. Brad's yell of 'what the fuck?' was almost comical. Beside me Erick placed an arm around me, now used to Grandfather's appearance and the effect it had on him.

"Good afternoon, Grandfather. I see you got my message."

I'd done as Erick had suggested and visited my round room of mirrors after I'd awoken. There I'd sent a message winging through the black door that held that ancient power within me hoping Grandfather would receive it.

"I did. It sounds to me that you are in a bit of a predicament. You know I can't fight this battle for you though, so why reach out to me?" Multiple voices melded into each other as he spoke.

Turning slowly to face him, I caught Brad shaking his head as though he were trying to clear it.

The poor bugger.

"Do you think you could pick a body and voice and stick with it? There is a mortal present, and your presence is proving overwhelming for him." I nodded in Brad's direction, and Grandfather looked at him in amusement.

With a slight shudder, his black cloak melded to his body as my grandfather morphed into a man who looked to be in his late twenties' early thirties. I observed the white hair and electric blue irises. I could see a lot of my mother in him, and myself too.

"I see where I got my hair, eyes, and nose from. Too bad I couldn't get the skinny figure and grace to go with it," I sniffed.

Erick shook his head as he looked between my grandfather and I.

"You have your father and a lot of your great grandmother in you. You are a creature of beauty, as is your mother. She got more from me, but her beauty could rival my Chavas."

His voice was melodic, yet there was sadness in there that broke my heart.

Gazing around the room, there wasn't a dry eye in sight.

His voice affects the emotions of those around him, much like Erick's and my wings. Now there's a nugget for the mental library.

"I didn't ask you here to solve my problems, Grandfather, I'm capable of doing that on my own. I asked you here because I need guidance in matters that pertain to your abilities. I doubt any of your offspring would or could help me."

Summoning my scythe, it appeared in my hand.

"I need to know if there is a way to keep this on my body without having to fashion a holster and without the mortals seeing it. I'm having difficulty summoning it during battle."

The scythe in question disappeared from my hand, only to materialise across the room in Grandfather's grip.

"Dear friend, it is good to hold you again." Grandfather greeted the scythe as though it were a living being. "You need to sharpen it. It's feeling dull to the touch."

"Okay, how do I sharpen it? You never left a care manual or anything," I replied grumpily as I crossed my arms.

"You reap." At my confused look, he continued on.

"The more you reap using the blade the sharper it will get. The souls sharpen the blade and fuel its power."

"Right, so on top of planning for Brian's demise, I need to go on a reaping spree. Awesome, this day keeps getting better. Let's say I feed the scythe, how am I supposed keep it on me at all times without scaring the mortals and immortals alike?" I stepped away from Erick to rest my hands on the back of the lounge as I waited for my grandfather's response to my predicament.

"When it's fully charged, it can morph into any weapon of your choice, or any object. If you need a sword while doing battle, it'll become a sword. You need a crossbow, that is what it will become. In Australia, it's illegal to keep a gun on your person unless you are in law enforcement or hold a license, so I wouldn't recommend carrying it around as a gun. It'd still require a lot of explaining. A knife wouldn't be any better. You can't have the mortal law enforcement touching it or they'll die upon contact. So, will many of the supernatural beings."

I fingered the scales I still wore around my neck, as we stood thinking of how best to disguise my scythe. And that's when it hit me.

"What about an ornament, or a piece of jewellery? Do you think I could replace my scale with it? I never take it off, and no one outside of this room would realise that I'd replaced the ornament itself." I looked to Erick, who approached me to finger the charm in question.

"That could work. Your scythe doesn't affect me, so there would never be a need to worry about taking it off," he murmured.

"Plus, she's not much of a hugger, so humans and supernatural creatures alike wouldn't be harmed."

This came from Ellie.

"There you go. You didn't really need me at all, did you?"

Grandfather smiled, releasing my blade back into my hand.

"Think what you want it to do and let's see if it works. I recharged it, in a manner of speaking, so it should be sharp for a while, but it needs to reap—and often, Evanee, or the only thing it'll be good for is cutting wheat."

I nodded my understanding and removed my necklace. Slipping the dainty pendant from its chain, I handed it to Erick, who held it tightly in his hand knowing how important it was to me.

"Righto, here we go." Thinking of my beloved pendant, I directed my thoughts at the scythe balancing placidly in my outstretched palm. It lay in my outstretched palm before shrinking and morphing to form the very pendant Erick clutched tightly.

"It worked. Look, it worked." I gazed up at Grandfather, proud of what I'd just accomplished.

"Of course, it worked. You have a strong mind Evanee, and a will of iron when you want to. Now is there anything else you need my help with?"

Grandfather cocked his head, his gaze piercing.

"There is one favour I was hoping you might consider doing for me."

The words came from Erick, and I looked up in surprise.

"And what is that, Tenebris?"

Grandfather stilled, and I wasn't so sure it was a good thing.

'Be careful what you say or ask for next, Erick. He may have a soft spot for me, but it looks like that's where it ends.'

Erick nodded cautiously, before looking back at him.

"Would you train Evanee for battle? She has trained for months with us, and made phenomenal progress, but I'm worried about her upcoming battle with Brian and the reaper we believe created him. She needs to be prepared for whatever comes her way once she assumes your throne."

Wow, I did not see that coming.

"Why not ask Reagan?" My grandfather growled.

"Because while she is a brilliant fighter, she doesn't have the powers you bestowed upon Evanee."

Sighing, Erick hesitated before saying what was weighing on his mind.

"I'm worried her powers are consuming her, replacing her. If this keeps up, the Evanee we know will be lost to us. It's already begun, they are merging, but I am worried at what cost? I don't want to lose her after I just found her."

Grandfather thought silently for a minute, finally giving his answer.

"They will inevitably meld, but I can see how that power might overtake some characteristics unique to our Evanee here."

Cunningness lit Grandfather's eyes and the smirk he directed at Erick twisted my gut.

"I will train her as you've requested, but you, Erick, will need to pay a price. You will join me in the ring before I train our Evanee. If you are going to be my heir's mate and the future King to my kingdom, you need to prove to me that you are worthy of the responsibilities that will fall into your lap. I will be back in a couple of hours for your first session, Evanee, so be prepared."

"I have things to do," I interjected.

"They can wait."

With that he vanished.

Nobody dared to move or even breathe.

"Erick, what the hell did you just sign yourself up for?"

The rest of us shared Jordan's astonishment and bewilderment at Grandfather's decree.

We all looked towards Erick as he stood immobile and stone faced. Without a word he turned and stormed out of the room.

Chapter 20

"Well, that was unexpected." I emerged from the rustling bushland, looking to where Erick sat atop the very boulder my father and I had shared so many years ago, staring at the bubbling water before him. Ahead of us, a waterfall thundered and pummelled age-old rocks that showed no signs of moving despite the ferocity of the water. When he didn't answer me, I tried again.

"I guess you, me, and my father now have one more thing in common." I stood where I was, not wanting to encroach on his space.

"How the hell am I supposed to beat your great grandfather? He's The Death. He's the boogie man from every little vampire's bedtime stories."

And there it is. It only took how many months for me to finally see a vulnerable side of you?

"The point isn't to best Grandfather, Erick. He doesn't want to kill you… at least I hope not." I was trying for humour, trying to ease his stress. "I'd kick his arse if he did."

"Evanee, a little seriousness would be appreciated right now."

Bending slightly, I propelled into the air, landing softly behind him. Sitting behind his hunched figure, I circled my legs around him and hugged his back.

"You are Prince Tenebris, mate and King to me, the supposed Queen of the Dead People. You have lived for over 500 years and you are still breathing, for a lack of a better phrase. Your job is not to kill Grandfather, but to show him who you are. Show him the man who dove waist deep into my mind, dragging me back to reality despite a supernatural mutated creature trying to attack him. You took me and my power on when you thought your best friend and brother-in-arms was being stolen by some temptress. That took balls."

His snort of laughter at my phrasing drew a smile from me. I was getting through to him slowly.

"Show him the man who has gone up against a petulant, bad tempered, and extremely stubborn woman. Someone who, at every turn, tried to push you away because she was scared she'd lose that smile that creases your eyes and makes them glow. The woman who has fought so hard not to drag you to hell every time she descends there. Show him that man."

I laid my head against his spine, praying I would get through to him. It killed a part of me seeing the man I knew as strong and confident doubt himself.

"So, you like my smile, do you?" I could hear his smile as he spoke.

"Are you serious? Out of everything I just said, the only thing you heard was that I thought you had a nice smile." I stood in mock outrage, hands on my hips. "That is the last time I try to comfort you, Erick Tenebris."

I moved to step off the boulder only to be yanked back into a solid wall that was Erick's chest, his arms capturing mine to hold them in front of me.

"I heard every word you said, and it meant more to me than anything anyone has ever said. I guess there was always going to come a time when I would need to prove to a male in your family that I was worthy of you," he confessed.

"That sounds so antiquated. Does that mean I'm going to have to bitch fight your mother and any sisters you have? Wait, do you have any sisters, because I know you have a brother."

"I had a sister. She was murdered decades before you were born. She was my older sister, and you have a lot in common with her."

The sudden sadness emanating from him made me turn and embrace him.

"Oh really? She was a genetic freak who had trust issues and a seriously bad temper?"

His shirt muffled my voice.

"No, she wasn't a genetic freak, but she was a kind woman and she had a bad temper. She once threw me off her bedroom balcony when she caught me going through her drawers. In my defence, I was seventeen and after a trinket she'd brought at the markets that day. She was a woman who, despite what life threw at her, picked herself up and kept on going." The respect and adoration in his voice warmed me.

"What was her name?"

"Sophia. She practically raised me while our parents were off completing their royal duties."

"I'm sorry that she was taken away from you." It was the only thing I could think to say. I knew no matter what anyone said, words offered little comfort when the person you loved so dearly was dead and gone.

"One day when you're ready, maybe you could tell me how she was murdered, but not today. We need to replenish our strength, rest, and then limber up so we can both have our arses handed to us in spectacular fashion by a man as old as Father Time. Hey, do you think there is a Father Time and that Grandfather knows him?"

Erick's head dropped back as he roared his laughter.

"Only you could think something like that. *Mic luptător*, you are the only woman who does and will always surprise me at every turn."

Hugging me tightly, we stood unwilling to leave this world we'd created together.

Eventually, I broke the comfortable silence, knowing we needed to return.

"My plan to run is still on the table you know."

A muffled whisper followed Erick's snort as he kissed my head.

"I may just take you up on that offer after Death's done with me."

~

The training room was rather full for a weekday. It appeared the mansion's grounds were running on minimal security this evening. Most of the faces were familiar to me as I had stumbled across them at some point, whether it was during guard duty or in the mansion. Tristan, Aunt Paige, Jordan, Ellie, and Brad stood to the side chatting away merrily.

"Awesome, I get to have my arse kicked in front of the entire household," I whispered to Erick who'd entered behind me.

"You? What about me? These are my people," he grumbled.

"Oh, I'm not worried about you. They're probably rooting for Grandfather to hand you your arse, considering not one of them has bested you yet. A little revenge and all that." I smiled back at him and he smacked my backside in retaliation.

A portal appeared in the centre of the room as my mother appeared, her ghostly figure floating through, her tattered dress rustling gently in a phantom breeze. Around her the assembled vampires hissed like a colony of feral cats being invaded by a human.

"Mother dearest, you are still in reaper mode. You may want to tone it down," I called out in greeting.

"Oh right. Sorry."

Addressing the rest of the room, Mum issued her apology.

"Sorry ladies and gentlemen, I forgot you're not all acquainted with my natural form."

Her ghostly form began to fade, as her tattered dress slowly morphed into tight black leather leggings with a pale pink shirt and a leather jacket. The gorgeous gold-plated high-heeled boots caught my eye and I instantly fell in love.

"Oh, she's been holding out on me. I am so going to sneak into her apartment later to steal those."

I eyed off those boots, knowing they were as good as mine.

"What are you talking about, baby?" Erick asked, confused.

"Her boots. She's been keeping those babies hidden I bet. I'll be stealing those later." I replied with a sneaky smile.

He only laughed before kissing my head and snatching my hand to drag me to the centre of the room.

"Mum, I believe you have been holding out on me." I greeted my chuckling mother with a hug and a kiss to her cheek.

"You like them? I picked these up last week. One of a kind unfortunately." Her devilish grin gave her little lie away.

"Oh, that's too bad."

"No doubt they'll be disappearing from my cupboard sometime soon," she drawled.

We laughed, only to cease at the disturbance in the air.

"He's here," she whispered with excitement.

A swirling mass of black appeared in the very spot Mum had appeared, and a cloaked figure stepped from within it. A full-length scythe in hand, he stood tall, observing his audience.

"Show off much?" I drawled.

Beside me, Mum laughed before she stepped around me to greet Grandfather. They hugged briefly before he released her to stand beside him.

"Grand-père, you'd better settle on a body before you scare your audience too much," she spoke softly.

"Very well," Grandfather murmured.

His billowing cloak once again melded onto his legs, so it clothed him in low slung black martial arts pants. He left his chest bare, his figure toned to perfection. His hair was once again a mass of pure white spikes, while his eyes swirled dizzyingly, never settling on one colour, unlike his previous visit.

"My word, that's Death?" a woman called from the crowd.

I watched, fascinated as the eyes of both men and women began to glow.

"You couldn't morph into some average-looking guy?" I rolled my eyes at Grandfather's husky laugh, the scent of desire drifting up from the crowd to greet us.

"Let's get on with this before you incite a bloody orgy," I huffed, following Erick from the mat.

"Why are there so many vampires in this room?" Grandfather asked inquisitively.

"They're here to see Erick have his arse handed to him, Sire," Jordan responded. "Few have had that pleasure, and only one in this room has bested him most recently."

"And just who has bested you, Erick?" Grandfather inquired.

"Recently there has only been one, and she's standing right beside me."

Is that pride in his voice?

Erick's face showed none of the emotion I thought I'd detected in his statement just before.

"Intriguing. Tell me, great granddaughter, what technique did you employ to defeat the great Prince Erick Tenebris?"

Beside me, Erick tensed as though worried I'd give away how I'd bested him that one time. He needn't have worried, I had no intention of giving Grandfather any advantage, no matter how small. I also knew if we were to battle again, he'd kick my backside hard and fast, avoiding my being able to use my other powers.

"Tsk, tsk, Grandfather. Now what kind of girlfriend would I be if I gave away my man's weaknesses? If he had any, that is. Surely you of all people should know better than to ask a question like that." Hugging Erick's side, he shared a smile I now knew he reserved only for me.

'As if I would tell him how I kicked your arse.'

'Gee, thanks for that,' Erick replied dryly.

'You're welcome, sexy.' Puckering up my lips, I kissed the air.

Grandfather laughed, and the room shivered in apprehension. He had that effect on those around him I'd noticed, but not me, Erick, or mum.

"She really is your daughter, Reagan. You've raised a fine young woman, and I look forward to bringing that attitude of yours down a notch, my girl," he finished solemnly.

"Try it, *old man*."

Baiting him was not a good idea, but when your insides felt like jelly, sometimes false bravado was the only way to go.

"Feisty, I like it. Now, let us see what this man of yours has to offer my family," Grandfather addressed Erick.

They stared at each other until Mum broke the silence.

"Would you two like to whip it out and measure, or shall we begin?" She cleared her throat.

"I will, if he will," Grandfather bared his straight teeth as he spoke.

"Oh please. You'd probably cheat anyway," I scoffed.

"I'd rather get this fight over with, if you don't mind."

Erick cut across as I spoke.

Nodding, Grandfather sauntered towards the sparing mat. I squeezed Erick's hand before I let it go as he followed. Both men were evenly matched in their 6'1" height. Their shoulders were equally broad, with Erick only slightly slimmer than Grandfather. They appeared at ease, their bodies graceful, heads held high, yet the looseness in their postures gave me pause.

My mother stood beside me, her smile no longer in place.

"This should be interesting. I've never heard of my grand-père purposely sparing with any person. I've heard of his great battles with the Leviathan, but he's not fought like this, well, not that I know of."

"Apparently, he wants to be sure that Erick is worthy of his kingdom."

Looking at Mum, I caught the faintest outline in amongst the congregated vampires. There in amongst the crowd stood a woman clothed in nothing but mist. "You've got to be kidding me. What the hell is she doing here?" I ground out through my teeth. Mum turned, as did Jordan, who stepped up beside my mother.

"Who is it, sweetheart?"

She peered into the crowd, looking for who had caught my attention.

"The bane of my damned existence," I hissed as I hurried past my mother. "I don't recall inviting you," I ground out, ignoring those around me. "And I highly doubt Grandfather would've either." I spoke boldly to the bitch who'd destroyed my life.

"Don't talk to me like that, little girl. It is an honour to be in my presence," Fate spat, irritated.

The two men stood in the centre of the sparing mat, forgotten by the audience surrounding them. Now everyone focused on me and the mysterious woman, they suddenly realised was standing amongst them.

"Like hell, Fate. Your conniving and meddling ruined my damned life, not to mention my great grandfather's life. All because you couldn't stand to be second best."

Her anger swirled around her, golden sparks flickering. My anger responded, obsidian and electric blue flames creeping up my arms. A sudden presence behind me had Fate smiling, and her power dampening instantly.

"Fate, I didn't realise you'd left your inner sanctum?" Grandfather's arm circled my shoulders, surprising me, yet, my flames refused to submit.

"I came to see you, of course. I caught wind that you would be here this evening, and I thought I'd pay you a visit, for old time's sake," she replied sweetly.

"I see. I trust you are not here to meddle, because I would hate to accidentally lose control during my battle and reap the wrong person."

The room grew heavy with his threat, shadows creeping up the walls that looked suspiciously like hands reaching from within.

"I am not here to interfere, but don't tempt me."

The sparks once again danced around her, and my cold flames intensified.

"Come, Evanee. Your mate would like for you to be near the ring during our battle."

Grandfather's large pale hand rested my forearm through the flame. With a gentle tug, he led me away from Fate.

"You shouldn't pick a fight with that one. She's as mad as they come, and only I can reap her, which would be a mistake. She has sisters, and they're as bat shit crazy as she is, with a touch of homicidal tendencies thrown in. You leave her to me, okay."

Pressing a tender kiss to my head, Grandfather squeezed me gently before walking back to the ring.

"Come here, baby girl. There are some battles we just weren't meant to fight. That is one of them."

My mother spoke gently as she hugged me tightly to her side. Listening to her, I wondered just who she was talking to—me or herself.

Nerves tightened my gut so hard I had to fight the urge to throw up as I looked at the ring before me. The room was silent, waiting with bated breath.

'You have this, Erick. No holding back like you did with me. You have nothing to prove to me. You'll always be my escape partner no matter what he thinks.' I had no idea if

he heard me, because the battle of wills began before he could even flick a glance my way.

I stepped away from my mother, my eyes never leaving the man who'd grown to mean so much to me. The man who'd stood beside me no matter my moods and temper tantrums.

Circling each other on light feet, the two beings assessed each other. Grandfather pounced first, his body a blur as his fist connected with Erick's jaw. My sharp inhale stuck in my throat as I fought the instinct to jump into the ring and defend him. Erick wiped at the blood trickling from the corner of his mouth. The redness barely had time to hit the ground before Erick was across the mat, a fist slamming hard into Grandfather's abdomen.

No one spoke, transfixed by the sight before them. Hit after hit landed as each man took his pound of flesh from the other. They danced around each other, their feet skimming the surface of the mat.

They were relentless, their punches and kicks blurs of pale flesh melding together. An ominous crack fractured the air as Grandfather broke Erick's rib, but Erick repaid in kind by breaking his rib on the opposite side. Neither said a word nor cried out in pain.

After thirty minutes of tit for tat, I noticed the infinitesimal twitch of Grandfather's wrist. Dread clawed at my heart as I knew what came next. It was something I did— when I summoned my scythe.

Time stood still for a split second. I spun toward where the shields stood at the back of the gym. My foot stepped forward and I was across the room a second later, ripping one the larger shields from its resting place. Flinging it across the room as though it were a Frisbee, I screamed his name.

"ERICK!"

Erick deftly grabbed the shield, and a resounding clang of a sword hitting metal sounded as Erick thrust the shield upwards to meet Grandfather's blow.

He dropped to one knee under the pressure. Grandfather gripped the sword with two hands, his upper arms flexing with the force he was exerting. Beneath Erick's knee, wood groaned despite the rubber mat holding steady under the pressure. Jordan disappeared for what felt like hours, but could only have been seconds, and reappeared at the side of the mat, Erick's sword in hand.

"Here you go mate, I think you might need this one," he mumbled, quickly passing the sword into Erick's outstretched hand.

Their swords clanged together, resonating through the room and seeping into my bones. Dropping the shield, I'd thrown, Erick brought both hands to his sword, meeting Grandfather stroke for stroke. I clenched my fists, biting down hard on my lip in worry.

Something's changed.

Grandfather had been holding back before, but he wasn't now. The sword he'd summoned was merely a newer and bigger version of my scythe, but the fact that he'd summoned it when this wasn't a life or death fight scared me.

Erick saw an opening and went for it, bringing his sword forward to strike Grandfather through the stomach. The sword lodged for a second before slipping through his now semi-solid form, dragging Erick down with it. Menace lurked in the swirling depths of my Grandfather's eyes as he reared back slightly and drove his fist into Erick's shoulder, his smile savage. Pale pink droplets of sweat dripped from Erick's brow, a white line appearing around his mouth, yet he didn't move.

"If this is all you have to offer, I'm not so sure you're worthy of being my great granddaughter's mate and heir to my kingdom," Grandfather spat.

"She's mine, and I don't give a fuck about your kingdom. I never wanted the title my father lumped on me, and I don't want yours," Erick hissed.

His sword forgotten, Erick ripped the taloned hand from his shoulder as gold and garnet flames erupted from his hand, his furious eyes glowing bright as golden lightening forked across them. A primitive grin lit Erick's face, and my lips drew back in a snarl mirroring his own. That ancient power within me drifted to the surface, intrigued by this new raw and primitive side of Erick. Every part of me wanted that for myself.

My eyes glowed, judging by the startled looks around me, and the crowd suddenly parted, giving me a wide berth.

Thrusting his blazing hand into Grandfather's abdomen, Erick hissed in anger. The black rubber mat beneath his bare feet melting. I shivered at the sheer intensity I was witnessing before me.

"That's better," Grandfather growled, his own sword disappearing before he lashed out, punching Erick in the centre of his chest, and sending him flying across the mat.

Erick landed hard and rolled to his feet, charging towards Grandfather. They met in a bone jarring tackle, the sheer force backing Grandfather up a step before he dropped backwards. Bracing his feet against Erick's abdomen, he kicked out. Erick landed back where he'd been only moments before. Giving no quarter, Grandfather leapt, his scythe appearing in his hand once more as he came to land atop of Erick. Erick froze.

Horror replaced the admiration filling me as I'd watched the two men battle. I knew what the scythe meant, and so did Erick as he stared unblinking in Grandfather's eyes.

His time was up.

Chapter 21

My body moved of its own accord, instinct and the need to protect what was mine taking over. My scythe appeared. I hadn't realised I'd summoned it. My training gear gave way to reveal the tattered dress I'd worn the night I'd received my powers as I blurred across the room. Hair streaming behind me, fog burst from beneath my feet as my arm reached down, the scythe merely an extension of it.

Obsidian sparks erupted as our scythes connected, the blast lifting the observers in the room off their feet. Teeth bared, I merged fully with that ancient part of me. Bending low, my talons puncturing holes in the mat to the left of Erick's head.

I was ready to play, but was Grandfather?

Pulling back his scythe, he hissed furiously. "You would dare come between me and my prey?"

"You issued the challenge the second you attempted to take my mate's life. You will deal with me now. Your fight with him is done." Mouth never opening, my voice crept from the fog now coating the room.

Straightening up, I stepped over a seething Erick. I could see his need to argue my interruption, but he remained silent at the concerned look I gave him.

"You dare to threaten me, fledgling." The room darkened at the corners, forcing the vampires still climbing to their feet to crawl forward and closer to the stage for fear of being consumed by that blackness.

"You should know by now, Grandfather, I don't threaten. I make promises and deliver them. You've lost yourself to the seduction of the fight. You challenged my mate knowing very well he does not possess the power you do. Well guess what great Grandfather, I possess those gifts. I protect those I love, and he is at the top of my list, so BACK THE FUCK OFF!" I roared, releasing my scythe back onto my necklace, silently setting the terms of our combat.

"So be it, little one. But you should know I was fully aware of what I was doing. You will know when and if I become seduced by battle."

The slightest flinch in his eyes contradicted his words. His own scythe disappeared, and we met in a clash of wills. Jordan's words of wisdom beat through my mind.

Fight dirty or go home in a coffin.

Nailing Grandfather in the balls with one swift kick, I delivered a roundhouse kick to his gut. My right hook obliterated the surprise and pain from his face when I hit him square in the jaw, obliterating it. I studied my great Grandfather as he reached up to snap it back into place. The speed at which he was healing was breathtaking.

A look of glee replaced his surprise. He stepped forward, extending his own leg at the last second. It landed solidly in my gut. I latched onto that foot, standing my ground. This wasn't a training session anymore; this was life or death—Erick's life.

A ragged gasp from my mother brought my head up only to come face to face with the last person I wanted to see—Brian. Fear hammered at the power coursing through me as Brian's face grinned demonically down at me. His fist smashed down and into my cheek bone. I dropped to the floor immobilised by more than the hit I'd just sustained.

Out of the corner of my eye I caught sight of Tristan and my mother holding Erick back as he roared furiously, fighting to be at my side. Jordan stood still, his fists clenched tightly, yet unwilling to move, knowing this was what I needed. The scales on his bicep swayed between life and death, never settling on either.

"Your weakness, *little girl*, is that you live in the past. Always moping and crying about the things that cannot be changed. You will die with those words engraved into your tombstone if you're lucky enough to get one. You are pandering to human weaknesses that have no right being in your new life." Grandfather taunted with Brian's voice.

"Evanee, get off your arse and nail him. You're not that naive girl you were in that parking lot all those years ago. MOVE!"

Mum bellowed at me.

There was anger in that voice, but I wasn't entirely sure who it was aimed at, me or Grandfather.

"Of course she is, Reagan. Look at her lying helpless like some pathetic human incapable of defending herself against some weak dying man. Should I do to you what he wanted to do to you? Tell me, will you lay there as I tear at your cloth…"

He never finished that sentence as a screech of fury erupted from deep within me.

I launched myself at him, my talons bared, and canines extended. Landing hard on his chest, I drove him to the ground. An animalistic rage drove me, my clawed hands slashing savagely at Brian's handsome features, and with it the anxiety that'd held me back for so many years. Decayed flesh stuck to my thighs, but I paid no attention to it.

I roared as flames emerged along my arms and feet. I fought to keep my wings contained beneath the skin on my back, unwilling to fight with them. Two large decomposing hands reached up to shackle my flaming ones, all the while Brian's bright blue eyes shone up at me.

I hated him. Hated him with every fibre of my being. I would rip his heart out and dance in his entrails once I'd finished gutting him. I would bathe in the bastard's blood.

Beneath me 'Brian' bucked, his legs rising to wrap around me. I slammed into the ground dissipating into mist, solidifying above his head, I smashed my fist down. Grandfather rolled at the last second, coming to his knees, but I was in front of him, latching onto his neck. My fist closed as he dissolved into a light mist, escaping my grasp. A fist reached out from that mist landing a solid punch to my left breast. Crying out in pain, I hunched over.

Straightening against the pain, I stared into the face of the man who'd broken me. The man who'd killed so many all because he had an obsession with my white hair and 'fuck me' eyes.

I charged at him, my anger blessedly free to wreak the havoc it had been longing to do for so long. Our talons slashed at flesh, some mine and some his. Chunks of decaying meat plopped to the mat, marking our path. Together Grandfather and I danced as only two beings of death could.

Disappearing into darkness and reappearing at will. Nobody moved or spoke, too busy trying to follow the fight.

At last I summoned my scythe, tiring of this. It appeared in the form of a knife, and I threw it with deadly aim, smiling as it landed just above his heart.

"You missed."

Grandfather taunted me in Brian's voice.

"Did I?"

Flexing my fingers, barbs shot out at the tip of the knife buried deep within his chest. For the first time Grandfather grunted in pain. Oh, I knew I couldn't kill him, but that didn't mean I couldn't inflict pain.

"Think what you want it to be, and it will be so. Isn't that what you said to me?" Appearing before him, I gripped the hilt of the blade as I spoke.

"So I did."

In all my cockiness, I missed the flick of his wrist. Erick's yell came too late as Grandfather buried a blade of his own in my side. I couldn't hold back my pained scream.

"They've trained you well, my darling child, but what you lack is a leash on that temper of yours. You're far too cocky for your own good," Grandfather whispered as he morphed back into the body he'd chosen when he'd first arrived.

"It's called faking it until you make it. False bravado," I grunted through the pain.

Behind me Mum and Erick moved as one to approach the mat.

"No, no, none of you move or the next thing I summon will be my hounds."

He has hounds?

"As for the rest of you little vampires, the show is over, so get the fuck out before I reap the lot of you."

He stood casually as though he didn't have a barbed knife sticking out of his chest, my hand still on its handle.

It took less than five seconds for the room to clear, every vampire sprinting for the door. I'd have laughed if I wasn't dripping precious blood onto the mat. When the last of our audience had departed, I dropped to my knees, my hand still gripping the hilt.

"Why have you not summoned your clipeum to assist you? Why have you not called to your mate?" Grandfather demanded softly.

"Because this isn't their battle to fight, it's mine. They are mine to protect, not to put in harm's way." I was panting now, the pain growing as Grandfather bent down, twisting the blade just a little.

"And there is your other problem. You were fated these two men for a reason. They are battle wise and hard to kill. I've seen both men in countless battles and reaped the ones they've slayed, and yet you would treat them as though they are mortal."

"I was raised to fight my own battles, not have others do it for me. My parents didn't raise a coward."

I spat, crimson blood landing against that pale chest before me. Twisting the knife in his chest a little in response to his twist.

"Oh really, so it wasn't you who was contemplating suicide the first night I visited you? It wasn't you who begged me to reap you when your beloved Bob died?"

Bastard!

"You're so willing to die, yet you forget that if you die every single person in this room follows you. Their kin will destroy the vampires here for what they consider treason. The reaper who seeks you will kill your mother. Ellie and Brad will fare no better, their alliance with you an automatic death sentence."

I looked to the side, as the people he was referring to gathered at the edge of the mat. Despair gripped me.

How do I protect so many?

"Get your head in the game and leave your heart behind, or the very people you've been trying to protect will be the ones you lose. I'll be back a fortnight from today to continue your training."

With that he disappeared taking his blade with him and leaving my own to drop with my arm. Releasing the blade, it settled on my necklace once more. My chin met my chest, exhaustion taking a hold of my body as blood squelched beneath my knees, sticking to me.

"Never ask my grandfather for another favour, Erick, or I'll cut off your balls," I grunted as the wound at my side began to heal slowly.

"I'll neuter myself before I ever ask for his help again."

Erick whispered softly into my ear as he hugged me from behind.

I really need sustenance.

"You two were spectacular up there. You held your own really well, Evanee. I'm so proud of you, baby girl," Mum whispered soothingly. "I'm not sure I've met anyone who's gone up against my grand-père and lived to tell the tale."

Pride shone from within the depths of Mum's icy blue eyes as she dropped to her haunches in front of me.

"Oh, there was one who held her own against that man," Fate's voice came from the corner.

"Shit me. You're still here?" I spat, clenching my fist hard against the need to pounce on her.

Fate continued gleefully. "I rather enjoyed the show. I'm glad I picked the two of you to fulfil my prophecy, and I'm guessing so is Death. Now, as I was saying before you so rudely interrupted me, there was one woman who held her own against that spectacular man."

"Let me guess, it was you."

Mum rose, her arms crossing as she refused to look at Fate.

"Chavas," I realised. "Your grandmother, Mum." Surprise lit her features.

"That's right. I may have cursed the day she came into his life, but she was the only one who ever got him on his knees outside of the bedroom."

"Ew, can we not have any bedroom references about my great grandfather. I don't need that image in my head," I choked out.

"It's too bad I cursed the bitch. My poor Death just hasn't been the same since."

I didn't hesitate as I summoned my scythe. Palming the handle, I spun on my knee and threw the blade at where Fate stood. The blade buried deep into the wooden floor alongside my mother's own blade. Fate had disappeared.

"Mother and daughter seem to have a lot in common," Tristan observed with admiration.

"Right, now that she's gone, I think I might just pass ou…"

My eyes closed before I finished, as darkness blanketed my vision consuming me.

~

The air-conditioning whirred softly through the vent in the corner of my office as I sat scanning the autopsy file for Abigail Lane. I was quietly impressed with the excellent and thorough notes our newest pathologist had typed. In the corner of the room, Jordan lounged reading today's newspaper.

"You know I have a ton of medical books you could read, if you get bored with the newspaper." I didn't bother glancing up from the report as I spoke.

"I'm good here. Thanks."

"The amount of emails and journals I have to get through is stupid. Who thought I'd still get emails when the office was a disaster zone? I mean it's been almost two weeks and I haven't made a dent in the pile." Huffing in exasperation, I knew I should respond to those numerous emails, but the need to know the results of Abby's autopsy constantly whispered to me.

Finally satisfied that she'd been in good hands, I made a start on the many pains in the backside requests. I seriously hated paperwork and there seemed to be even more now that I'd stepped up the office ladder.

"That's what comes with being the boss lady. Now me, I just go around bashing skulls in while I look menacing. My life is simple and uncomplicated, which is how I like it."

"Uh huh, but really you're one big cuddly teddy bear. Just you wait until your mate comes along. She'll knock you on your arse so fast you won't know which way is north or south." I grinned evilly at him.

"You are the only person I know who would call me a *big cuddly teddy bear.*"

Giggling at his eye roll, I noted he avoided the rest of my statement, and I let it slip. Putting my head down, I continued to make my way through the numerous emails clogging up my inbox.

The piercing scream of a terrified woman roused me, and my head snapped up. It came again, and my chair shot backwards as I catapulted over the desk, reaching for the door handle only to be stopped by Jordan. He shoved me unceremoniously behind him as he pulled at the door, slowly opening it. His dense and dark power flexed outward, searching for the threat. When he couldn't detect anyone in the hall, he nodded, motioning for me to stay behind him.

Together we stepped lightly into the hall, with me at the rear. The morgue, viewing room, and loading bay sat behind us. The cry came again, and my body tensed with dread as Helena, a recent transfer, came sprinting towards us.

"There's something at the front door." She gasped out in panic. "At first, I thought it was a man, but then he looked at the camera and oh his face. Oh my word, his face."

The poor woman looked as if she wasn't sure whether to pass out or throw up.

"Helena, listen to me. I want you to go into my office and stay there. Don't leave it no matter what you hear. I'll deal with this. If you could please phone the police and ask for Detective Bernard. I need you to tell him what you saw. Do not tell anyone else but Detective Bernard, do you understand me?"

Her body shook slightly as I forced her to focus on my face and what I was telling her.

"Ye…yes Dr. Sheperd. Call Detective Bernard."

I grabbed her shoulders and turned her toward my office before nudging her forwards. Her hurried steps echoed through the empty hallway and she rushed into my office, shutting the door and locking it for added measure. The poor woman had no idea no lock would keep her safe from the creature lurking outside our doors.

Jordan and I approached the reception desk looking at the monitors. Cursing long and low at the body sprawled in front of the doors, I knew Brian's calling card when I saw it. The young woman's body lay broken and twisted as though he'd dumped her on the floor without a care for how she landed.

"I have to say, at least he's constant in his obsession with you. I've called Erick already. He's rallied the troops and they're on their way." Jordan's gaze never wavered from the screen.

"I guess it's time to face my ex again. Although, I have to say this all reminds me of the stray cat, Mr Crowley, I was trying to befriend at my house."

Stepping back from the screens, we approached the metal doors.

"Oh yeah? How so?"

The pop and crackle of Jordan cracking his knuckles in anticipation of the fight ahead skittered up my spine.

"The darned thing used to bring me dead birds every now and again. I wonder if Brian expects me to eat the bird on the other end of this door. No pun intended." Loosening up my neck, my fingers flexed as I readied myself for what would come next.

Grandfather had been right when he said I needed to get my head in the game. My heart would be nothing but a hindrance in this battle.

"Shit, I hope not. There is nothing more disgusting than coagulated blood."

Flashing his canines at me, my respect for Jordan kept rising. He knew I needed to keep focused and allowing my feelings of guilt and sorrow for the woman on the other end wouldn't benefit me or her right at this moment.

I slapped my ID card against the security pad, and the doors hissed open slowly. The scene before me worse than it looked on the monitors. A pool of blood seeped steadily around the young woman, who looked to be in her mid-twenties. Her blonde hair lay afloat the pool of blood, a stark contrast.

"I was wrong, the body's fresh. You could still eat her, not that I'd advise it," Jordan observed sombrely.

"Look at her eye sockets, or what's left of them. He's smashed his fists right through her skull. His rage has taken over, and it's making him far more careless than before."

Skin ripped from her temples exposed the white bone of her skull beneath. He'd fractured the bone badly from the sheer blunt force he'd used to extract her corneas. The amount of blood pooling around her body suggested he'd not even bothered to drain her as he had the others, which suggested she was bait more than a pleasure kill. Looking closer with that part of me that called to the dead, my gut churned as I noted the absence of her soul.

"I think he's devoured her soul. It's missing. He usually leaves a fragmented thing that I have to release, but there's nothing here. He's fed the reaper side of him and ignored his vampiric instincts to drain her."

Stepping over the poor girl, Jordan and I took a left, moving towards the security gate.

The hairs on the back of my neck rose, and I looked around the area trying, but failing to see him.

'He's watching there in the shadows.'

Jordan murmured telepathically, and I fought the urge to turn and look at where Jordan had sensed him.

'Do you think he'll take the bait and follow?' Lifting my ID card to the security panel, we exited, approaching the silent street behind the hospital.

The power surge behind us answered my question, as I realised our mistake too late. Strong arms grasped me around my waist, pulling me backwards and away from Jordan. Jordan spun, and I reached out for him in desperation, but he was too late. Brian's portal snapped shut on his cry of fury.

Chapter 22

My black joggers emitted a high-pitched squeak as they dragged along the ground. Brian's arms dropped from around me, and I landed hard on my backside with a wince. Climbing to my feet, my head darted from side to side trying to figure out where Brian had teleported us to. Grey concrete floors stretched as far as my eyes could see, interrupted intermittently by white lines and numbers highlighting designated parking spots.

Right, okay I'm in a parking garage, but which bloody one?

The lack of windows made it difficult to tell whether I was ten stories up or two stories down but suggested the parking lot was an old one. The elevator in the corner was useless, the 'lift' sign hanging haphazardly, the black buttons unlit and cracked.

Brian's wet, hacking cough drew my attention to where he stood, studying me.

"You're going to die tonight, Evanee, but not before you lift the curse you placed on me."

Bile rose in my throat. Helena hadn't been all that delirious in her heightened state of panic. Brian did in fact look like some hideous creature that'd crawled from the very depths of the grave, half decomposed and rotted. Large chunks of skin dripped from his face, revealing empty cheek sockets, only to partially heal and repeat the process all over again.

The curse has worsened. He's not fully regenerating.

"Brian," I greeted. "I'd say you look like death warmed up, but that'd be an understatement."

Brian's grotesque body stiffened with anger and hatred. "You did this to me, and now you're going to fix it. *He* can't, even though he promised he could."

"Who is *he?*" I asked. "I need a name if I'm going to laugh at the fool who thought they could lift a curse I inflicted." I stood immobile, waiting patiently for Brian to decide just whether he was game enough to reveal the name of his master and creator.

Waving his finger at me, I winced as the tip dropped off, revealing white bone beneath.

"Tsk, tsk. I don't think so, Evanee. You won't be getting his name out of me so easily."

"What a shame. I'll just have to persuade you then. Though, I'd rather been hoping for a less messy night. These are my good work clothes." I shifted my legs ever so slightly apart as I taunted him, grounding myself for the attack he would inevitably spring on me.

'Erick, are you there?'

'I'm here, mic luptător.' Erick reassured me.

'Brian has me in a parking garage. I can't tell which one or even what city I'm in.'

A series of curses erupted through my mind as Erick seethed at the situation. He wasn't in control, neither of us were, and it was doing his head in.

'I am working with your mother and Jordan, but neither of them can get a lock on you. None of us can. Reagan seems to think something, or someone, is hiding you.'

Frowning at that last part, I hoped Brian would assume I was simply frowning at our conversation. My eyes darted around the sparsely light garage, but nothing caught my gaze. Flexing my power ever so slightly, I searched the garage for what might be shielding my power. I highly doubted Brian had the brains to pull something like this off.

There!

Clocked by shadows in the furthest corner of the garage stood my Grandfather.

'It appears Grandfather wasn't all that impressed with my fighting skills. I guess I'm on my own for this one.'

When Erick didn't reply, my shoulders slumped before straightening once more. I hated Grandfather in that moment. There was no doubt in my mind that this was a test.

He doesn't think I have it in me to beat this arsehole. Well, he'd better think again, because he has another thing coming. Only one of us is walking out of here tonight, and it sure as shit won't be Brian.

"Did you like my gift?" Brian queried.

He was hoping no doubt for some emotional reaction on my part. Truth was, if he'd sprung it on me three weeks earlier, I might have given him the reaction he hoped for, but not anymore. Grandfather had successfully wormed his way into my head, beating at the anxiety I'd harboured. Brian no longer held the title of the Boogie Man for me, and he never would again.

"I thought your work was average as per normal. Smashing her eye sockets like that Brian, really? Although, I was rather impressed you siphoned her entire soul this time, but wasting all that precious blood is a bit of a rookie move. Funnily enough, I was just saying to Jordan how you reminded me of my feral cat, Mr Crowley. That cat loved to drop dead birds at my back door."

I waited for what I'd said to sink in.

"You're comparing me to one of your stupid cats?" Brian spat as he stepped forward.

"No Brian, I compared you to a single feral cat. Weren't you listening?"

Four, three, two, one.

Right on cue, a bellow of rage shook the ground beneath me. I wasted no time calling to that ancient part of me. It rose swiftly and settled below the surface of my skin, ready as I faced Brian's charge unflinching.

Foot slipping back slightly, I braced myself for impact. There was no trace of the scared and broken woman who'd been carried from that parking lot in Brisbane all those years ago. She was dead and buried and would stay that way. In her place was a jaded bitch who would wade through the blood of her enemies if it meant protecting the ones she loved. Brian was merely a serial killer who was in desperate need of a one-way ticket to whatever hell awaited him. Personally, I was hoping for the same torture he'd inflicted on his victims—only tenfold.

I caught Brian as he barrelled into me. Spider web cracks radiated from where my foot refused to budge any further.

In a split-second decision, my back foot swung forward slamming into Brian's gelatinous midriff. Bile clawed its way up my throat at the squelching, but I ignored it. Toppling backwards, Brian took me with him, his arms losing traction thanks to the gore now coating my lab coat.

I somersaulted off him, only to come face to face with Brian's booted foot. Moving swiftly, neck craned to the side as he slammed his booted foot down hard, the ground fracturing.

Talons erupting, I shackled his ankle before rolling slightly, releasing one hand to slash that tender spot behind his kneecap. His bellow of pain above me went unnoticed as I once again rolled to a crouch. Brian stood where I'd left him, and I cursed, rising from my crouch.

Must slice deeper next time.

Shrugging off my lab coat, I now faced Brian in my scrubs.

"You destroyed my life, you bitch. Fix what you've done, or I'll take you to the grave with me."

Brian launched off the ground, his clawed hand shackling my throat as he drove me into the nearest wall. Gripping his wrist with both hands, I held onto him as tightly as his rotting skin would allow.

Leaning closer, he whispered into my ear, and I fought my roiling stomach as the pong of decay slapped me square in the face.

"You can't kill me remember, you tried that already. The night I took your precious Bob from you. I, on the other hand, can kill you, and nearly succeeded that night."

He inhaled deeply, and I imagined him savouring some perverted image that popped into his grotesque mind.

His clawed hand slamming into my abdomen was not something I'd calculated for, and I grunted as the pain washed over me.

"That's better. Your pain is better than any orgasm I ever had. If I still had the ability to get an erection, I'd be rock solid and buried balls deep in you right now," he crooned.

"Well, thank fuck I neutered you then," I whispered hoarsely as I reached down to yank his claws out before I shed my corporal body.

Tiny red droplets dripped from my slowly healing wound as I drifted to the centre of the room to land lightly, reappearing once more.

A slight breeze against my neck heralded Brian's presence. I summoned the scythe from around my neck, gripping the Fairbairn-Sykes fighting knife as I spun. I drove the sharp-pointed blade forward, so it lodged just below his heart. I watched uncaring as Brian stared down, shocked at the handle now sticking out of him. I gripped the knife's handle harder as he staggered back withdrawing it from his body. The blade released easily, but I knew better than to let Brian recover.

He dropped to his knees, gripping his wound as it trickled blood lethargically. Stepping around him, I grabbed a handful of his blond locks, tugging hard so his neck arched back painfully. I stared down into his shocked face.

"Here's the thing Brian, I'm moving on with my life, or should I say death. I've allowed my fear of you to consume my living years, but I'm done. I can't protect the ones I love if I'm too busy living in the past. Someone powerful taught me that."

A disturbance in the air a few feet from Brian and I heralded Erick's approach as he stepped through a portal, only for it seal shut instantly behind him.

"Nice of you to join us, gorgeous," I murmured, looking up briefly.

Erick scanned the parking garage before eventually settling on the scene before him.

Letting go of my hold on Brian's head, it dropped forward and stilled as he caught sight of Erick. Pride at the man who'd fought my Grandfather so hard to stand beside me, and who'd battled tirelessly with me so I would let him love me, swelled within me.

"Remember me, arsehole?" Erick snarled, appearing suddenly before Brian. "I held back at Evanee's house the other evening, but tonight... Well, that beautiful woman standing behind you has agreed to stand back while I torture the shit out of you until you tell us exactly what we want to know. Personally, I hope you clamp up, but honestly it won't matter if you sing like a canary or not, I'm still going to have a little fun with you first."

"You're not getting Jack shit out of me, wanker; torture away. I've had that many needles and knives slice my skin during and after my conversion, there really isn't anything you could do that would be any worse," Brian spat.

"I'll be getting out of here shortly, and I'll have Evanee's eyes as my trophy."

"Oh, I highly doubt you'll be leaving alive. The only reason I'm here is because Death willed it, and I doubt very much that he will let anyone in or out unless it benefits him. As for claiming Evanee's eyes as a trophy, that won't be happening either. I like those, what did you call them again? Ah, yes—'fuck me' eyes."

Leaning forward, Erick grabbed Brian by the shirt, and I watched as he leaned forward to whisper in Brian's ear while his heated gaze met mine. "I've thoroughly enjoyed staring into those beauties as I buried myself deep in my beautiful mate."

I had the sudden urge to slap my forehead at Erick's taunt when I noticed Brian's rigid body waver.

Moving to intercept Brian, I stopped short when a deep masculine murmur came from beside me. "Oh, no you don't, you slimy little prick."

A ghostly taloned hand shot out of thin air, burying wrist deep in Brian's chest. Startled, I stepped aside as the tall silhouette of Grandfather materialised beside me.

"There will be no escaping this fate. I may have been forced to stand back and watch as you hurt my precious little girl, but tonight you will face the consequences of your actions," Grandfather hissed, menace dripping from each syllable.

"Um, I was a grown woman at the time."

"You have and will always be a young girl in my eyes. Now don't distract me, I'm in tough Grandfather mode here."

Snorting at him in disbelief, I looked down at my gut, happy to see I'd finally healed. Circling behind Erick, I trailed my hand over his taught backside with smugness at Brian's narrowed eyes.

"Quite the predicament you're in here, Brian. The Grimm Reaper at your back and a hybrid at your front," I taunted. "So, here's what's on the menu this evening. You either tell us the name and every detail that pea-sized brain of yours can remember about your master, or Erick here will make good on his promise."

"Screw you, whore," Brian spat.

"Are you sure that's the response you want to go with Brian? I should probably tell you that Erick's well over the 500-year mark." Squatting so I came down to his eye level, I sighed. "I've been inside that intriguing mind of his, and the number of barred doors in there can make a girl grow wet just thinking about what could be behind them." Puckering my lips up at Erick, he grinned down at me.

"My baby knows his stuff, trust me. I watched him take on Death himself and stand his ground."

"What, couldn't he beat him?" Brian laughed wetly.

Erick's grip on Brian's blood-stained shirt tightened and the sound of it ripping ever so slightly, reached my ears.

"No one beats Death you moron. You can only hope he grants you a swift death or spares your life," Erick snarled.

"True, young prince," Grandfather agreed.

I could see the moment Brian registered who stood behind him. His eyes widened, as he tried to turn his head to face Death.

"Who the hell are you?"

Why he bothered to ask the question when he knew the answer was beyond me.

"That would be Death, and consequently my great grandfather." I smiled sweetly. "What? You seriously didn't think I just appeared on this earth with a crown strapped to my head. No, it's being passed down from him." Head jerking in Grandfather's direction, I addressed him. "You haven't exactly told me why you're here and why you're only now deciding to help me."

"Relax, darling child. I am merely here to see him on his way when you're done. I am also very interested in who's behind the attacks on my two favourite descendants. Whoever it is, they've found a way of hiding from me too. I'm most intrigued as to how they accomplished this."

A black leather throne appeared to the side of us, and Grandfather extracted his hand from Brian's back, a thin thread of mist following his hand to settle against his bare chest.

Does the man ever wear a shirt?

"What did you just remove from him?" I queried inquisitively.

"The reaper essence whose power he stole. He should stay put for now."

Grandfather approached his throne, seating himself gracefully upon it.

"Oh! Thank you. Nice throne. What leather is that?" I grinned.

"Human and various supernatural beings' skin, beaten and sewed together. The legs are the bones of the Leviathan I conquered centuries ago. It is comfortable."

Erick's mind shuddered violently, and I felt it through our link.

Nausea rose within me as I realised of where we both stood in the grand scheme of things. We were but insignificant creatures floating through this universe.

Dismissing Grandfather, Erick addressed the man he still held. "What's the name of your master?"

"You think I'm scared of you idiots?"

Are you kidding me? Why can't he just bloody cooperate? I don't want to see him tortured. I'd much rather just kill him and be bloody done with it. I have a job to get back to, and a crime scene come to think of it.

Erick's fist was a blur as he drove it into Brian's soft gut. His pained screams echoed throughout the garage, and I forced myself to harden my heart.

'You are doing well, mic luptător. I believe we are killing two birds with one stone here,' Erick encouraged.

'What do you mean?'

'Death is watching you closely. I think he's not just here to escort Brian to whatever afterlife awaits him. I think he's come to see if you have what it takes to finish the job.'

What he said made sense, considering Grandfather's observance during our battle moments before.

When the garage was once again plunged into stillness, I faced Brian once again. "I don't want this, Brian. You've haunted me for the longest time, and now I am ready to move on. I will grant you an instant death, but I need the name of the reaper who created you. I know he's the head of Aeternum, but I need a name. Tell me the bastard's name, and I'll deliver a quick death."

"Not going to happen." His eyes blurred slightly before he sighed. "We could've been great together. I could've grown to love you, instead you forced me to hate you, just as I hate her."

Fire blazed along Erick's arm as Brian finished speaking, and I didn't turn away as Erick jammed a blazing clawed finger into Brian's left eye. His shrieks washed over me, and I let them slide off as water would off a duck's back.

"Speak to her like that again, and I'll take your other eye, and light what's left of your balls on fire," Erick roared.

"His name, Brian. I want his name." When he remained silent, I shook my head.

"So be it. Do what you need to do, Erick."

Nodding, Erick slammed Brian into the floor before he knelt down beside him. Palming the Fairbairn-Sykes knife

I still held, I handed it to Erick, resigned to what would come next. Brian's screams came long and hard, as Erick burnt, sliced and plucked appendages from Brian's regenerating body.

Pleading for mercy between wet gasps, Brian panted. "Enough, fine, I'll tell you what you want to know."

Erick stepped back, revealing an exhausted and haunted Brian. I crouched down beside him, at a safe distance, nodding for Erick to stand with Grandfather. The shape Brian was in, he wouldn't be moving, not for a long, long time.

"What's his name, Brian?" I crooned. When I missed the name he whispered, I leaned forward just that little more.

"Seb... Sebatien. His name is Sebastien Moissonneuse. He's supposed to be part of some big-shot family in France," he gurgled almost incoherently.

"What else can you tell me?" I asked softly.

"He has a basement full of supernatural creatures. Some I never even knew existed. He has a hard on for some woman who he reckons screwed up his life." His speech became more and more slurred the longer he spoke.

Pulling back to look in his single eye, it horrified me to realise the terrible truth. The man who took so much pleasure in causing pain to so many women was broken not only on the outside, but on the inside too. Someone had broken him long before tonight.

"Who broke you so badly, Brian? It can't have been an ex-girlfriend because you and Desmond have been who you are for a long time. Who broke the little boy within you?" I drew closer to him as he closed his remaining eye.

"Like you give a crap about my childhood." Blood dripped from the corner of his mouth.

I edged closer. "You're right, I don't give a shit about your childhood, but I'd still like to know what fucked you up so badly that you felt compelled to rape and torture women."

My hand reached behind me, and the knife Erick held appeared in my palm, a scythe once more. Palming my scythe, I rose, slowly moving to the top of Brian's head.

"Not all women are nurturing and caring, and not all women were made to be mothers. My mother and aunt were sisters who should never have had kids. Being rich doesn't mean shit when your mother is the one peddling you out."

Grief gripped my heart at the realisation the woman meant to protect and nurture him had in fact helped create the monster before me. Would he have gone down this road if he'd had a better mother? It would be another mystery never to be solved.

"I hope you find peace, Brian. I hope the restless and tortured soul of that little boy within finds the peace it should have had when you were a child. Thank you for your information." Not waiting for his response, I moved. Grabbing a hold of his head, my arm plunged down in one forceful motion, my scythe slicing cleanly through skin, tissue, and bone to land hard on the concrete beneath.

I stared hard at Grandfather as I stood, tossing Brian's decapitated head so it landed wetly at his feet. "He may have been a monster now, but he was once a scared and helpless child, and that part of him deserved a quick and painless end. You may think I'm weak in this moment and I really don't give a rat's arse. I was once human, and it's that human part of me who remembers humility and empathy. I will not disregard it because I am now 'other'." Looking to Erick, he appeared beside me, and we clasped hands.

"I have work to do. Do what you want with his body and soul."

Summoning a portal, Erick and I stepped through. I didn't look back. I couldn't look at the grotesque scene I'd helped to create.

Grandfather had been wrong. I needed to gaze back at the past from time to time. The past was a double-edged sword. It could guide and encourage us, or it could trap us in an endless cycle where we'd repeat our mistakes.

Chapter 23

Erick and I returned to work only to be confronted by officers cordoning off the entrance to the mortuary. My new, well, ex forensic assistant now, stood crying hysterically beside a perplexed-looking Jordan before she'd spotted me and screeched at me for leaving her alone while some psychopath roamed the hospital grounds. I was about to roll my eyes at his theatrics until Detective Bernard excused himself and rushed towards me.

"What happened? And why are you and Erick covered in… what the hell is that?" Bernard asked in a hushed and nauseated tone.

"Brian happened. This was his invitation to come and play. But you won't have to worry about him anymore. We took care of him." My haggard murmur raised Bernard's eyebrows.

"Should I send a party to a certain location to retrieve his remains?"

"That won't be necessary, Detective," Erick reassured.

I dropped Erick's hand to rub at my pulsing temples. Sighing, I stared around the area frustrated by the sight before me.

"Bernard, you know as well as I do that the human authorities will be required to undergo an identification process. His family wouldn't be able to identify him with what my curse did to him. He was also missing an eyeball the last time I saw his head. The main issue, though, is his altered DNA. Testing would prove futile and would only raise red flags. So, let's just dub him the new Jack the Ripper and let him disappear."

No one said a word as we stood observing the human officials going about their duties. The ramifications, had the general population become aware there were beings less human walking amongst them, was all too real.

~

Winter was here, and I was in heaven. Sitting beneath a full moon, the scents of tea tree and eucalyptus drifted lazily along the fresh crisp air. My toes wriggled against the heat emanating from the burning logs in the fire pit. Snuggling deeper into the embrace of the outdoor lounge, I mulled over the events from the evening before.

"You've been quiet since we returned, *mic luptător*. What's bothering you?"

Erick placed a glass of Shiraz in my hand and sat in the free spot beside me on the lounge.

"How am I any better than Brian?" The fire continued to hold my attention, the flames swaying hypnotically.

"You are nothing like Brian, Evanee. He was a sadistic psychopath who took pleasure from torturing and raping women."

"Sociopath," I whispered. When I could feel Erick's eyes on me, I drew my eyes from the fire. "Brian was a sociopath. I thought he was a psychopath, but what I saw at the end changed my mind."

"You haven't said much about what he said towards the end. He spoke too softly in those last moments for even me to hear," he prodded gently.

A single tear dropped at what I'd seen and heard before I'd delivered Brian unto my Grandfather.

"I saw an innocent child with a soul fractured beyond repair. I didn't see it in Desmond because I was too preoccupied with revenge. Brian's and Desmond's mothers were monsters who created a new generation of monsters." Sipping at my wine I allowed what I'd said to sink in. "I forgave him. Looking at that broken part of him really hit home."

"You have a good and big heart, *mic luptător*. Sometimes it can be too big for your own good, but that's what makes you you."

Looking into Erick's concerned eyes, his arm reached across at my small smile and he drew me to him.

"I wonder what Grandfather did with his body?" I resumed looking at the fire, wriggling my toes against the heat once again.

"Incinerated it I believe. Reagan returned to the area and found nothing but a pile of ash." I nodded my understanding but kept quiet.

"The name he gave for his creator—Sebastien Moissonneuse, I can't help but wonder who he is and what he has against me and my family?"

Erick drank his wine silently, allowing me to air my thoughts.

"But I am more concerned about the basement full of supernatural creatures. Whatever his plans are, they go beyond just wanting to kill me." Scooping up my phone, I thumbed a message to my mother.

"Who're you messaging?" he asked.

"My mother. If you could please call Jordan and Tristan, I'd appreciate it."

~

Erick tossed a few more logs onto the fire, embers sparking up into the night as Mum, Jordan and Tristan filtered in.

"Thanks for coming guys. Take a seat." I nodded towards the lounges scattered around the fire pit.

To distract myself, I sculled the last of my wine, the burn at the back of my throat pleasant and welcome. I stared at my empty glass for a second before handing it to Erick, who placed it on a side table. Gripping his hand, I held it tightly as I studied the members around the fire.

"I won't bore you all with the unnecessary details of the other night, but you should know that before Brian died, he divulged who the head of Aeternum is, and a few other concerning issues. We were right in assuming he is a reaper, and judging from the sound of his surname, he's French."

"So Brian gave up his name then?" Mum asked.

"Yes, he did. Tell me, mother, does the name Sebastien Moissonneuse ring a bell?"

She sat straighter, her shoulders stiffening, and it hit me then.

"Mum, tell me that Sebastien is not the full version of Bastien? Tell me we aren't hunting for the fiancé you jilted to run away with Dad." I already knew what the answer would be, but I needed to hear it from her.

"Yes, that would be the same Bastien," she said wretchedly.

"Fucking hell." Jordan rubbed at his raven spiked hair.

"Shit, so this was never about Evanee or the prophecy. It was about you, Reagan, this whole time," Tristan said, fitting the pieces together.

"I'm so sorry. I never thought he would do anything as depraved as this," Mum stuttered.

Standing, I paced along the uneven paving.

"Evanee? Tell me what you're thinking, beautiful."

Erick's hand on my thigh stopped my pacing.

"Brian said that Sebastien was pissed because Mum took the opportunity for him to be great from him. I'd say there's a strong chance he was only marrying my mother to inherit the title that would one day pass to her if she didn't die before her relatives." At his confused look, I continued.

"Both Grandfather and Mum mentioned the mysterious deaths of the direct descendants in the Mors family. I know the Mors family hoped Mum and Sebastien would produce a child as my mother was the last child born to the family at that time. But, what if the accidents that have been killing the Mors family members haven't been freak accidents? What if he purposely orchestrated them?"

"But most of these deaths happened before you were born." Mum interjected.

"Yes, but you're not accounting for the fact that he wanted power, Mum. By killing off Grandfather's direct descendants, he backed you all into a corner, so he dangled the idea of new descendants to get his foot in the door. Then there's the prophecy. Who's to say he didn't know about it? Grandfather said he thought you would be the one to fulfil the prophecy, until you ran away with Dad and had me." Facing Mum, I stared at her.

"The night Dad died; the reaper got a glimpse of me in the back seat. What if it was him that killed Dad? It would have been the first time he became aware that I existed. You, and I'm going to go out on a limb here, and Grandfather have shielded me from the supernatural community until recently. The fact that he wasn't aware you'd had a baby wouldn't be that farfetched."

Mum nodded. "What you're saying makes sense," she said.

Beside me, Erick stilled.

"What?" Tristan and I asked at the same moment.

"Until that night at your house when Brian brought you Abigail, Sebastien thought of you as the offspring of John. His goal was to get rid of you so that he could get to your mother. That was before you sent Brian back to him with a message."

Dread filled me as I stared into Erick's concerned eyes. "Shit."

"Now he knows Reagan isn't the woman in Fate's prophecy," added Jordan, "which means she's dispensable or bait. Erick, we need to stick guards on Reagan at all times. We can't risk him getting to her."

Jordan stood, the scales on his bicep moving. They were weighted to one side — death.

"Jordan, I have lasted over 3000 years, I highly doubt I will need guards," Mum huffed irritably. "Not to mention Bastien has no idea I still retain my power. As far as he and the rest of my family knows, the power has been dying off slowly." She spoke with care.

'Are you seeing what I'm seeing?' I asked Erick silently.

'He is agitated at the thought of your mother being a target.'

There was humour in Erick's response, and I tried not to grin.

'It would appear I'm not the only one in this trio with a particular attraction to a beautiful blonde woman with electric blue eyes and a particularly bad temper and stubborn streak.'

I laughed at this, and he grinned at me.

'I'd pay to be in the same room as the two of them during an argument.'

Giggling at Erick's dry expression, I drifted towards him, and he pulled me onto his lap.

"Heaven help us all and the house if that were to happen."

He spoke aloud, stroking my hair softly.

"What the fuck are you two talking about? We have a crisis on our hands and you're screwing around," Jordan bellowed. Looking to where a stunned Tristan sat, it didn't take long for a shit-eating grin to spread across his handsome face.

"I would say you need a sparring session, my old friend. You seem to be carrying a lot of tension," Tristan cajoled a fuming Jordan.

Fearing bloodshed, I addressed Jordan's concerns.

"We'll work on a plan to keep my mother safe. For now though, perhaps you could watch her? I have Erick to watch my back, and you would know if I was in mortal danger thanks to our link. I also think Sebastien would dismiss you as just another vampire. He wouldn't be aware of our connection." I smiled at Jordan and watched in relief as he began to relax.

"Just what are you up to, Evanee Sheperd?"

Mum knew when I was up to mischief. Standing with her hands on her hips, she looked at me as though she could read my mind.

"Not a thing, mother dearest. I think it'd be best if you stayed with us at the mansion until after the ball. After that we could decide how best to move forward. Wouldn't you agree, Erick?"

"A fantastic idea, *mic luptător*. Jordan, perhaps you could get Reagan settled in a suite closest to yours in case she finds herself in trouble."

Mum's look of astonishment at Erick's request was comical. Tristan snickered as he tried but failed to keep his laughter to himself.

"That's a great idea, Erick," Jordan agreed. "Reagan let's go. I'll show you to your room."

My mother crossed her arms stubbornly, and I bit my lip at the look she shot at Jordan's turned back.

"Move your arse, Reagan," Jordan bit out, "or I'll put you over my shoulder and carry you."

Mum's hands dropped to her sides before she looked at each of us. Jordan turned to her, daring her to test him, not moving a step further until she conceded.

"Go give him hell, Mum." Giving her a double thumbs up, her look of thunder preceded the finger she threw at each of us in turn before stamping after him.

We waited until they'd disappeared into the house before we broke down in fits of laughter. It was sometime later before any of us could say a word, and even then it was broken by deep bellied-laughs.

"Did you see the look on my mother's face? She is probably thinking of every possible way to make his death look like an accident." I laughed as I recalled the stubbornness highlighting her slightly pointed jaw line.

"Heaven help the poor bastard. He has no idea what he's getting himself into. You Mors women are a breed all your own. If he succeeds in taming her, I'll eat my sword."

Erick grunted at the elbow I threw at his ribs.

"Oh, he is well and truly screwed now. Wait until it finally dawns on him. The karma he has coming to him is not enough, but I'll be sure to help it along."

Tristan wiped at his eyes, and it was the first time I'd seen him look anything but the stoic vampire he usually portrayed.

Settling back, we each watched the flames dancing happily as curlews called lovingly to their mates in the distance. I looked back at Tristan, his loneliness drawing a frown from me.

"Where's Ellie?" I asked.

"She's visiting with her brother. She thought it best I didn't come with her while she tried to garner support for you guys." He shrugged it off, but I knew he was smarting at not being introduced to her family.

"Ellie and her family have had a tough relationship since I've known her. I wouldn't be surprised if she told them she was planning on introducing you to them at the ball. It's what I'd do. The buffer would be as much for you as for herself."

"You think?"

His uncertainty clawed at him, and I realised I'd gotten used to having him around. He was part of the family; the cranky uncle everyone left alone, but from who they sought advice.

"Definitely. Ellie being away comes at the perfect time. If Erick's okay with it, there is one job I'd like you to do for me."

Looking to Erick, he nodded, as surprised and as curious as Tristan was at my request.

"I need you to take care of something for me. I'd do it myself, but I don't trust myself to stay the course."

Frowning, Tristan sat forward. "What is it you need me to do?"

"I need you to kill Mrs Turner and her sister." My eyes never left his.

"You want Tristan to kill Brian's and Desmond's mothers?"

Erick's astonishment didn't change what I knew needed to be done.

"Yes, I want them both dead. And Tristan, I want video confessions of what they did to their sons' left with the bodies. I don't care how you get it out of them, but the truth needs to come out. They created monsters from years of abusing their sons. They hid their sons' crimes, and their own. I don't want them to get their hands on any more innocents." Staring straight into Tristan's lavender and blue eyes, he nodded, understanding why I felt I wouldn't be able to do it myself.

"I can do that for you. I'll take the jet and be in Brisbane within a couple of hours."

Standing, he nodded to each of us. As he moved to leave, I snagged his arm.

"No one is to know about this but us. No one would understand why I'm giving the order, but I need justice for the broken children hidden within Brian and Desmond. Make it look like a murder-suicide, or suicides all around."

Nodding, he left without a word. Together, Erick and I sat in silence before I whispered. "Don't judge me, please." My head dropped lightly against Erick's chest.

"There will be no judgment from me, Evanee. I know it isn't revenge for yourself you are after, only justice for the suffering of the innocent. I have to say, I think you're stepping into the role of future queen well. I'm looking forward to watching you blossom into the fair and just queen I know you'll be."

Lifting my head, I looked up placing a tender kiss to his lips. "With you by my side?" I asked cheekily.

"Damned straight, woman. You're stuck with me, so you better get used to it."

"You're such a charmer. Do you think my mother has killed Jordan yet, or do you think she has him strung up by his toes?" The thought of the semi-giant man hanging by his feet from the ceiling drew a laughter from us both.

"I don't know, but either way we should probably run interference. Not to mention I believe my aunt has arrived from her visit to my family. I guess she'll want to get to work on the party, especially considering it's scheduled for two months' time."

I made a face, not wanting to ruin my evening out beneath the stars. Rising into the air, Erick grinned devilishly.

"But I think everyone else can wait. I believe you and I need a date night."

Circling my arms around his neck, happiness filled me. "What did you have in mind?"

"Dinner and a swim. I hope you're wearing something a little more daring than the first time we went for a dip."

He tickled the underside of my breast and I laughed. I had indeed chosen a rather risqué ensemble from my vast Victoria Secret collection.

"I guess you'll have to wait until after dinner to find out," I murmured coyly.

"Right, I've changed my mind. Swim first, dinner after."

Erick scooped me up in his arms and my laughter drifted into the roaring wind as Erick sped towards the falls.

I'd gained a man who would have made not only my father proud, but Bob too. The bizarre family I'd acquired loved and supported me despite the storm brewing on the horizon. We were a weird concoction of banshees, vampires, reapers, and vampers; but we were family, and that was a win in my book as far as I was concerned. Now to win over the rest.

Acknowledgements

Thank you to all my readers who have supported me from the first copy of Moribund right through until now. I don't think I will ever be able to put into words just how grateful I am to have you along for the journey. A shout out to a certain high school student who helped me achieve one of my goals as a writer. Thank you for picking up Moribund more than once. I hope I can continue to inspire you and give you new worlds to escape to.

To Amanda Pillar of Smoking Hot Cover, as always, your cover designs are works of art. I am incredibly lucky and grateful to have you as a cover designer. Thank you, Dannielle Line, for your brilliant and quite frankly, mad editing skills. Danielle Cook, as always bestie, you have supported and helped me when I needed it the most. Thank you.

And finally, Helen Walton. Wow am I lucky to have met you. Your guidance and support have been phenomenal. Your coaching and laughter have pushed me on when I was ready to throw my computer out the window. Thank you from the bottom of my heart.